D0441447

"Ann Hazelwood's prose is both charming and engaging, which makes for enjoyable reading."
— Josh Steven, Reedy Press, St. Louis

"I found myself immersed in the tale of this extended family and this wonderful quaint town. I wanted to move there immediately. You will laugh, cry and share in their hopes and dreams. I think I fell in love with the main character. It will remind you of a simpler time and place. Ann makes us feel so much a part of the story and so close to the characters. She knows how to tug at your emotions. You will love the characters, but let me give you a warning that Grandma has some surprises for everyone."
— Randy Davies, Community News, St. Charles, Missouri

"This is a family story as warm and cozy as your favorite quilt."
— Vicki Erwin, Main Street Books, St. Charles, Missouri

"Ann Hazelwood has written a delightful book that weaves romance and mystery into a wonderful quilt of a story. Ann certainly knows about quilts and the bucolic Missouri setting; her years as a quilt shop owner and author of Missouri travel books shows through. Luckily we can now share her gifts as a story-teller too!"

—Jeff Fister, Virginia Publishing Co.,
St. Louis, Missouri

"Quilters have an immediate connection to the main themes of this book; family, friends, and community. Ann Hazelwood has captured this connection in an intriguing story that quilters will love. The story and place will be familiar to the reader. This is a novel a quilter can call her own."

—Chris Stergos, Patches Etc.,
Quilt and Button Shop,
St. Charles, Missouri

"Ann Hazelwood knows a few things about the human spirit, family and dreaming big. Add a mixture of the love of quilting and all the things Missouri historic and otherwise; you will experience the words and passion of this unique and gifted author. Enjoy the experience!"

—Tom Hannegan, Streetscape Magazine,
St. Charles, Missouri

The pattern for this block is available at:

**http://www.americanquilter.com/
grandmothers_fan_hazelwood**

The Basement Quilt

Introducing the Colebridge Community

a novel by

Ann Hazelwood

American Quilter's Society

PO Box 3290
Paducah, KY 42002-3290
americanquilter.com

Located in Paducah, Kentucky, the American Quilter's Society (AQS) is dedicated to promoting the accomplishments of today's quilters. Through its publications and events, AQS strives to honor today's quiltmakers and their work and to inspire future creativity and innovation in quiltmaking.

EXECUTIVE BOOK EDITOR: ANDI MILAM REYNOLDS
GRAPHIC DESIGN: MELISSA POTTERBAUM
COVER DESIGN: MICHAEL BUCKINGHAM
PHOTOGRAPHY: CHARLES R. LYNCH

All rights reserved. No part of this book may be reproduced, stored in any retrieval system, or transmitted in any form, or by any means including but not limited to electronic, mechanical, photocopy, recording or otherwise, without the written consent of the author and publisher.

This book is a work of fiction. The people, places, and events described in it are either imaginary or fictitiously presented. Any resemblance they bear to reality is entirely coincidental.

 American Quilter's Society

PO Box 3290
Paducah, KY 42002-3290
americanquilter.com

Additional copies of this book may be ordered from the American Quilter's Society, PO Box 3290, Paducah, KY 42002-3290, or online at www.AmericanQuilter.com.

Text © 2012, Author, Ann Hazelwood
Artwork © 2012, American Quilter's Society

Library of Congress Cataloging-in-Publication Data

Hazelwood, Ann Watkins.
The basement quilt / by Ann Hazelwood.
p. cm.
ISBN 978-1-60460-045-2 (alk. paper)
1. Quilting--Fiction. 2. Missouri--Fiction. I. Title.
PS3608.A98846B37 2012
813'.6--dc23
2012021253

Location: Colebridge, Missouri

Narrator: Anne Brown
29, slender, blonde, the owner of Brown's Botanical Flower Shop; she lives with her mother, Sylvia.

Sylvia Brown
Anne's mother, 54, a homemaker with black hair, widowed, a retired librarian; she is sister to Julia and Marie.

Aunt Julia
Youngest of three sisters, 48, a freelance editor with reddish-brown hair; she is unhappily married to her husband, Jim Baker.

Aunt Marie
Oldest of three sisters, 65, gray-haired, retired teacher and widow.

Sue Davis
Daughter of Uncle Ken, brother of the three sisters; he lives in Ohio and is married to Aunt Joyce. Sue is full-figured, 32, light brown hair, single, a secretary; she grew up in Colebridge and still lives there.

Ted Collins
Anne's boyfriend, handsome, dark-haired; he is a CPA for his father's company, Collins & Collins.

Sarah Baker
12, blonde, bright; she is the daughter of Julia and Jim.

John and Martha Davis
The siblings' mother and father; deceased.

Wendy Lorenz
Ted's former girlfriend.

Sally Freeman
Part-time student and employee at the flower shop.

Sam Dickson
Single, Jim's colleague; he is tall, dark, and handsome.

Dedication

I dedicate the first book in this Colebridge series
to St. Charles, Missouri.
This is where I have enjoyed my love of business,
romance, and most of all, family.
Its quality of life has been very good to me.
Thank you, St. Charles!

FROM THE AUTHOR

Colebridge, Missouri, is a charming, historic town with the kind of wonderful quality of life that everyone likes to read about in a storybook. The Missouri River in all its beauty and strength runs along the town's manicured edge. Everyone knows everyone. The town is proud of its preserved architecture and amazing parks. It is a great place to do business because of its tourist trade and proximity to a metropolitan area—St. Louis.

It is the scenery and charm for which I tell a story that takes place in a colonial two-story brick home on 490 Melrose Street. It was once the home of John and Martha Davis, now deceased. It is now inhabited by their middle daughter, Sylvia, and her twenty-nine year-old daughter, Anne Brown. Sylvia, a widow, is pleased to have Anne still living with her after college, which also helps Anne support her business—Brown's Botanical Flower Shop in downtown Colebridge.

The Davis' had two other daughters, Marie Wilson, the oldest of the sisters, and the youngest, Julia Baker. They had one son, Ken, married to Joyce; they now live in Columbus, Ohio. Their only child, Sue, moved to Colebridge to be closer to the rest of the family. She is thirty-two, single, and a secretary; she sometimes helps out in the Brown's Botanical Flower Shop on the weekends.

This family story is told by Anne Brown, who observes and lives through a period of time when the family discovers who they really are, when they share a task originated by her Aunt Julia. There are paranormal activities and mysterious occurrences that entwine around an ongoing romance, uncovered secrets, an unexpected death, and an unhappy marriage.

The family members have always been close and in touch. When Aunt Julia presents her desire to finish a quilt, they do not hesitate to respond, even though Julia's history of behavior is to never finish what she starts. The conversations and actions are warm and intriguing; however, there seems to be an unknown family member who is unannounced and present.

Visiting Colebridge and Anne's family will shed light on your own town and family relationships. Discover what you will learn about business, death, love, quilting, and loyalty, and guess—who will be the uninvited guest that shares it all?

CHAPTER 1

For most folks in Colebridge, Missouri, the high point of Sundays was an afternoon nap, followed by a nice fried chicken dinner. Their lives geared down to neutral after the excitement of attending church and reading the Sunday paper.

For me, after sporadic church attendance with my mother, it was back to my serious career as owner of Brown's Botanical Flower Shop. Since all the shops on Main Street were closed on Sundays, I treated myself now and then to bringing work home to our kitchen table, where I could spread out my catalogs to order from on Monday morning. That allowed me to munch on some of Mother's chocolate chip cookies and delicious leftovers from Saturday evening's dinner.

Mother always made a practice on Sundays of creating wonderful smells in the kitchen, smells that could be tasted that evening and which would last the rest of the week. We did not eat out much since she enjoyed cooking. That was fine with me since I had many rushed meals throughout the week and had no particular interest in cooking.

It was just she and I living in our 1920 brick, colonial, two-story home. It had looked the same all my life. Each spring the same geraniums would be planted in the flower boxes out front, next to the green shutters. In the fall and winter, the same seasonal wreaths appeared on the doors. Mr. Carter, our aging handyman and neighbor, kept our house freshly painted and well maintained. Before his death, my father was not handy and spent most of his time practicing law at the office of Brown and Caldwell.

I had lived here all my life of twenty-nine years, and could not imagine living anywhere else unless I married someday. My two-year relationship with Ted Collins didn't seem to be headed that direction, thanks to me, so I didn't see me leaving anytime soon.

The phone rang, which interrupted me from making a decision on whether to order more red glass vases for the holidays than I did last year. I hated using standard vases and pots for everyone, which seemed so impersonal. I loved collecting containers from estate sales and flea markets that had potential in unique flower arranging.

On the third ring, I figured it must be Ted calling early to see what my plans were for the evening. I picked it up to find it was Aunt Julia, Mother's youngest sister. She sounded more upbeat than usual, said she had just finished a quilt top, and was now going to have to quilt it. I was impressed, and asked her to repeat her accomplishment because this was not a skill I knew her to have. She went on to say she was not going to tell the family until the top's completion because her mother said she could never finish anything. Now she needed our help.

"What on earth can we do?" I asked.

"I have Grandmother's quilting frame that takes up an ungodly amount of space, and wondered if you and your mother minded if I set it up at your house?" Still a bit puzzled, I told Aunt Julia to hang on while I mentioned her dilemma to Mother.

I placed the phone down on the end table and went into the kitchen, where she was peeling carrots. I explained who was on the phone and what Aunt Julia was asking.

"Oh my, what an unexpected surprise this is!" Mother said. "The only place we could possibly accommodate it would be in the basement, if we moved some things around."

I thought it was a good suggestion, as we had used the basement for all sorts of things as I grew up, plus there was an element of this request which made us think that it might not actually happen. "Sure Aunt Julia, we'd be happy to help you out, but Aunt Marie is the only quilter in the family," I reminded her.

Her response was joyful, and said she would bring it over Wednesday evening after work. Her twelve-year-old daughter, Sarah, was willing to come with her and help.

Later that evening I helped Mother rearrange a large space in the basement. It was sort of fun, anticipating if such a quilting event would happen. We laughed at some of the odds and ends stored here and there, wondering how they settled there in the first place. Mother remembered playing under the large quilting frame when she was a child. She always wanted to help stitch, but they would never let her.

"Well, Mother, you may get your chance. Aunt Marie will have to teach us all, I suppose."

CHAPTER 2

I couldn't rush home fast enough after work on Wednesday to see if the quilt frame would arrive. I walked in to find Aunt Marie already there, helping Mother prepare some small sandwiches and vegetables. Right on time, Aunt Julia and Sarah walked in with arms loaded. Sarah carried in the quilt top, which we could not wait to unfold. It was beautiful. Julia had chosen all pastel colors and a simple pieced pattern she called Grandmother's Fan.

It took a bit of skill to get the pieces of the frame assembled, but with the help of Aunt Marie, we were ready to pin the three layers of the quilt. Lots of compliments made Aunt Julia beam with pride. "Mother would be so proud of you, Julia," Aunt Marie said with a big smile on her face.

"Well, I wish she was here, but then I'm glad she's not, because she would be telling me how to do each and every step, which would end in some hurt feelings," Julia said.

When we finished basting around the edge of the three layers,

Mother told us to take a break, sip some wine, and nibble on her tasty treats.

"I suggest we go to the den so red wine will not appear on this lovely quilt," she said.

We toasted Aunt Julia's success and quickly ventured back to the basement with much anticipation.

"Show us some stitches, Marie," Aunt Julia said eagerly.

Aunt Marie went through the basic drill of explaining the process of a running stitch and then told us all to be fitted for a thimble from the many in her decorative assortment.

"A thimble," I said with a questionable tone. "Do we have to use this thing, which no doubt will get in my way?"

"Yes, indeed you do," Aunt Marie answered. "We don't want blood on this quilt, and we don't want sore fingers, Anne, especially if someone has to handle delicate flowers all day!"

I sadly nodded my head and said I'd be a good sport.

"There's someone missing that really needs to be in on this project," Mother said, tilting her head in concern. "Your cousin Sue needs to be a part of this family experience, especially since her immediate family is not here. Her mother would want us to include her."

Sue was my Uncle Ken and Aunt Joyce's daughter. She was in her thirties, single, and had chosen to live in Colebridge after she finished college. She got a secretarial job, and was not keen on making changes in her life. She was overweight, understated in her appearance, and never dated, as far as we knew. We tried to include her when we could, and I asked her to help out at the flower shop on Saturdays.

"Great idea, I will call her tonight," Aunt Julia agreed. "Can everyone make it back tomorrow night? I will bring chili instead of soup or something, if you'll put on a pot of coffee, Sylvia."

We all looked at each other to see if that would work, and then we separated, as each had their own tasks to do for the evening. As we approached the door, Aunt Julia remarked, "Well I sure got us into a hornet's nest." We all laughed and went our separate ways.

The next day was a hectic one at work and included one of my most difficult customers, Pete Jennings. He gives me plenty of business but is always demanding with each and every order. It kept me from arriving home around my usual time, so I was late for the special quilting night.

Aunt Julia, Sarah, Aunt Marie, and even Sue were all there enjoying some of Aunt Julia's favorite chili. Aunt Julia also brought a heavenly layered chocolate cake that captured my attention. "I think a glass of merlot and your cake will do me just fine, guys!" I said. "There is nothing better than chocolate and merlot!"

"Not before we make some stitches," Mother said. "We need to get started, and the cake will be our reward for our very first quilting. Marie said that years ago this would have been called a "quilting bee," and food was always part of the activity. Grandma Davis had the ladies from church over at least once a week."

Off to the basement we went, as I grabbed some napkins and coasters. We all seemed to know where to sit and Aunt Marie checked our thimbles and made sure we all had enough light.

"I am so glad you could join us, Sue," I said, all excited. "Except for Aunt Marie, we are all beginners so we will all learn together."

"I don't need one of those thimbles," said Sue.

"I think you will find out that you will!" said Aunt Marie in a firm voice.

"Who is this quilt for?" Mother asked Aunt Julia.

"It's for me!" Julia proudly announced. "Of course it'll be Sarah's someday, but I want to look at it every day, and I think the colors will do fine in our guest room." She paused, and then said, "Why do I feel our mother is looking over my shoulder?"

"Well, I wish she could see this moment," Mother said. "Hey, hold that pose all of you, I am going to get my camera. We will have a before and after 'Kodak moment,' as we say around here."

Off she went, and the moans and groans of the stitching began, as each of us became disappointed by the uneven sizes of our stitches.

"Isn't this supposed to be for old people to do?" asked Sue, straining over her work. "This is hard. How in the world can they go through all those layers?"

"Yeah, Mom, I could be doing more fun stuff than making my needle do things it doesn't want to do," said Sarah.

"I want your stitches in this quilt, Sarah, and when you are older, you can point to them with pride," said Aunt Julia.

"Well, that's all for me!" said Sarah as she disappeared into the den to watch TV.

I took a break to run up and put coffee on for that scrumptious cake for which I was salivating. Coming down the stairs, I announced it would be a short time before the coffee would be ready. To my surprise, not a head looked up. Everyone was intent on their task of creating stitches. I wanted to laugh at how everyone looked as if they were in pain, but couldn't stop the process.

"Look, look," Aunt Julia cried. "I finished this whole line, and isn't it beautiful, Marie? What do you think?"

"I think it's pretty good Julia, but we'll have to see if the stitches went through the three layers, or you'll have to take them out," Aunt Marie explained.

"Out, no way," Aunt Julia cried. "Anne, crawl under and see if the stitches are coming through."

I reluctantly made my way under the quilt and called, "I think they're fine."

"Well, then we need to celebrate and enjoy some of my cake," Aunt Julia declared.

Everyone happily placed their needles aside except Sue, who was determined to finish the outline of one of the fans. We all went upstairs and gathered around the kitchen table.

The chatter and pride of getting in the first "quilting" was enjoyed along with the cake. I indulged in two pieces, making up for an absent dinner. In no time, everyone had left and Mother told them they could all come back anytime that suited them. Aunt Julia could not thank everyone enough for coming. I could tell there was already a sense of satisfaction in starting the last step to completing her quilt.

I was feeling like I had overindulged with calories and wandered down the basement stairs. As I turned out the three lamps, I glanced at each one's contribution to the evening. I was certainly not pleased with the size of my stitches. Sarah's, Sue's, Mother's, and Aunt Julia's were all pretty bad, too. They were all uneven and large, to say the least. Aunt Julia's were surprisingly the worst! It was her quilt after all, though, and she seemed pretty pleased. None compared to Aunt Marie's tiny stitches, of course.

My hand smoothed over the quilting stitches as I treasured the picture in my mind of our family gathered around the frame.

When I came up the stairs I said, "What if they don't come back, Mother?"

"Well, then, you and I have a big job to do."

CHAPTER 3

Two days passed and no word was heard from any of the quilters. Then a week had passed and the weekend was approaching. Friday night was usually "date night" for Ted and me, but he had called earlier and said he'd have to work late. He asked if a movie would be in order for Saturday evening. I'm not sure I really answered him. I was tired from a long, busy day, so I was pleased I didn't have to rush home to freshen up.

It had been a long time since I was excited about seeing Ted. I liked him well enough, but I always felt guilty when he wanted to talk about the future. I had much to do to secure the flower business' success, which took many hours of my day. I continued to be worried that Ted would really resent my time devoted to the business as well as my civic involvement with our historic district. He had job security since he worked for his father, so he conveniently kept his hours from nine to five. His father was connected civically, serving on many boards, so he did not have the same sense of obligation that I did as a small business owner. Ted didn't complain often but I always knew how he really felt. I was determined to stay focused, however, despite any discouraging clues from him.

He was a pretty straight and narrow accountant, so he knew he had a job whether he worked hard or not. His family liked me for sure. I got plenty of hints about their wanting me to be part of the family.

I got home, put on my favorite jeans, grabbed some pretzels, and ventured down to the basement. I went to my same spot at the frame, right next to Sue's. I turned on the floor lamp and rethreaded my needle.

"You want some company?" Mother called, coming down the stairs.

I jumped like I had just been caught with one hand in the cookie jar. "Oh, sure! I was just thinking how making these stitches relaxes you, and lets your mind wander. I would like to get as good as Aunt Marie, but she said it will take practice."

We both stitched in silence for some good period of time before Mother said, "I never thought I would be stitching on a quilt with my daughter. You should be out on a date; it's Friday night. So what's going on with you and Ted?"

"Not a thing. He had to work late for a change, and I could care less. I guess what I'm really saying is that I really didn't feel like getting dressed up after my long day. It's just good to stay home and relax."

"You know, we should be planning to make a quilt for your trousseau, don't you think?"

"Save your stitches and time, Mother. It won't be needed for a long time," I responded. I was grateful she did not question me any further.

Silence continued until she said, "You know Julia always tried so hard to please our mom. Even with our mother gone, she still seems as though she has something to prove."

"What about you, Mother? Do you feel like that, too?"

"Well, I was the middle sister. You might say I sort of got lost in who did what first and last, which was fine with me. In a way, I felt special because mom was usually upset with Julia or Marie. Julia, being the youngest, was wilder, braver, and not good about obeying the rules. Marie was the overachiever and had really good grades. Our dad was quiet and never seemed to involve himself in our "female disputes," as he called them. When Dad died, Marie and I were not living at home anymore, so a lot of responsibility fell on Julia. She probably resented a lot of it, although she never complained too much. I'm sure Mother's frustrations as a widow were often taken out on Julia."

"Is that what it's usually like, having sisters?" I asked, looking directly at Mother for a reaction. "There's times it sure would have been nice to have had one. Sue is just too different to be very close to. Outside the shop goings-on, I have little in common with her. She is very tight-lipped about her work and even Uncle Ken and Aunt Joyce."

We were interrupted by the doorbell.

"Who could that be at this hour?" I asked. I ran up the stairs, taking two steps at a time, and opened the door to find Ted, who was wearing a big smile.

"Oh good, you are still up," he said with a big flirty grin that usually got my attention. "I saw the lights still on so thought I'd drop by to see if you would be up for having a nightcap somewhere? I feel like I deserve it after a long day. What do you say?"

"Well, I suppose," I responded unenthusiastically. "Mother and

I were pretty settled in the basement quilting on Aunt Julia's quilt."

"You quilt?" Ted joked.

"I do now," I bragged. "Come on in and take a look for yourself."

We made our way down the steps, and, of course, Mother greeted Ted in a cheerful manner as she always did.

"Please explain this all to Ted while I put on some shoes and fix my face. I'm not sure Ted even knows what a quilt is! We are going to go have a drink."

After a few minutes we were off to Charley's Place, one of the popular spots on a corner of Main Street. It was a comfortable sports bar/restaurant where I could go alone to enjoy a drink or have a quick lunch. It had three floors of comfortable seating and unique artwork. Since it was a half block down from my shop, I recommended many folks eat there, and they were never disappointed.

"So, I saw your quilting stitches and I am impressed!"

"It is bizarre, I know, Ted, but you should have been there when all the family was sitting around trying to help Aunt Julia accomplish something that was important to her," I said. "This quilt may be living in our basement a long time, but that's okay. I wish Grandma Davis could see us all quilting. She would never believe this in a million years!"

Two drinks arrived, a merlot for me and a Jack Daniels on ice for Ted.

Ted leaned over to kiss my check and whispered how good it was to end his day with me.

I smiled as always, hoping he would not suggest coming over to his condo for a longer evening. It was getting more and more difficult to keep our relationship casual. I could hardly take more than a few hours with Ted. I didn't know if it was boredom or guilt about being away from my shop. I kept telling myself I needed the balance of the two. That's what my friends kept saying, anyway.

John Cummings, a friend of Ted's, and his girlfriend, Sheila, approached us for conversation. He also worked at Ted's firm, and Sheila was in from out of town for a visit. After a half hour of useless chatter, I looked at my watch and told Ted I needed to get home, so we left them at our table, still talking.

CHAPTER 4

It was a busy Saturday morning, with a big wedding order to deliver. At 2:00, all finished, Sue, the delivery guy Kevin, and I looked at each other in relief. We settled in for a late lunch, and I reminded Sue that Sunday afternoon everyone planned to quilt again.

"Oh, I just don't know if I can make it. It's my only day off and I have so many things to take care of. I need a wife, right? Forget a husband. That would be just another thing to look after."

"Well, you're not the only one," I said. "Look at it this way: Mother always cooks up something yummy, and you have to eat. It's a good excuse to see everyone. I'm kind of looking forward to it. By the way, have you told your mom and dad about the quilt and our get-together?"

"I said something to Mom, but she did not have much of a reaction. Remember, she and Grandma Davis did not always see eye to eye, and she never really got to know Aunt Julia. I guess

Grandma was not the best mother-in-law. I think Mom might be surprised Aunt Julia really did make a quilt top on her own."

"You don't regret living here by all of us do you?"

"Of course not, it's really more of a family than if I were living back home," she smiled at me with affection. "I probably would never see them, as they are always so busy. I guess that's why I wonder why they only had me and no other children. Do you ever wonder about that Anne? Do you ever feel lonely as the only child?"

"Oh, sure, but Mother always said she had trouble getting pregnant, and I was not an easy pregnancy, so I guess that took care of that."

"Come to think of it, there was a little mention of that the other day so maybe that's the reason," Sue commented, like she wanted to console me. "At least you were given a good reason. I usually made up my own reasons for being the only one. There were times growing up that I wondered if they were sorry they even had me. They were both so busy that a lot of the conversations in our house seemed to be about who was going to take care of me when. I guess that's silly. But, still, I think it may be part of the reason I wanted to stay here in Colebridge."

As I locked the door promptly at 5:00, I yelled out to Sue, as she put on her coat, "See you tomorrow, anytime you want!"

Aunt Julia and Aunt Marie arrived right after the late church service. They brought oatmeal cookies and a healthy-sized blue cheese ball.

"Where is Sarah?" I asked looking outside the front door.

"She is with a friend at the mall, so I hope she'll be home about the time I told her to be back," Aunt Julia said. "I don't know this girl's parents, so I hope they bring her home when she said they would."

"Have any of you been quilting since we were here last?" Aunt Marie asked.

"Mother and I put a few more stitches in, but not adding much improvement."

"Well let's get down there and take a look," Aunt Marie said.

We walked down the stairs, turning on all the lamps to get the best lighting. It was another dreary winter day, which seemed to beg for a fire, hazelnut-flavored coffee, and quilting. I turned on the gas fireplace in the corner that had kept out many winter chills through the years.

Everyone went back to the chairs where they had sat before, except for Aunt Julia. She walked around looking at the quilt strangely as if she were going to grade everyone on their stitches. "Didn't I sit here by you, Sylvia, and quilt around these fans last week?" Aunt Julia asked. "Look, you can see where I stitched, but the thread has been taken out," she exclaimed with a hurt look on her face.

Mother said quickly, "Well, that's impossible, Julia!"

"Are you sure you didn't remove them before you left?" I asked.

"Why would I take out my stitches?" Aunt Julia asked. "I know I'm not very good, but I didn't take them out or remove anyone else's!"

I was quick to comment that it was just Mother and I quilting since then, and assured Aunt Julia that we didn't dare take out any stitches.

"If any stitches should be removed, they're mine," I said.

Aunt Julia sat down and did not say another word.

The doorbell rang and I quickly left to go upstairs and answer the door, leaving a very uncomfortable situation in the basement. I was happy to see it was Sue, who came in her jeans, sweatshirt, and with her dog, Muffin, whom she rarely left behind. She was a tiny Chihuahua that never left her heels, so she was a pretty tolerable guest.

"Leave your coat and head downstairs. We are about to get started poking our fingers. Hi there, little Miss Muffin!"

Everyone greeted Sue and Muffin except for Aunt Julia, who was still quiet and hurt.

"Sue, just to fill you in, Aunt Julia's stitches were taken out of the quilt since she was here last and none of us have an explanation."

"That's crazy, obviously someone did." Sue said. "Mine should have been taken out for sure!"

"I wish someone would just tell me if my stitches are unacceptable instead of removing them," Aunt Julia said with some hint of anger. "They didn't just disappear on their own. This is my quilt, and I will be happy with anyone's stitches."

She was nearly in tears, but no one knew how to respond.

Finally, Mother spoke. "Okay, this is my house and I know when people come and go here," she said. "I know that it's just been Anne and I quilting since last week, and we would never, ever do anything like that, so let's just all calm down and think this through."

With that said, I went upstairs to put on the coffee. "Perhaps I should bring down the vodka instead!" I said trying to warm the frigid air.

I was so puzzled; I simply didn't know what would happen next. Would Mother actually do something like that without saying anything to me? I could see why maybe Aunt Marie might want some improvement on the quilt, but she had not been there to do so. There was no chatter going on, so I thought I had better suggest we take a break and have some supper. I came down into the basement, and stares came my way, like I was going to admit to the crime.

"Well I'm starved, so I'm going to help myself, will anyone join me?" Sue announced.

Surprisingly, they all said they would quilt awhile before taking a break. That was the mysterious thing about quilting; you couldn't get yourself to stop easily. You always wanted to quilt just a little more to complete an area.

"Are everyone else's stitches where they should be?" Aunt Marie half-jokingly asked. "Sylvia, have you ever had any ghosts here in this house you haven't told us about? Anne, what about it? Better speak up if you and Sylvia are aware of any spirits!" With that said, we all laughed a bit to ease the tension in the room.

"You know, our mother made a quilt for Anne when she was little," Aunt Marie smiled. "It had fairies on it, remember, Anne? I helped a little bit with that, so she taught me a thing or two about quilting."

"I know I do," said Mother. "I remember she was determined to wait to see if you were a girl or a boy before she would start one. I kept telling her you would be a girl. I just knew it!"

"I loved that quilt and had it on my bed for a long time. It had a different fairy on each block. I would play a little game and name each one of them."

"Do you still have it?" Sue asked.

"I guess so. Mother, where would it be, do you know?"

"I think I might. Give me a minute and I will check that chest in the guest room."

Mother went up the stairs, and I asked Aunt Marie and Aunt Julia about Grandma's quilts. "Do you all have any of the quilts Grandma Davis made?"

"I certainly don't," Aunt Julia snapped. "Your mother and Marie do, however. They somehow had many things from our mother that I never had."

"You were younger," Aunt Marie consoled. "We were setting up housekeeping and you were still in school. You were not that interested at the time."

"So it seemed. You have been kind enough not to mention that Mother never thought I could take care of anything, nor could I do anything to please her, so it's no wonder!"

Mother coming down the stairs with my quilt was perfect timing. No one had to reply to Aunt Julia's accusations.

"Look what I found!"

Everyone stopped quilting to take a look, and I made sure I commented about how special the quilt was to me growing up.

"Getting pregnant with Anne was a big deal if any of you can remember how long it took us to achieve that," Mother said.

"Now that you found it, I think I'll keep that at the end of my bed just to look at," I smiled.

"Look at your grandmother's stitches, Anne," Aunt Marie said. "They are so tiny, even, and small. She must have had a lot of practice. I know when I was learning, she was so picky about my stitches and took them out at the end of the day when I wasn't looking. I would come to the quilt and want to brag about my stitches and they were gone! I felt like Julia here!"

"Yikes," said Sue. "This is sounding mighty familiar, you guys!"

We went silent and looked at one another. I think everyone was thinking what I was about to say.

"Well, Grandmother, we wish you could see us and join in, but taking out Aunt Julia's stitches is really spooky," I laughed.

Aunt Julia got up from the quilting frame and said she needed to get on home.

"Oh, Julia," Mother pleaded. "Please don't get upset. We're just joking around, and the soup is ready upstairs."

"No thanks, I can't digest all this," Aunt Julia pouted. "You all enjoy and decide who's going to come clean about tearing out my stitches."

Off she went upstairs and out the front door, before we could respond. This was a Kodak moment I hoped would not be remembered. She offered no thanks to Mother and no further good-byes to any of us.

CHAPTER 5

Days passed without anyone calling or talking about when we would be quilting again. I could tell it was bothering Mother, even though she didn't say anything.

I was finishing up my morning coffee and toasted English muffin when I suggested that we give everyone a call to quilt that evening.

"We'll just have wine and cheese," I said. "Aunt Julia has to come back sometime; it's her quilt." Mother offered to call her, so I said I would call the rest.

"I bet by now she realizes how silly it all was," I said.

"Well, think about it, Anne. Wouldn't you be a bit hurt if someone pulled out all your stitches?" she asked.

"So where did the stitches go? You can see where she had stitched, or I would have guessed she just thought she had quilted there, but really didn't."

The day passed quickly and everyone I called said they could come. I was anxious to find out whether Mother had luck with

Aunt Julia. I left the shop as soon as I could. I had already decided that if a customer came in during the last ten minutes, I was going to tell them I had a family emergency. Certain customers had to drop in late because they, too, were working hours like mine, but I had a few lonesome souls who knew I would be working on the drawer at the counter around closing time, and came to bend my ear. You can bet it was never on anything positive. It was usually political or an unhappy shop owner with a list of folks to blame because he or she had a poor day.

On the way home Ted called me on my cell phone, and I gave him a quick explanation why I had to get home. I said that I would call him later. No doubt he was calling to get together, but I did not let him get that far in the conversation. I was in an impatient mode and sidetracked with thoughts of Aunt Julia. There was no need to fill Ted in on the details, as he was used to my phone calls being answered on the run.

When I got home, the house was quiet. "Hey there, anyone home?" I yelled.

"I'm down here, Anne," Mother answered.

I hung up my coat, grabbed a soda from the fridge, and went down to the basement to join her.

"Anne, come here. I have something to show you." There was concern in her voice. "You won't believe this, but my stitches were taken out from where I quilted this week!"

"Come on, this is not a good joke, let me take a look."

"Look right here." She pointed to a row of stitches she had sewn along one of the borders. Sure enough, there was evidence of where her stitches had been, but the stitches themselves were gone.

"This is crazy and weird, Mother! Did you call Aunt Julia and tell her?" I looked over the area where her stitches had been.

"No, I just discovered it when I sat down to get a head start

22

on the others," she sounded as if she were testifying in court. "Besides, Julia said she had a meeting, and wouldn't be here. She wasn't talkative and cut me pretty short, so I didn't prolong the conversation."

The doorbell rang before I could respond to Mother. I went up the stairs to let in Aunt Marie. Sue was just parking her car, and I waited for her and Muffin to get to the door and then took their coats. The first words out of Aunt Marie's mouth were, "Is your Aunt Julia coming?"

"No. She has a meeting; at least that's what she told Mother. I'm going to take the glasses downstairs. Sue, would you bring that cheese platter and bottle of wine?"

"Now, Anne, I thought the food and drinks were supposed to stay upstairs so we don't get the quilt soiled?" Sue joked. "Aunt Julia will not appreciate us messing up her quilt, especially with her not here!"

"Not tonight. We are going to really need this wine for sure when you hear what has happened."

Everyone carried something down the stairs and Aunt Marie said, "Sounds like we are going to party tonight, Sylvia. Anne, let's have some of this wine."

"Yes indeed, good idea, Anne. Pour us a glass as quick as you can."

"Oh, you have my favorite kind." said Sue. "I never met a merlot I didn't like, but I can never afford fine wine or fine dining, so this is awesome. Thank you!"

"I'll take whatever you have uncorked," said Aunt Marie. "So, what's up, Sylvia?"

"See this?" Mother pointed to the part of the quilt in front of her.

No one said a word, not knowing what she was trying to say or show.

"My stitches from a few days ago are gone! Gone like Julia's! All gone!"

Everyone had a look like there was a joke to follow, but no one wanted to laugh prematurely. I took that to mean that they didn't know if we were joking or if indeed we really had a problem.

"Unless Mother took them out herself, we have a situation here," I said. "I haven't been down here since you all left."

Finally, Sue sighed. "Aunt Julia is not going to believe this, of course. She'll think you all just did this to make her feel better."

"So does this mean we need not bother stitching if someone, whoever that is, is going to take out our stitches?" Mother asked. "Who is going to be next?"

Before she could get a response, the doorbell rang. I sprang from my chair and wondered who could be arriving at this late hour. Ted knew everyone was coming over so it wouldn't be him. I opened the door to my surprise to find Aunt Julia.

"Hi," I said in astonishment. "I thought you couldn't come! I'm so glad you decided to."

"My meeting was very short and I was feeling guilty knowing you were all here and working on MY quilt," she said.

"You'll be glad you did, because we need your help, especially tonight." I gave her a little hug. "Will you have some wine? We took it downstairs tonight, and I told them all they better be careful. Here's your glass."

As Aunt Julia came down the stairs, no one knew quite what to say, so I made the first comment. "Aunt Julia got finished early, so she decided to help us tonight after all!"

"How come no one is quilting?" she spoke into the silence. "Are you taking a break, or just enjoying the wine?"

"Okay, I'll be the one to fill her in," I offered. "Mother came down to quilt today and her stitches were removed, just

24

like yours were. Here, see for yourself." I pointed to the row of stitches taken out.

Aunt Julia's look was peculiar; we all waited for a response.

"Good story, you guys," she laughed.

Mother then said, "I'm serious Julia; it's so weird."

"Look, it is what it is. Who the heck knows what's going on, but I want this quilt quilted, so let's all get busy," Aunt Julia commanded as she sat down at her place.

We all resumed our seats and Sue passed around the cheese tray. She also changed the subject by telling us that she had made a point to look for a quilt that she had as a child, and was pleased she found it.

"The thing is really worn." She pulled it out of a large, used shopping bag. "I guess it shouldn't have been washed so often. I have always loved this so much. I even took it to college and kept in my dorm room. I took another look at it now that I'm such a quilting connoisseur, of course, and those darn stitches are pretty tiny. I don't know who made it. Do any of you?"

No one responded. I thought it a bit odd, since everyone knew about my fairy quilt. I wondered what was going though Sue's mind with this dead silence.

"Well, whoever gave it to you would be pleased to know you love it so much," said Aunt Marie. "You know I've told you and Anne before that I have something quilted put aside for whoever gets to the altar first, but no one seems to be in a hurry."

"Don't even bring it up to me," said Sue. "I am not Anne, and may never get married. I don't even date, nor do I really care. I see so many unhappy married people, and then unhappy divorced people that I always say to myself how glad I am that I don't have their problems. I am a professional bridesmaid, not bride material, I'm afraid."

"Don't feel bad about any of that, Sue. No one is going to rush me down the aisle, just ask Mother and Ted."

"I think you girls are smart," said Aunt Julia. "Just between these walls, I don't think I would do it over again, except then I wouldn't have Sarah."

"Julia, how can you say that?" Mother asked.

"Well, it doesn't take long for the honeymoon to be over, and then before you know it, you are not the apple of his eye any longer. Frankly, I almost don't care. Let the next person in his life deal with him!"

"Julia!" Aunt Marie said sharply. "You don't mean that." She paused, "Or do you, and why would you say such a thing?"

Aunt Julia got up from her seat, moving over to refill her glass. She had her back to us and when she turned around she had tears in her eyes.

"Shoot, I don't know why I brought it up, but I guess I am tired of pretending everything is okay when it's not. I have suspected for some time that Jim has been seeing someone. But then he'll be his own self for a while, so then I think I must be making it all up in my head. I guess most of the time I'm in denial; it's just easier that way."

"Have you ever confronted him?" I asked.

"One time I did, and he really flew off the handle, to where it scared me. He said to never bring such a thing like that up again. He said if I was that insecure, it was my problem and not his."

"How mean is that?" stormed Aunt Marie. "It isn't just your problem; it's a problem that involves two people in the marriage."

"Of course it's never the man's fault, right!" I said. "The problem always seems to be with the person who brings up the problem. I hear it over and over at the shop."

"Oh, my God, Julia, what are you going to do?" Mother worried. "I can't believe Jim would do such a thing. I thought he was always crazy about you. You know we'll support any decision you make, but just make sure about what really may be going on."

"If he will not talk to her about her fears and concerns, he's hiding something," I said. "This is something none of us can advise you on, because we want it to be what's right for you. I, however, don't think anyone should put up with an affair. I know I wouldn't."

"Don't be so hasty there, Anne," Aunt Marie said. "Fred got off the track early in our marriage with some young hussy at work, and when he confessed it all to me, I forgave him. He was not the sort to get involved like that, and come to find out, more than one person at his work succumbed to her flirtatious invites. After that, it seemed like our marriage was even stronger, and I learned to trust him again, and was so very glad I did not throw him away! Everyone makes mistakes!"

"Gosh, Marie, you never told us that," Mother was not the only one who was astonished.

"Why should I have? We worked it out, and I didn't want anyone holding that against Fred. I really felt he was sorry! Everyone liked Fred. He really was not a womanizer, as they call men like that now."

"Good for you, Marie, but I'm afraid no one is sorry for anything at this moment in time, except me, that is," Aunt Julia declared.

"We will not share any of this with anyone," said Sue. "What is said in this basement should stay in this basement. I feel badly for both of you. Is there anything we can do?"

"Forget we had this conversation," Aunt Julia was firm. "I will give it my best shot, and we'll see what happens."

"Hey, you all, I think we can roll this one end of the quilt now,"

Mother claimed. "This is great! We are moving right along. Can we do that Marie?"

"Not tonight," I interjected. "We're all tired and mentally challenged, so I think we need to call it a night, and meet up Sunday afternoon if anyone can come."

One by one, we all hugged Aunt Julia and Aunt Marie and went upstairs to say our quiet good-byes.

CHAPTER 6

It was two days later before Mother and I had a chance to visit about the conversation that took place when our quilting group last met. I was taking my time getting to work that morning because I didn't have a busy day and knew I would be covered. Mother poured my second cup of coffee and offered me another slice of toast.

"So what do you think will happen with Julia?" Mother asked. "It's been on my mind constantly. I'm sure she is also thinking about what our mother would be saying right now."

"You mean she would be blaming Aunt Julia instead of Jim?"

"Yeah, I'm afraid so. She is probably thinking about how she must have done something wrong to drive Jim to another woman. Julia is an easy person to take advantage of and I'm afraid Mother was hard on her for some reason, which just made matters worse for Julia. Little things like trying to help her succeed with this quilt would be a good thing for her."

"Well, we will all help make that happen. Let's stay focused so it does indeed get finished. I am glad she confided in us, aren't you?"

"Yes, I guess, but I would feel better not knowing, especially if and when I see Jim again. I will definitely plan on giving some time to the quilt on Sunday afternoon."

The next night I promised to meet Ted at Q's Seafood and Grill for dinner and a movie. Why I felt it was my duty to make time for him I don't know. Why did I not get excited to see him? He was handsome, easy to get along with, came from a good family in town, and had a good job. I told myself I had to wait on long term commitments right now because I was trying to build my business, and I resented having to spend my time socializing.

He walked into the bar just as chipper as always. I have to admit the gentle kiss and hug were a welcomed touch. "I've missed you!" he said. "I know it's been crazy, but I have to tell you I am looking forward to some good salmon, what do you think?"

"Sure, I'm up for it." I answered.

"So what's keeping you so busy, sweetie?"

"We have had two funerals this week. Do you remember Sam Wood from Wood Chemical?"

"Not really."

"Well, people are calling in from every state to send flowers. I knew his daughter, Darlene, and she was one of many kids they had. He died quite suddenly from a heart attack, so it shocked a lot of people. I am thrilled with all the business, but tomorrow is the drop dead date to get it done!"

"Literally, speaking, right?" Ted joked.

"Yes, indeed, mister! We are also trying hard to give Aunt Julia some time with getting her quilt quilted. Everyone was over last night and it was an interesting evening to say the least!"

"What do you mean?"

I waited until we received our drinks, and then went over in my mind what I really wanted Ted to know and not know. "I may as well share with you something that's been happening, that has truly been a mystery to all of us. Promise you won't laugh?"

"No, I can't promise that because it may deserve a good laugh." He smiled.

"Go ahead, call us crazy, but this has happened two times, so there's something going on. Aunt Julia made some quilting stitches in the quilt, and when she returned on her next visit, they had been taken out and none of us did it! Then, the next time we got together, Mother started to quilt where she left off, and her stitches were all removed on the border where she had been quilting."

I knew by the look on his face he was not taking me seriously like I wanted him to. "Well, it seems to me that someone doesn't like what's being done or how it's being done, and they want the person to start over. You just haven't figured out who is not willing to come forward and confess."

"Ted, you don't understand. No one, no one, did this. No one would ever do this, and no one else has been in the house, much less the basement!"

"Did you ever read the book *Gone Again* by Richard Welling?" he asked.

"No, I haven't. Tell me about it."

"It's supposed to be a true story. They were talking about it at work when it came out, and I have to admit that I couldn't put the book down. I won't tell you the whole story line, because you may want to read it. It tells about things disappearing, and they were supposedly taken by anyone who disagreed with what was occurring. It doesn't necessarily have to be a live person. Things were taken by some sisters who all died in this house. They took the things after they had died. There was a murder and all sorts of occurrences with the new owners of the house, and each sister was protesting in her own way by driving the owners nuts! If you're so certain it's none of you, then I suggest you question the dead."

"Ted, I can't believe you are telling me this! Do you believe in ghosts?"

"I do after reading this book. Others read it when I did, and many had their own ghost stories to tell. It's hard to discount what people say is true, just like you can't question your quilters on what they tell you. Hey, we're going to miss our reservation, drink up! We can take up this subject later."

The restaurant dining room was dark and relaxing. I did not bring up Ted's ghost remarks until we had ordered our dinner. I couldn't help but be impressed that he was open to the idea of ghosts. He always seemed so "straight arrow" in politics and career decisions. I leaned over to give him an unexpected kiss, and finally responded to his remark about missing me.

"You are a sweetie," I softly said in his ear. "I missed you, too. I am so pleased that you understand my time choices; I know most guys would not!"

He smiled at me. "So who do you think your ghost could be?"

"I don't know who lived in our house before, so that's no help. I've lived there all my life, and no one has died there. My dad died at the hospital."

"Do any of you have any enemies who would object to what you are doing? Dead enemies, that is?"

I couldn't help but laugh.

Our dinner was served, and although my mind was preoccupied with Ted's question, we changed the subject to a planned trip that he had to go on with his boss. It was a struggle to have to listen to all his concerns when I was really thinking about who might be upset with our quilting bee.

Ted dropped me back at my car at the shop. As always, I declined a short stop by his apartment, telling him I had to get up early the next day. In spite of myself, I had to admit that it was a great visit, nice dinner, and some interesting insight into our mystery at home.

CHAPTER 7

Friday morning I left to get an early start at the shop. Luckily, I did not wonder the night away thinking about all our dead enemies! Maybe they weren't enemies, I thought.

Sue came in on her lunch hour to add ribbons to our afternoon deliveries. "Sue, have you ever read the book, *Gone Again?*"

"No, but I have heard of it."

"I'm going to stop at the library after work to see if I can get it. Ted recommended it last night, and I think it may be helpful regarding our stitch stealer."

She laughed. "Are you serious?"

"I'll let you know. Do you know if Aunt Julia or my mother had any enemies growing up?"

"What kind of question is that?" Sue gave me a strange look.

"Think about it, okay?"

With that, Kevin came in to take the delivery and I reminded Sue that we were still on for Sunday afternoon. "I'll bring my delicious chocolate brownies, would you like that? Around 2:00, would that be a good time?"

"You bet. Would you call Aunt Marie and Aunt Julia to remind them? Be sure to include Sarah. She will love your brownies."

"I'll call them when I get home," Sue said.

I didn't get out of the shop till 6:30 that evening but the library was open till 9:00, so off I went. I planned to put on my pajamas and hunker down with the intriguing book for the night. Mother would be reading when I got home or she would be out with friends. Mother was always reading. She was a librarian for many years, and I grew up with books, books, and more books.

Gone Again was now in my hands, but the long day had taken a toll on my ability to stay awake. I read till I dropped off to sleep, getting through about one hundred pages. When I woke up the next morning, I wanted to take the book with me to work to catch a few pages during lunch.

When I came downstairs, Mother said Sue already called to say everyone could make quilting on Sunday afternoon. "Great. Did Sue tell you she would bring her delicious brownies? That is Grandmother's recipe, isn't it?"

"Yes, I believe it is. I have it also, but never think to make them, like I did when you were younger. I guess some things you don't outgrow, huh?"

"Mother, do you know if there is anyone from the past in Aunt Julia's life who would want to harm her in any way, or would want to haunt her?"

"What kind of question is that, Anne?"

"Just think about it; I have my reasons for asking." I could tell it had upset her, so I said I was leaving. I wished I hadn't asked, but it was certainly on my mind.

CHAPTER 8

Sunday came and a cold and cloudy fall day it was. I went to church with Mother, and we heard the weather report was calling for snow showers.

"I'm sure it won't keep anyone from coming this afternoon," I said. "Besides, I can't think of anything better than to make some coffee, eat a good brownie, share a little gossip, and quilt!"

Mother laughed. "If they don't come, you and I will do just fine."

Sue was the first to show up, I was glad to see. "Just so you know, I'm a big chicken with snow. If it gets bad, I am out of here!" she said.

"Just leave your brownies!" Mother took the container of goodies into the kitchen.

A few minutes later Aunt Julia and Aunt Marie showed up, shaking the snowflakes off their coats. "I need that coffee now!" Aunt Marie said to Mother.

"It's hot and ready, so take it on down to the basement."

We all chatted away, found our usual chairs and then sat down. "Oh Sylvia, we would have helped you roll the quilt. You didn't have to do this by yourself, or did Anne help you?" Aunt Julia asked. Mother and I looked at each other, waiting for one or the other to respond.

"Julia, neither Anne nor I rolled the quilt," Mother said slowly.

I could not believe my eyes. The quilt indeed had been rolled. Mother, I know, could not have done it alone. I didn't do it and I sure didn't help her.

"Here we go again!" Sue said.

"This really isn't cute and clever you know," Aunt Julia fumed. "The two of you are the only ones around this quilt. Maybe I'm missing something, but I don't see the humor in these little stunts."

"Okay, everyone calm down. I was telling Ted about these occurrences the other night. We definitely have something going on here that we can't explain. That means, whether we believe it or not, something of the supernatural is happening. We don't see the humor in this, believe me, Aunt Julia. Ted told me to read a book called *Gone Again*. It is supposed to be a true story. Things happen to people like us if there is someone from the past that is trying to communicate with us. It could be someone with good feelings or bad feelings. It sounds like it is someone who has close connections to Mother and you, Aunt Julia."

"We do not have a ghost in this house," Mother was adamant. "At least we didn't until this happened. It can't be a bad spirit; at least no one has been harmed. It must be someone trying to communicate something. It appears to me that someone wants to be a part of this quilting process."

"Well, if I ever!" Aunt Marie shook her head. "I never believed in all that nonsense."

"I do," said Sue. "I think it's Grandmother Davis trying to communicate with us. She was a quilter, and maybe she's just trying to show us how to do things."

"Then she's still looking over my shoulder," Aunt Julia said slowly, her voice hollow. "If it is her, I wouldn't be surprised. She isn't convinced I can't do this without her. She still has to criticize and be in control, gosh darn it!"

"Oh, Julia, that is a bit much," Mother frowned.

"What else did the book say when and if this happens?" Sue asked.

"Well in this story, some sisters died in this home. As the former owners, they were upset and were trying to send the new owners messages," I said. "They weren't harmful, but until they were acknowledged, they kept doing things."

"So, how did the new people acknowledge the ghosts?" Sue asked.

"They calmly decided they weren't bad people, tried to understand the sisters' concerns, and then actually started talking to them."

"Boy, I'm glad I didn't bring Sarah today. Do you think it's our mother, too, Sylvia?"

"Mother, can you think of anyone else in your life who would want to communicate with you?" I asked.

"Our mother didn't bother me much like she did Marie and Julia. I was in the middle and ignored more than noticed."

"I don't like to go there. It's pretty silly if you ask me, but who else would it be?" said Aunt Marie.

"Look, Sue and Aunt Marie are the only ones getting some quilting done," Aunt Julia said. Everyone still was not focused on the quilt, but we reluctantly started quilting.

"I think I'll get the brownies before everyone runs away from the basement ghost," Mother laughed. She went on upstairs, and when I turned to check on the others' quilting, I noticed that Sue was still not using a thimble, and seemed to be hurting; she kept switching fingers.

"Why don't you wear a thimble, Sue?" I asked. "Aunt Marie has some to try on, did you not do that?"

"I did try them, and if I have one on, it gets in the way so I use another finger."

"Someone told me at the shop that if we get a drop of blood on the quilt, our own spit will take out the blood, but no one else's will," I offered. "Mrs. Johnson, who comes in the shop, told me that when I told her I was a beginning quilter."

"I'm sure it will happen eventually, so it's good to know," chuckled Aunt Julia.

Mother, who had brought down the brownies, said, "Be careful everyone, I don't think your spit is going to take out chocolate stains. A little spit never hurt anyone."

"How are things at home, if you don't mind me asking?" Aunt Marie turned toward Aunt Julia.

"Jim is quite puzzled about why I continue to come over here so often even though he knows darn well it's a legitimate reason," she mused. "He always wants to know when I'll be home and where he can reach me. I wish it was because he really cared, but unfortunately he needs to know these details to fit into his secret schedule."

"Do you have any idea who it is he could possibly be seeing?" Sue asked.

"I'm sure it's someone at work, because it's easy, and there are many young beauties to choose from," Aunt Julia said.

"Have you confronted him?" I asked without being sure I really wanted to know.

"Nope. I'm not up to it, frankly. Besides, this could pass. I even wonder if I'm so blasé about it because I may not even love him anymore. I dread the thought of this coming to a head because of Sarah. She adores him, you know. I guess most daughters are like that with their dads."

"What if he admits things and says he is sorry? Would you forgive him?" I asked.

"I don't know right now, Anne." she answered sadly.

I looked at the clock and realized it was nearly five o'clock. The snow flurries had stopped, which eased everyone's minds. Ted was coming by to pick me up at six, and I needed to change clothes.

"You know, I have plenty of leftover lasagna, if you all want to stay for dinner." Mother offered. "We've wasted time trying to solve our mystery and didn't get much quilting done."

"Well, Sarah is spending the day with her friend Angie, so I'll call and tell her that I'll pick her up a little later. She will love the idea."

"Hey, I won't turn down a free meal," Sue said, getting up from her chair. "No one's waiting for me to get home, so if you'll let me help you, Aunt Sylvia, I'll stay."

I thought to myself how sad it must be for Sue not to have anyone special in her life. She didn't have many interests to speak of. She was lazy at times with her appearance and was a hot fudge sundae away from being too plump.

Mother and Aunt Marie went upstairs, but I couldn't pull myself away from the two that were left to quilt, plus I wanted to finish the design I started with. "I think I'm getting a tad better," I said. "What do you all think?" Aunt Julia was the first to respond and echoed my observation.

"Did you say you were getting together with Ted tonight?" Sue asked.

"Oh my goodness, I guess I won't be changing clothes. We're just going over to watch a game at his friend Andy's house. They're having food and we're bringing the wine, so it's no big deal. Frankly, I would rather have Mother's lasagna."

"He is so easygoing, isn't he?" asked Aunt Julia.

"Yes, and it's a good thing he is or he would not be able to be in my life."

"I just love him, Anne; you better not screw things up!" Sue grinned.

I could hear voices upstairs and realized Ted had arrived. As he walked down the stairs, he joyfully greeted us. "So this is the 'basement quilt' I've been hearing so much about!"

"Yes, indeed," Aunt Julia answered.

"What do you think of our quilt, Ted?" I rose to greet him.

"I don't know about these things, but it's very colorful!"

"Aunt Julia did the whole top herself, which is a lot of work," I said.

"Well, I have a little something for you, Anne," he said. "Your quilting buddies might enjoy it as well."

"I love presents! What is it?" I took a prettily wrapped package out of his hand.

I tore off the lovely paper, and inside was a very large and colorful quilt book, entitled *How to Make a Beautiful Quilt*. "Oh my, I didn't know they made such beautiful books on quilting! I thought it might be the book *Gone Again*. I went to the library by the way, and picked it up. I am halfway through. I was telling everyone about it this afternoon."

"Let me see the quilt book," Sue reached for it.

Mother and Aunt Marie came down to join us and started to admire the book. It had everything you would ever want to know from what fabric and notions to buy to how to finish a quilt. The colorful quilts were quite beautiful, but out of my league as a quilter right now. The thoughtful gift was just like Ted to do such a thing.

"Anne said someday she may make her own quilt, so I wanted to encourage her," Ted teased.

"We will hold her to that," Mother smiled.

CHAPTER 9

———⌘———

The next morning, I came down to the kitchen to find Mother looking through my quilt book. "Aren't these amazing quilts?" she asked.

"Yes, I spotted a lovely pattern that would be perfect for my flower shop."

"Flower shop? That's a bit strange. I think most of these are for beds. Wouldn't you want to have something for your future or even one for the bed you have now?"

"A lot of the quilts are wall quilts," I defended my idea. "I spend many hours in my shop, and what a great conversation piece that would be if I had a quilt on the wall with flowers on it. I was going to show it to Aunt Marie and see if she knew how difficult it would be. I hate Mondays," I continued. "My most difficult salesman is coming in today, and there's no getting rid of him. He just hangs out like he has nothing else to do."

"Will you be home for dinner?"

"Yes, and I shouldn't be too late if I don't have interruptions.

They sure enjoyed the lasagna last night didn't they? There isn't any left for my lunch today, I noticed."

"Yes, indeed they did. It was pretty late before Marie left."

"Really, why was that?" I asked.

"Oh, we sat in the living room by the fire and had a nice talk. She is quite worried about Julia. She has always looked out for her since Mother died. She was the oldest sister, and Julia could easily get into trouble. Marie had to go through an affair early in her marriage and she never, ever talked about it until with us here the other night. Years ago, you didn't talk about such things, plus, it was embarrassing. I don't think even Julia knows much about it other than she knew there was a time Marie and Fred didn't get along. I think she would have divorced him if divorce was as accepted back then as it is today. She stayed with him because our mother said once you made your bed, you sleep in it. I know Marie doesn't want Julia to have to go through that pain. Boy, I hope this affair is just Julia's imagination. Soon after Marie found out, Fred got cancer and she had to take care of him all those years till he died. I sure give her a lot of credit for hanging in there, but as a result, it cheated her out of many years of happiness. I am sure all that is going through her mind as she listens to Julia talk about Jim."

"For heavens sake, I had no idea." I sat down to digest this news. "Poor Aunt Marie. Grandmother was quite demanding with everyone, it sounds like. I see why Aunt Julia feels she never quite measured up. What would Grandma say now if she knew about Aunt Julia and Uncle Jim?"

"She would give the same advice, I'm sure. Our dad was much easier going. Your grandma definitely ruled the house."

"Oh, my, I need to get going, Mother." I put on my coat. "Have a great day, try not to worry, and I'll see you for dinner."

As I got in my car, I couldn't help but be preoccupied with what Mother had told me.

I was making great headway at the shop for a Monday. That's because Mr. Johnson cancelled his appointment. It allowed me to accomplish a great deal, and Mondays were generally slower to begin with. I worked on an ad that I wanted to come out before Thanksgiving. From now till Christmas Eve, it would be busy, busy, busy in my little shop, I hoped.

Sue came by on her lunch hour since she was running an errand nearby. "Is anyone quilting tonight?" She stood in the open doorway.

"I don't believe my ears." I looked up from the colorful floral display on my counter. "Like someone said to me recently, what is a young, single girl like you doing at a quilting frame?"

"I know, but I think I'm really enjoying my contribution to the quilt and being close to the family," Sue said, finally closing the front door behind her. "I don't date, have very little social life, and you all are so good to me."

"Well, how about we meet at the house and you have a bite to eat with us? Mother would love it."

"Oh, I couldn't possibly take advantage of her good food two nights in a row."

I reassured her we always had plenty and called Mother. She decided to call the others just in case they were available. After Sue went back to work, I got to thinking how if she lost twenty pounds and got a new hairstyle she could certainly get someone's attention. But who could ever say that to her? It would not be me if I wanted to keep a cousin and a very good weekend employee. I used to keep an eye out for anyone I could fix her up with, but gave up with my busy life and her disinterest in the matter. Besides, I myself hardly had time to date.

CHAPTER 10

————⊙⊙⊙————

Mother was delighted to have Sue join us for some of her wonderful meat loaf. "I heard from Julia, and she can't join us for dinner, but she will come later after she goes to a school thing with Sarah. I haven't heard from Marie, which concerns me a bit."

After a delicious dinner, Sue, Mother, and I went downstairs. Mother turned on the lights, and we went to our places. "I'm so tired." I dropped into my chair. "I hope I can muster up some stitches."

Sue said, "Oh look, someone forgot her thimble. I wonder whose this is? It's where I sit, but I don't use a thimble. Look familiar anyone?"

"That doesn't look like any of ours." I studied it.

"Let me see that." Mother held it up to her eyes. She looked at it closely, as Sue and I started quilting.

"This is your grandmother's thimble," Mother slowly announced. "I haven't seen this since she died. We have looked for this everywhere. Has Julia or Marie been using this?"

"I don't think so but you can ask them when they come," I said. "I know Aunt Julia is using a brass one, because she commented on the design of it on the edge."

"Why would it be where I was quilting?" asked Sue like it was placed there on purpose.

"Okay, it must be Marie's," Mother said. "Maybe she found it, which would be great. I always admired it. Mother always wore it, and told us it was sterling silver. At the funeral, we even discussed putting it on her finger before we closed the casket."

"Oh, my word, Mother! Why would you do that?"

"Because we hardly ever saw her without it, that's why. She always had a quilt in the frame. She used to brag about having the prettiest thimble in her quilting group at church. She likely got it from her mother."

"It is very beautiful, Mother, but are you sure that's really hers?"

"Oh yes, no mistake." She got up from her chair. "I will put it here on the table so we can ask Marie."

Another half hour passed, and Mother was getting antsy because she hadn't heard from Aunt Marie. "I'm going to give her a call; this is not like her."

"Here, use my cell phone." Sue handed it to her. Mother waited for Aunt Marie to answer to no avail.

"Now I'm really getting worried." She paced the room.

The doorbell rang, and Mother ran upstairs, hoping it was her older sister. It was Aunt Julia. She was pretty soaked, as it was pouring down rain. Mother filled her in on the concern of not hearing from Aunt Marie.

"She probably had another event to go to, and didn't get your message," Aunt Julia said matter-of-factly. "We'll give her a call in an hour or so."

When Aunt Julia got downstairs, Mother didn't waste any

time asking if she had her thimble. "I sure do. I was thinking about getting one of those necklaces that holds a thimble. Have you seen them?" With that, she reached inside her purse.

"Do you know whose thimble this is?" Sue held up the one she had found at her place.

"Oh that looks like Mother's thimble, doesn't it?" She smiled.

"I think it is Mother's," said Mother. "Do you know if this belongs to Marie now?"

"Well if it does, she doesn't use it. She uses one that has that ridge around it, so your needle doesn't slip. I could never use one of those, but she seems to like it."

"Do you remember when we thought about putting it with Mother in her casket, but couldn't find it?"

"Yeah, I kind of do," Aunt Julia said thoughtfully.

"We found this thimble sitting where Sue sits when we came down to quilt this evening," Mother said. "I know this is her thimble. I would know it anywhere, and this was not in the selection of thimbles that Marie offered to all of us."

"You're right, I don't remember it," Aunt Julia nodded.

The phone rang and I made a dash to answer it. "Aunt Marie, we're so glad to hear from you, did you get our message?"

Moments went by as I listened to her explain why she had not come over. "Are you alright? Are you sure? Here, let me let you talk to Mother."

Mother anxiously took the phone. While she was talking, I told Sue and Aunt Julia that Aunt Marie had been having chest pains in the afternoon. She felt it best to be checked out at the emergency room. They looked her over, believed it was indigestion, and after keeping her for awhile, decided to let her go home.

Then I heard Mother ask her, "Marie, remember the silver thimble Mother had all the time, and how we looked for it when she died?" I could tell from their conversation that Marie had not seen the thimble, even after all the questions Mother asked her. "I have it here. We found it on the quilt when we came down tonight. It was where Sue sits."

We could tell from Mother's conversation that Aunt Marie had some reservations about what Mother had told her. We had to laugh when she asked Mother if any stitches had been removed. "Take care, we love you," Mother said as she hung up the phone.

"Is she okay?" asked Sue.

"Yes, at least for now. I am not surprised at her chest pains after our long night of talk last night."

"What was that about?" asked Sue.

"Oh, just old time talk from years back, I guess you could say."

"So the thimble does not belong to her?" asked Aunt Julia.

"No, she hasn't seen it since Mother died," Mother said in disbelief.

"Oh, my dear, here we go again," Aunt Julia said. "Let's see, who could be helping us with our quilt again, Anne? Was Mother's thimble here all along and we didn't notice? Is this all really happening?"

"Anne, why don't you just keep the wine down here so we can help ourselves?" said Sue, swallowing the last from her glass.

"I'll be right back." I went up the stairs to get the wine and glasses. I thought to myself that Sue had a very good idea when she suggested I set up a little bar in the basement so we could have our wine or coffee anytime.

When I came back down, I could tell Mother and Aunt Julia were upset about the thimble, which Sue just took in stride. "So who is going to take the thimble home?" I asked.

"I think it should stay here somewhere, in case anyone wants to use it," said Sue. "You never know, it may disappear on us, just as easily as it appeared."

With that Mother broke into tears. "This is part of her," she choked, putting her hands to her head. "She is here with us, I just know it. God, I miss her."

I moved over to console Mother and hugged her. "I can imagine how you feel. I would feel the same way, if that were you! I remember Grandma, too, and I can't help but think she would be so proud that we were not only all together as a family, but that we were quilting, just like she did."

Now we had Aunt Julia in tears. "You know I have taken all this activity so personally, but really, it's not just about me," she wiped tears from her cheeks. "She took out your stitches too, Sylvia. She wanted Sue to use a thimble so she provided her with one. She even helped us roll the quilt, so it's all not bad, and it's all not about me!"

"Well, this is all good, and we have more important things to think and pray about, like Marie," Mother reminded us. With that, we decided to call it a night. A very long and weary night it was!

CHAPTER 11

Almost a week had passed, and I was reminded by my shop calendar that Aunt Marie would have a birthday in a couple of days. I called Mother from the shop and suggested we all get together and take Aunt Marie to lunch. Mother thought it was a great idea, and remarked that her sister loved Donna's Tea Room on Main Street. "I will call Marie and Julia, if you'll call Sue at work, because I don't have her work number," Mother said. "I will tell them 12:00. Will that work for you at the shop?"

"Yes, as a matter of fact it will. You might tell her to invite that nice neighbor that she has, or anyone else she wants, as far as I'm concerned."

"That's a good idea," Mother agreed.

Aunt Marie was thrilled, although she thought everyone was just making a fuss because she had made a trip to the hospital. She and Fred never had any children so she felt very close to our small family. She was always very attractive and her dark hair was slow to gray. When I think back, I wonder why she never found anyone to remarry. Fred left her with financial freedom so she didn't have that pressure to bear on finding someone. She often hinted that things that I admired might be mine someday.

I arranged for some flowers, of course, which was my usual practice. I tried to keep a pretty detailed birthday calendar of family, friends, and good customers so I could remember them with a flower or two. I also made notes on what their favorite flowers were. I checked on what I had been sending Aunt Marie. She loved yellow roses.

She was in luck, as I had some in stock.

Donna's Tea Room always made our visits very special. It was Victorian style, but Donna Howard, the owner, had good taste, and didn't give you that "funeral home" feeling when you ate lunch there. Her seasonal touches in décor were amazing every year, and her coconut cream pie and soups were always my favorites. Mother made the reservations, and we all showed up on time. Everyone looked pretty fashionable compared to the casual clothes we wore while quilting.

"Aunt Marie, you look wonderful. Have you had any more pains?" I asked as she approached our table.

"No, thank goodness. I have a new hairdresser, did you notice?"

"Maybe that's what it is," I exclaimed. None of us asked her birthday age, but Mother and Aunt Julia knew, of course. Sue seated herself next to me, and seemed to be in a pretty good mood.

"Whose birthday is next?" Aunt Julia asked.

"You'll never know it's mine," said Sue.

"Oh yes, we will, Sue, remember our calendar at work?" I joked. I'm amused by how some love to have their birthdays remembered and enjoy the attention, and others feel it is nearly a death sentence and do not want to be reminded. I thought Aunt Marie was enjoying every moment.

"Say Sue, you seem in a pretty good mood today, what's going on?" I asked.

"Well, since we don't seem to have any secrets between us, I have to tell you that Mark Hampton asked me to have a drink with him last night."

"Oh, my gosh! He's in your office right? How did it go?"

"He went to school with you, didn't he, Sue?" Aunt Julia asked.

"Yeah, he knows my mom and dad, and I had a little bit of a crush on him in high school. We just had a nice visit, talking about old times, and then the status of our new boss, Mr. Cook." She paused. "He made the comment that I always heard growing up—that I sure didn't look like either one of my parents."

"So what?" Mother quickly said. "A lot of people don't. I don't think I looked like either my mother or father."

"Oh please, Sylvia, you look exactly like Mother," Aunt Julia claimed.

"Absolutely, Sylvia, we have always thought that," chimed Aunt Marie.

"Who do I look like?" I asked them.

"Your father, I think," said Aunt Marie. They all nodded.

"She's got his personality, too," Mother grinned.

"I kept asking Mother if I had a baby book and she said she wasn't sure," Sue said.

"Who doesn't have a baby book?" I asked. "Do you have your birth certificate here in Colebridge? Maybe it's with that."

"I have a great picture of you and Sue together when you were around three," Aunt Marie said. "You have seen that on my fire-place mantel, haven't you Sue?"

"Yes, weren't we darling?" Sue laughed.

"Having baby books back then is not like it is today, Sue," Aunt Julia said. "Today these young mothers are scrap booking like crazy, and video taping, etc."

"I was the only child, for heaven's sake. You would think there would be a big fat book somewhere! Do you have a baby book, Anne?" Sue asked.

"Yes, I do," I answered proudly. "Mother has always been artistic, so I can see why it was fun for her to do."

"Hey, don't forget, I'm a little younger than you. I'm going to call home tonight and find out where all my things are." Sue said this as if she were going to do it that minute.

The lunch was wonderful as usual, and Aunt Marie was delighted. Sue gave her a gift certificate to our local quilt shop, Isabella's. She couldn't wait to tell us what she might purchase. Mother gave Aunt Marie a lovely scarf, and the rest of us showered her with gifts as well. Donna brought out birthday cake for everyone. Of course, she offered her special pie, too. Aunt Marie blew out the candles, and we all wondered what she wished. Most of the group had to leave, so many took their cake to go. I could not resist the coconut cream pie, so I ordered it to go to have another day.

Sue and Aunt Julia were the first of the family to leave. "Boy, that was a bit uncomfortable, huh Marie," Mother said.

"What are you talking about?" I asked.

"Sue's inquiries about her babyhood are not good," Aunt Marie said. "It will just turn out to be painful for her."

"What in the world do you mean by that?" I was totally in the dark.

"You never told Anne?" Aunt Marie asked Mother.

"Told me what?" I had to wait through a surprising moment of silence before Mother answered.

"Sue was adopted when she was one year old," Mother said. "Ken and Joyce decided not to tell her because they took her from an unfit and unmarried cousin from Fred's side of the family. The mother was a drug addict and had a record of getting into trouble. Ken and Joyce were having trouble getting pregnant, so they fell in love with the idea right away. This practice was not unusual back then."

I was stunned. "For heaven's sake, what a horrible secret to keep from a grown-up adult who has every right to know! How could you all get by with this for so long?"

"It is not our place to tell her, Anne," Mother said firmly. "Every parent makes these choices."

"I wouldn't be surprised if Sue presses them now on some details," I said with concern. "She might put two and two together. I feel so bad for her. She feels lonely enough in this world right now. I hope she doesn't blame all of us in any way when she finds out!" I found it all to be very unsettling, and I worried how Sue would handle such news.

"Thanks for the roses, Anne," Aunt Marie said as she was leaving. "I will be over this weekend to get back to quilting."

Mother, too, put on her coat, and said good-bye.

I sat there for a moment alone, finishing my coffee. How was I going to deal with what I knew, especially if Sue found out that everyone knew but her. How was I, also, going to handle all this, if no one ever decided to tell Sue? Would I be able to keep the secret along with everyone else? Gee, I wondered if any secrets were kept from me? I didn't like secrets and I was uncomfortable with surprises. I liked to be in control and know all the facts. I was beginning to wish they had not shared what they knew with me.

CHAPTER 12

———⊸⊷⊷⊶———

Thanksgiving was just a week away. Aunt Marie generally had all of us over to her house, but there was no mention of it thus far this year. Sue was going home to Ohio to her parents, so that was going to be quite an eye-opening trip. There was no doubt in my mind she would be bringing up questions about her birth. It was certain she would have to share her news with us because we were all so close. She was scheduled to work at the shop the following Saturday, so I knew that would be newsworthy!

The shop was extra messy today. I didn't know how I would clean it to my satisfaction by closing time. My part-time helper, Sally, worked most days but she also went to school part time at night, so today it was up to me to clean up. I didn't mind seeing the mess, however, because it was a sign of a pretty good day! The counter and floor were covered in bits and pieces of happy flowers versus funeral bouquets. The surprise flowers for the Morgan's twenty-fifth anniversary party were bright colors in lovely glass vases that the family brought in to match the other decorations. It was going to be a happy night for all of them. I loved working on special occasions and celebrations instead of arrangements that sad family members would be viewing in the funeral home. How do you balance lovely with sad?

I didn't finish till 6:30 and called Mother and told her I was going by the bookstore and then grab a bite to eat somewhere nearby. Pointer's Book Store on Main Street was just a few blocks from my shop, so I went there often to grab a quick coffee, scope out the latest best sellers, and dream that someday I would be one of those authors. Mother loved the place as well. When I was younger, it was a treat to go there and pick out one book to take home.

They had sandwiches and pastries in their little coffee shop, so I decided it would serve my dinner needs tonight. It was hard not to be interrupted once I got home. Mother always wanted to hear about my day. Unless I could stay awake before bed to read or do my writing, there was rarely a moment to myself. There were times this was comforting and times I wished I had my own digs to vanish to. I was around people all day, so a quiet apartment of my own seemed very tempting at times.

As I entered Pointer's, I saw Harry Stone, the manager. He stopped a minute to ask me how business was. I had known Harry for a long time. He was now working for Vicki Pointer, the daughter of the original owner. His loyalty and love for books and Main Street helped to build the store's business by offering many unique events such as the authors' lecture series each winter. He had been part of their business for many years, originally working for Vicki's father. Harry was always visible and ready to help in any way. He knew I loved to write, so he often guided me to the latest self-help book on writing.

"How's your mother doing?" he asked. This was a question I was asked daily, because most people knew I lived with my mother.

"She's great and always keeping busy. I want to get to a few of your lectures, but it seems like there's always something going on! I'm sure Mother will be attending most of these."

"Sue Davis was telling me there is a quilt in your basement that's requiring a lot of social time."

I laughed and shook my head. "It really is a small town, isn't it, Harry?"

"That's right, so behave yourself!"

With that, I wandered down the aisle of the sale books, which were my weakness. My eyes went right to the gorgeous garden books that I wished I could sell in my shop. I could only imagine how hard it would be to sell such books at full retail price. How could Harry be making any money by selling these so cheap? I was thankful it was not our way of doing retail, however, he probably didn't throw away fresh greenery and flowers like I had to everyday.

As I got closer to the coffee shop, I saw a person who looked just like Ted. Not to make a mistake, I got closer and noticed it really was Ted. He was very engrossed in conversation. When I looked to see who he was talking to, I realized it was Wendy Lorenz. Ted used to date her before me. I had to stop and move to the side of the aisle and raise my book towards my face in order to grasp what I had just seen. How and why he would be with her, I didn't know.

Was he with her or did he just run into her? I took another look only to see flirtation definitely going on, especially coming from Wendy. Her sexy, thick, black hair with her natural dark skin was such a gift. I bet she woke up looking just like this every morning. Ted never said who broke up with whom, but I bet it was her responding to a better offer. This was definitely a flirtatious meeting with her chest within a half inch of Ted's lean body. He wasn't backing off at all, either. He was flirting right back with those deep dark eyes of his that twinkled when he smiled.

With a pang of nausea in my stomach, I backed up and headed to the front door in hopes neither Harry nor anyone else I knew would see me. For one brief second I thought maybe I should pretend that I hadn't seen them and just casually go up to them. If I did that, it would only give Wendy some pleasure, knowing I had seen them together. Nope, I was out of there!

I got in my car, still with stomach pains intact. I tried to calm down and make sense of what I saw. I should be able to trust Ted; at least I thought so. I wouldn't go out on him, especially after seeing him for about two years. I never thought that he might go out on me. Was he seeking her out because I was too busy and never available? Was I taking him for granted? Was he getting tired of being put off when talking about marriage? Was he getting discouraged? Was my imagination getting away from me? What was he doing in the bookstore, anyway?

My car automatically went home as it so often did. I was anxious to hide and be safe from this hurtful experience. When I pulled in the driveway, I saw Aunt Julia's car parked in front of the house. The last thing I wanted was to share with anyone what had just happened, so I needed to compose myself and give myself an excuse to head to my room. I was a big girl, after all, and whatever I found out, I told myself I could handle it.

"You're home already?" asked Mother when I came in the front door.

"Yeah, I've got a headache, and just didn't feel like going to the bookstore."

"Have you eaten?"

"No, I had a late lunch and snacked on some cookies, so I'm fine right now."

"Julia and Sarah are downstairs," Mother said happily. "Sarah is even quilting. You may want to check on them before you go to your room."

I knew it would have been rude and odd if I did not say hello, so I went downstairs to find them both involved in their stitches.

"Oh, Anne, come see what I did!" Sarah bragged. Sure enough, she had made her mark with pretty long stitches, but not much worse than any of ours.

"I'm proud of you girl! I think you're better than me."

"Mom said she was not going to take out the stitches because I made them." She grinned.

"Oh, did your Mom tell you sometimes stitches disappear?" I joked. No one said anything. "So everything was okay today when you came down here tonight?"

Mother had a funny look on her face, and said, "Well, I must be losing my mind because I put Mother's thimble on the mantle so we wouldn't misplace it, and there it was again, right in front of where Sue quilts." She scratched her head. "No one has been down here in days. I came down to turn on the lights when Julia said she was coming over, and there it was."

I laughed and said, "Well, I guess someone thought Sue would be here. I guess not everyone knows that Sue will not wear a thimble! That reminds me, Mother. Sue left for Ohio for Thanksgiving, so what are our Thanksgiving plans, do you know?"

"I think we'll just have it here or go out to eat, because when I talked to Marie today, she wasn't feeling so good. I don't want her going to all that work. Did you ask Ted to join us?"

"No, not really. I didn't know what we were doing."

"Maybe he would like to have you go to his parents for a

60

change, Anne."

"Right now, I really don't care what happens." I put my hands on my forehead. "I need to lay down for a while and get rid of this pounding headache. Is it anything serious with Aunt Marie?"

"She wouldn't say much," Mother said. "She just said she was feeling really tired and needed to rest."

"Sorry, Aunt Julia, I'll catch up with you another time." I headed back up the stairs. "Maybe Sarah can take my place for tonight."

I didn't waste any more time and made a dash for my room. As I took off my clothes, I kept taking deep breaths, telling myself I was overreacting. I thought for two seconds about calling Ted and putting an end to this mystery, but then what if my call was interrupting a cozy evening with Wendy?

I curled up in my favorite blue sweatpants and a long-sleeve, white t-shirt that felt like butter melting all around me. I had been wearing these clothes for years. Then I grabbed my robe to add another feeling of warmth. Textures were becoming more and more important to me as I got older. Maybe I was turning to good old standbys as a comfort system instead of running into my mother's arms, like when I was little. It said to me that everything would be all right, no matter what. My chenille bathrobe was nearly paper thin. I had a new plush robe in the drawer that Mother had given me for my birthday, but it wasn't my robe; the robe that I nearly grew up with. I wore this old thing for comfort, not for warmth. No one but Mother saw me wear it, so I kept my fancy one for travel.

I've been a spiritual person ever since I could talk. In grade school we learned many prayers that still clung to me every evening when I shut my eyes. They told me God was always with me in time of need. Ever since I could remember, I had talked to God throughout the day, for one thing or another.

As an adult, I often referred to God as the chairman of the board of my business. I tried to always remember to thank Him. I was taught that, too. Mother always made me write thank-you notes, and my Sunday school teacher made a big deal about how we should give credit and thanks to what came our way. As I thought of this greater power, I gradually became calmer, putting God in charge of this petty romance matter, and I began regaining my senses.

I was trying to remember when I had talked to Ted last. I really wasn't sure. Many times when he called, I blew him off. I just could not marry him. I loved him, sort of. Yes, I loved him, but I would resent marrying him now. Then be strong, I said to myself. Not everyone your age is married, and most who are complain constantly.

Suddenly there was a knock at the door. "Anne, are you okay?" Mother whispered.

"Come on in, I'm just trying to lie still to let this headache subside." I rolled over with my back to her.

"Are you sure you're not hungry? It might help your headache if you ate a little something. Did Ted reach you on your cell?"

"No, did he call here?" I asked, turning towards her now. I grabbed my cell to check for missed calls and noticed the phone had been turned off. Ah—I remember doing so in the bookstore. "What did he say?"

"I told him you were not coming home till late. I told him you were stopping by the bookstore and would not be home for dinner."

"I'll call him later or tomorrow morning." I buried my head back in my pillow. "I'm sure it was nothing important."

My sense of relief was like a rock was lifted off of my head.

Did he call wondering if I saw him, or did he call because he felt guilty? I knew there might still be a problem. It would be very hard for him to explain Wendy being there, but if they really were together, he certainly would not be calling me. I said again to myself, be a big girl, Anne!

Hunger suddenly appeared with a surge of urgency. I ran down the stairs to open the fridge, hoping to find the leftover ham I remembered being there. I didn't bother with bread. I managed to find a large dill pickle and some potato chips. After that, I thought cookies or ice cream might make me feel better. Mother had already gone to bed, or she would have thought I had smoked pot or something, the way my appetite was so demanding. With a very full stomach, sleep could not come fast enough.

CHAPTER 13

It was a slow start to the next morning. I could have used a few more hours of sleep, but instead wasted precious hours wondering about Ted and Wendy. I came down the stairs much slower than usual and meandered to the den where Mother was drinking coffee with her newspaper in hand.

"Is your headache gone?"

"Oh, yes, I just can't seem to get going this morning," I sat down and stared out the large window overlooking my herb garden in the side yard that was now frozen over and dry. I longed for my own greenhouse some day. "I can't wait till I can dig in that dirt again, yet winter has barely begun," I sighed.

"Speaking of the winter, I decided we would have a little Thanksgiving celebration here for whoever is available. I just do not want this to be bothersome to Marie. Is there anyone you want to invite like Ted or anyone at work? It's not a hard meal to do once the turkey is in the oven. Julia said they would be here and she would bring a couple of pies."

"I'll let you know in a day or so, but I probably won't invite anyone. Oh, the time is flying, I'd better get with it! I'll bring some nice fall flowers from the shop for a centerpiece. You are sweet as always to think of others, Mother." I didn't give her a chance to question my not inviting anyone.

When I arrived at the shop, Sally was already on the phone taking an order. When she was finished, she said I should call Ted. "He said you should turn on your cell phone." Boy, she was stern!

"Oh, yeah, I turned it off last night and forgot to turn it back on. I had a headache and went to bed early."

I wasn't up to talking to Ted just yet. I still wasn't sure how I would respond. Would I just act like nothing was wrong and see if he mentioned seeing Wendy? Did I really want to ask him for Thanksgiving, which was just days away? Did I even want him in my life at all? Was I bored with the relationship? Was that a jealous reaction in the bookstore or was it just a shock that Ted would still be interested in someone like Wendy Lorenz?

Taking a string of requests for floral arrangements interrupted my thinking, and before I knew it, my stomach was growling for lunch. I just then remembered that I had gone off without breakfast. At that moment, Sally handed me the phone and told me it was Ted.

"What's up with not answering your cell? Are you okay? Your mother said you came home with a headache and went to bed."

"Yes, she's right. I turned off my phone while coming home at some point and crawled into bed as soon as I got there, but I'm fine today."

"Well, then, I take it you'll be up for lunch at Charley's?"

"I guess that would be okay, if I don't stay too long." Did he hear the hesitation in my voice?

"I'll meet you there in fifteen minutes or so, okay?"

"Sure." Not taking a moment to think, I grabbed my coat and scarf and flew out the door before I changed my mind.

The aroma at Charley's was welcoming. There was Ted, waiting for my arrival. He got up from the bar stool at the lunch counter and kissed me gently on the lips, and said, "Hi sugar," which he often called me.

"I'm hungry for one of their French dip sandwiches," I said as I joined him. I didn't want this short time at lunch to turn into a major discussion, so I stuck to the topic at hand, which was food.

"Hey, that sounds pretty good, but I'm going to add a bowl of their white chili," Ted said.

Making small talk with the waitress took up some amount of time. My mind was racing with how I was going to proceed in conversation. "So what's been going on with you these days?" I asked, hoping that might lead in to last night's activity. Major discussion or no, I was too anxious to know something more about what was going on with him to leave the question alone.

"Well, it's been pretty busy. I've had to handle a few client things for Matt, who has been out sick the last couple of days."

"So you worked last night?" I asked bravely.

"Yeah, last night and the night before," he answered between swallows of water. "I tried calling you last night, but couldn't get through, so I left a message with your mother."

This was not the answer I expected to hear, so I gave him another opportunity to bring up his going to the bookstore. "I wanted to stop by the bookstore and cleaners on the way home, but with my head pounding, I just decided to crash." He said nothing.

The food was brought and I couldn't eat fast enough. It was really dawning on me that his encounter with Wendy was not going to be brought up. That was not a good sign.

"What are you doing for Thanksgiving?" Ted asked.

"Mother just told me this morning that she was going to cook because Aunt Marie has been feeling poorly," I answered, hoping he would not be so bold as to invite himself.

"My mom is trying to convince me to go with them to my Aunt Claire and Uncle Ed's house. They live in Dover, which is a good couple of hours from here. They could sense my reluctance, but then they suggested I bring you along, which is an offer you might consider, so what do you think?" He tilted his head as he smiled the question.

"Oh, that's sweet of you Ted, but I need to be here giving Mother a hand. It's been a while since she's prepared a big meal for a group of more than three." I reached for my soda so I wouldn't have to look at him.

When I did see the look on his face, I think he had realized he was not going to be getting an invitation from me, which meant he would and should go alone with his parents. The good news was that he did still want to be with me for Thanksgiving, but there was something not right about it all. I was convinced I gave him the right answer.

I changed the subject to tell him Sue was out of town for the holiday and that we were all curious as to whether her parents would tell her she was adopted.

"When did that surface?"

"Well, we were quilting, and the conversation went to baby quilts and baby books, of which she had neither."

"That basement of yours is turning into quite a gossip town, isn't it?" He smiled. "Do you tell secrets and ghost stories?"

"I think it's been good for all of us in many ways." I answered seriously, ignoring his humor. "I've learned a lot about my family and even myself, plus I can now call myself a quilter! I don't think anything we talk about is gossip like you suggest. We share our worries, our joys, and, yes, sometimes our life secrets."

"What have you learned about yourself?" Ted moved closer to me and looked me right in the eye.

"I think I have learned that despite my age difference with the rest of my family, I share their everyday concerns. Plus, I've found that my family history is pretty interesting. And the beauty of making something appear with those stitches is something I have taken pride in, just like the others have. The repetition of the stitching is therapeutic for me after a long day of retail and the pressures of creating when you sometimes don't feel like it. Aunt Julia was even teaching Sarah how to quilt, and Sarah took to it like she had been doing it all her life. Aunt Julia said her large stitches would remain in the quilt, for her to examine at a later age in life. I think that is pretty cool, don't you?"

"Yeah, I guess," he said unenthusiastically. "What's going on with the mysterious spirit that you all feel is present?"

"It's still there. Grandmother's thimble keeps showing up at Sue's quilting spot no matter where we put it each night."

"I know a way to fix that. Sue needs to start using that thimble, even if she complains. I bet that would take care of that!"

It was the first smile and laugh I had during our lunch. "I'll make that suggestion, but Sue is pretty adamant about not using any thimble at all!"

The waitress brought our check. I grabbed it away from Ted and said it was on me this time. He never liked when I did that. There were fragments of my independence he was not comfortable with. Maybe I was feeling angry over his explanation of the night before and feeling guilty in not asking him to Thanksgiving dinner.

"When will you leave for Dover?"

"I—I haven't decided if I'm going," he stammered.

"Well, I've got to run, Ted." I put my coat on. "Thanks for reminding me to eat!"

"At least I'm good for something," he shrugged, giving me a quick peck on the cheek good-bye.

I walked quickly down the street in the cold wind. As I walked towards the shop I kept saying darn, darn, darn in my head. I was no further along in my problem solving than when I went to lunch. Getting back to work was a way to immerse myself with customers and the live color and beauty of the flowers. It was always a good distraction for me. It provided a great sense of satisfaction in a world that I had created and loved.

As the day got closer to 5:00, I started thinking about Ted again. I realized I had not decided how to gauge his visit with Wendy, and noted that Ted had not asked me to see him that evening. In my heart, I thought I really hurt his feelings by not asking him for Thanksgiving. I did decide I had an answer for Mother if she asked if I invited Ted. I would tell her about his visiting his aunt and uncle.

I was extra busy in the shop on Wednesday as the holiday approached. Customers were all in a good mood, looking forward to their day off and the holiday meal ahead. If I said "Happy Thanksgiving" once, I said it a hundred times. I didn't want to work too late because I wanted to be of some help at home. I was always grateful for a profitable day at the cash register, but I knew Mother would need all the assistance she could get. I could at least set the table, get out the silver and china, and then center the gorgeous rose and burgundy mums I had chosen and arranged for the centerpiece. I had noticed that Mother had pumpkins on the porch as she did every year, and our special wreath of fall leaves on the door was in need of a new ribbon. I grabbed a roll of fall plaid print ribbon and put it in my purse to take home for the finishing touches.

It was 4:00 and people were still picking up last-minute table arrangements for the next day. In walked someone I had hoped to never confront. It was Wendy Lorenz with her sister, Candy. I wanted to head to the backroom looking very busy, but I was caught a moment too late.

"Hi, Anne," Wendy called. "Do you have anything left from your Thanksgiving arrangements that will suit for a nice table arrangement?" I didn't respond but just stared at her.

"Have you ever met my sister, Candy?" She walked around the shop scouting each shelf and corner, as if she were doing a mental inventory of my worth.

"I don't believe I have," I said in my professional voice. "Nice to meet you, Candy."

"I've heard about you and your lovely shop, Anne," she said. "We're trying to help our mother pull together dinner for tomorrow. We're having more guests than we thought so we need to fill in the very long opening in the center of our table. We just need it to look a bit like autumn, but it doesn't matter what colors."

"Sure, I think we can supply that." I used my courteous voice. "Sally, would you show them some of the things we just put in the case this afternoon?" I wanted to get away from the two of them as fast as I possibly could. "If you'll excuse me, I need to finish something for a late delivery. It was nice to meet you Candy."

I immediately headed to the powder room towards the back of the shop. I closed the door and did not know whether to laugh or cry. Wendy no more would come in my shop to buy anything unless she wanted to send a message, which I think I caught loud and clear. Would it be too wild an idea to think that Ted would be going to Wendy's house for Thanksgiving? Why didn't she go to Collier's Florist, my competitor?

I appeared at the counter in time to see Sally lock the door. "I'm sorry I disappeared on you like that, Sally. I couldn't stay one minute longer around those two without ruining a very good sale for the day. You probably had no clue who they were, but one was Ted's former girlfriend. I know she would not step in this shop unless she had another mission."

"Hey, don't worry about it," she shrugged. "We got a great sale out of it, and they were nice to me. We had a really, really good day!" Sally was always so positive and customers loved her. "I'll balance the drawer tonight, as I know you have to get home. I have no plans, and I have a nice sleep-in planned for tomorrow morning."

"What are you doing for Thanksgiving dinner?" I asked, thinking I should have asked her sooner.

"I had an invitation from my aunt, but frankly, I'm looking forward to doing nothing tomorrow."

"Well, I think you should appear at our doorstep around 5:00 tomorrow evening, and enjoy a nice dinner with us. You can sleep in all morning. You'll be hungry, and you'll probably know everyone. I would feel so good including you, for all you do for me."

"I think you may have an idea there," she smiled. "I'll bring some wine or champagne, how's that?"

"Great! Mother will be thrilled to fill our large dining room table. Thanks for balancing the drawer, and I'll see you at 5:00 tomorrow."

I drove home through endless traffic. Where was everyone going and why was I hitting every stoplight? I wondered about Sally's lonely life at such a young age. She had hopes of finishing school majoring in physical education. She never had money and valued every dime she made at the shop for her schooling. Her family had basically told her to get lost after she graduated from high school. I really gave her credit for staying focused on her education. She never dated and had an appearance as though she didn't want to be noticed by anyone. She was turning out to be quite a good floral designer and a good self-starter, which every employer loves to have. This kind of experience did not seem to be directly related to her future plans, but it appeared she enjoyed it as well as pleasing the customers.

I didn't think of Wendy and Ted till I walked in the door to announce to Mother that we were going to be including Sally on our guest list.

"Oh, that's wonderful, and Julia also called and asked if they could bring a work friend of Jim's who did not have an invitation for Thanksgiving. So we need to add two more place settings. It's times like this I am so pleased to own large sets of china and have this beautiful dining room. Young people don't care about those things anymore, but when you are using family china that has many memories, it's so special."

"Was this set from Grandmother Davis?"

"It's better than that; it was her mother's china. The pattern is called 'Moss Rose,' which is a fairly common pattern by Haviland. I fell in love with it when I first saw it at your grandmother's house. I wasn't even married to your father then. I asked a lot of questions about it. I never dreamed it would be on my table one day! Over all the years, I think there is only a cup or two missing. Do you like it, Anne?"

"I never thought about it. It's just always been in the china cabinet. It's pretty fancy, but I do love roses, you know, and it's actually pretty sweet in appearance when you look really close."

"Well, my hope is that you will come to love it because it will be yours one day, and I want you to be able to capture memories just like I have."

As I spread out the tablecloth and arranged the china, I wasn't focused on the beauty before me but on how stressful my day had been. Placing each cup and plate helped me have time to think. Was I sad that Ted would not be at our table this year? Was I upset that he had not called since our lunch? Was I angry over Wendy's visit? Did I really think Ted would be so cruel as to just start seeing another person without breaking up with me?

CHAPTER 14

O n Thanksgiving morning, Mother put the turkey in the oven at an early hour so the yummy smell was heavenly even as I awoke. As I pretended to be of help, my appetite seemed to be first on my mind, even though I reminded myself that there still hadn't been a call from Ted. I didn't know whether I had gone too far. Should I make a call to him? I felt lonely and didn't really know how to fix it.

I finished a raspberry muffin, refilled my coffee mug, and wandered on down to the basement to quilt for a while. I needed to think. I was alone at the frame, which was unusual for me. Glancing to my right, I saw the fancy silver thimble sitting at Sue's place. I didn't move it. Sue could move it when she came back to quilt. I had to smile at this paranormal reminder. Suddenly, it didn't seem like a big deal!

I got up from my chair to stretch and walked over to the wall phone. I wanted to relieve my guilt and call Ted. I called his cell but only got a message. Well, whatever he was doing and wherever he was, there would be a record of my calling to wish him a Happy Thanksgiving, so there!

It would be interesting to see if he returned the call. Something told me he did not go with his parents to Dover. If he went to Wendy's, our relationship would truly be over.

Mother called me to help her open a jar and I went back upstairs to be of more use before I decided to change my clothes for dinner. As I looked in the mirror, I made a mental note to try a new hair-do and maybe lose a few pounds. I knew I was snacking more lately and I attributed it to my troubles with Ted. Wendy's shape was slender and she was very tall. It was obvious that she would never have a problem getting a guy. She had more free time than I and probably had her own personal trainer. She surely would be a lot more fun than I had ever been for Ted. In spite of my ambivalence toward Ted, I could not get her flirtatious look at him out of my mind.

I put on a favorite black dress that fit quite well to my figure instead of one of my daily shop outfits, and finished it off with a pretty red scarf that I purchased at the Main Street art fair last summer. Cute, sort of, maybe even pretty, but I still needed to make some changes. Red lipstick and fresh nail polish would be an added plus for this holiday dinner. I needed to take a little more time to look like a young woman, not just a shop owner. I wasn't sure I was even sexy. Ted, perhaps, thought so, but his compliments were almost predictable and no longer effective.

I could hear chatter coming from the entryway. It was Aunt Julia, Uncle Jim, Sarah, and another man's voice. I then heard Sally's voice join them. I took one last look in the mirror and hurried down the steps to greet the arrivals. Aunt Marie had also just come through the door carrying her special cranberry salad that we enjoyed each year.

"Hello and Happy Thanksgiving everyone," I said joyfully. I helped take everyone's coat; one of them belonged to a handsome man I assumed was Uncle Jim's guest.

"Hi, I'm Sam, Sam Dickson," he said in a deep voice. "Thanks so much for letting me crash your dinner party. Jim insisted that there would be plenty of food, and he wouldn't hear of me dining alone."

"He was right," I said. "You are most welcome. Mother is a very good cook. I'm good at arranging the centerpiece and setting the table, but that's as far as I can brag. What can I get you to drink?"

"Since I'm told we are having wine with dinner, may I have some of that hot cider I smell?" he asked.

"Sure. I think I'll join you."

So this was the Sam that I would hear Uncle Jim and Aunt Julia mention now and then. I filled a glass for most everyone, including Mother. I saw Sam look about the house, and out of the corner of my eye, he seemed to follow every step I made. I tried not to stare, but he was indeed striking, tall, and very pleasant, to say the least.

"Before we start dinner, Sam, I want you to come to the basement to see the quilt that I have made," Aunt Julia said. "All of the family is helping me quilt this, and it has turned out to be such fun! We only have a few more turns on the frame, and it will be done."

Everyone but Mother followed Aunt Julia down to the basement to see and hear Sam's reaction. To my surprise, Uncle Jim, the stinker, was pleasantly gracious and complimentary about the quilt.

"This is beautiful," Sam said. "I know all about quilts. I was raised with them and my sister is a professional quiltmaker. She wins all kinds of awards and a fair amount of money with her talent."

"Where does she live?" asked Aunt Julia.

"She lives in Tulsa, but we see each other fairly often, as I occasionally have to fly there on business."

"I've seen pictures of some of those famous quilts in some of the books and magazines," I said. "She must be very talented. Who taught her to quilt? Your mother?"

"Yes, she did, at quite a young age I'm told."

"Did you hear that, Sarah?" Aunt Julia said to her daughter. "You could be a famous quilter one day!" Sarah gave her mother one of those "Oh, Mother!" looks.

"I have quite a few family quilts and I love them," Sam said.

"When we all came together, the only one who knew anything about quilting was this lady right here, Sam," Aunt Julia explained as she put her arm around Aunt Marie.

Her sister blushed with delight as she gave Aunt Julia a quick peck on the cheek.

"I am so proud of all of them," declared Aunt Marie. "Julia will have a wonderful heirloom with many family memories and we all have enjoyed helping her."

Well, a guy who knows about quilting was pretty impressive, I thought to myself. I hoped this would help Aunt Julia in her explanation to Uncle Jim on why she needed to be at our house so much. I was pleased she was proud of her accomplishment and willing to show it off.

Mother was encouraging us to move upstairs as the turkey was about to make its debut. Sam positioned himself to walk up with me and said, "Jim tells me you have a successful flower shop down on Main Street. That's a beautiful area."

"I try. It used to be a gift shop, and every time I shopped there, I would admire the large windows looking out at the street and the beautiful river. I don't think the owner realized what a treasure she had. When I heard she wanted to retire, I could immediately see the transformation, and I offered to take over her lease. I do love it, despite the work commitment."

"Oh, I'm sure," said Sam. "I admire your energy and work ethics at your age. It's cool to know what you like and what you want to do with your life. I admire people who really go after their dream. Will you be open tomorrow?"

"Yes, of course. Funerals, births, illnesses, anniversaries, and special occasions continue on after the holidays, and thank goodness that they do!" I smiled.

What a nice compliment to hear from a man! He said to go after your dream! Hmmm.

Mother had place cards on the table, which I had not helped her with. She was so good with details and had added this touch because of two new guests joining us. The candles were lit and I had to admit the table was gorgeous. My rose and burgundy mums blended nicely with the china as if some floral designer had planned it that way. Ha!

I sat between Sally and Sam. Sally was quite chatty with Aunt Julia and Sarah. Sam was extremely mannerly and complimentary to Mother's spread of food laid out on the table. She made sure we joined our hands and said a prayer of thanks.

After the wine was poured, Sam made a toast to the gracious hostesses, which included me as well as Mother. It was followed by another toast by Aunt Marie, who wanted to toast the basement quilters.

"I wish Sue were here to join us," Aunt Julia said. "I think we should call the family later, don't you, Sylvia?"

"Yes, that would be a nice thing to do. I sure hope their gathering will be a happy one."

"She's coming home tomorrow, because she promised to work

on Saturday," I said. I explained to Sam that our cousin Sue lived in town, but was in Ohio to visit her parents. I told him she helped me out on Saturdays and was a surprisingly good quilter.

"Sally, have they twisted your arm to help quilt?" Sam asked her.

"No, they know better. I'm not good at such things."

"She is becoming an awesome floral designer," I bragged. "I don't know what I'd do without her. Someday she will finish school and be teaching physical education. It scares me to death to know she won't always be part of Brown's Botanical Shop. I will be lost without her."

"I hope to teach here in the region," Sally said. "I really like Colebridge. I feel I've met just about everyone in town at the flower shop."

Moaning and groaning began as everyone finished their plates. The turkey had been perfect, as were all the trimmings. Mother was always pleased when second helpings were had. It was another Kodak moment with the wonderful food, happy chatter, and picturesque table setting.

"How about having dessert and coffee in the living room?" Mother suggested. We all agreed. I was helped out of my chair by Sam, which was so gracious. I imagined that he must have come from a well-balanced and formal family. Why was he still single, I wondered. Maybe he had a girlfriend out of town. Why did the presence of this handsome visitor take my mind off of a longtime boyfriend so quickly? Why was I hanging onto his every word?

We left the table and went to get comfortable in the living room. It was perfect for just such an occasion. Mother did have good taste, picking out classic pieces of comfortable furniture that went nicely with some of our family antiques. Jim had helped build a fire in the fireplace, and it kept a healthy flame while we enjoyed our dessert. Sam again seemed to follow my movements as we all got comfortable in our chairs.

I placed myself on a footstool near Jim and Sam. "What do you actually do in your travels?" I asked Sam, looking directly into his dark eyes.

"Jim, do you want to answer that question or should I?" Sam answered with a grin. They both laughed.

"I'm in charge of sales in a five-state territory. I'm hoping to be through with the travel at some point and stay in one location like Colebridge, settle down, and have a family someday. I like it here. This travel is hard to manage when there are other people in your life."

"I can only imagine," I said, wondering about his current personal life.

I didn't want to stare, but his face and body had incredible lines that seemed too perfect. His build was solid, as though he worked out every chance he could. He reminded me of a movie star visiting Colebridge who had wondered into our house by mistake. He probably did have a person waiting in the wings for him, or maybe he had just lost a person close to him. I was impressed with his analysis of what he felt he wanted in the future. He liked Colebridge and quilts! This was all too good to be true for a guy this polished and handsome, I told myself. Mother always said if it's too good to be true, it likely is not true. Hmmm.

"Sam is in line for VP at Martingale any day, so his travels will likely end soon," said Uncle Jim.

"Well, that's pretty cool," I said. "Where do you live now?"

"I have a loft in the restored Foundry development. It can't be that far from your shop. I have an incredible view of the river from the top floor. I was also attracted to the tall ceilings and the amazing kitchen they designed for it. I love to cook, so I'm enjoying it very much."

"That used to be an old car foundry, but I guess you know all about that, right?" I asked. "Mother could tell you about folks she knew who used to work there. I know it took a long time to get some of the buildings there developed. I knew condos would do nicely with that view and location."

"Yes, and having the art center and coffee house in the same area is a bonus," he agreed.

"I do know Mrs. Corbin who lives there," I said. "She's a good customer and we have made many a delivery there. I think she must entertain quite a bit."

Mr. Sam Dickson must be a pretty well-to-do bachelor to live in that building, I said to myself. I had heard the lofts were quite pricey for our community. So he loves to cook, too? So far, Mr. Perfect had a perfect score. Hmmm.

Sally and Mother were starting to clear the table so I joined them. As soon as Aunt Julia came with some dishes into the kitchen, I asked her about Sam's love life.

"I've only been around him a few times. Jim sees him a lot and feels he'll be president of the company someday. I know he is single, but not much else. When I've been around him, there hasn't been a serious girlfriend, but he most likely has someone, don't you think? He's pretty impressive, and I see where you're observing his every move. Am I right?"

Before I could answer, she asked, "I noticed Ted was not here today, so what's the scoop on that?"

"He was going with his parents to his aunt's house in Dover."

"Did he invite you to come along?"

"Yes, he did, but I wanted to be here to help Mother."

"Ted just can't quite pull your heartstrings, can he?" Aunt Julia began loading the dishwasher.

"I'm learning more and more about Ted. I can't go into it now, but it's making me rethink my future with him."

"Well, I'm coming over Tuesday night to quilt, so you'll have to fill me in."

"Find out more about Sam if you would," I whispered. "He seems like a guy too good to be true. By the way, you and Uncle Jim seem to be acting pretty normal, considering your suspicions about him."

"He's been extra nice lately, which makes me extra cautious. He's going out of town Tuesday and I would almost bet there is a side dish to this trip."

"You say it so calmly." I wiped the counter. "How do you handle even the idea of him being with someone else?"

"Over time, one loses the urgency and passion over such behavior," she said. "Your focus is on family, your house, your income, and frankly, I don't want another failure in my life!"

I was quite taken aback by that statement. I interpreted that to mean she would turn her head until she had to deal with the problem directly. Boy, did I feel green when it came to relationships! Aunt Julia and I really did need to talk.

Sam walked in the kitchen just then and brought in some dessert dishes.

"Thanks Sam, you don't have to do that," I said trying not to look at him as intently.

"I'm happy to, and want to extend my thanks for a wonderful meal and great conversation," he said with an incredible smile. "I hope I didn't impose on your family. Jim is a lucky guy to have family here like this. I need to leave to take care of some last minute things tonight, but I'll stop by your shop tomorrow perhaps to check it out."

Uncle Jim walked in to say he would leave with Sam, and Aunt Julia could stay longer if she liked.

"No, I'll leave as well, as long as you'll forgive me for leaving you with these dishes. Sarah needs to get some homework done. Is she ready to go?"

"Yes, I think so," Uncle Jim said. "I'll go get her away from the TV in the den."

Aunt Marie left as well, but dependable Sally stayed around to help us finish up in the kitchen.

"Okay Miss Anne, fess up to showing a lot of interest in Mr. Sam," Sally said.

"I noticed how he kept looking at Anne," said Mother. "He was quite a handsome gentleman, I have to admit."

"Okay, you guys, you're right," I said. "He is quite handsome and I like his focus on what he wants. I'm pretty sure he has someone in his life, according to some of his comments. He mentioned that it was difficult to do with all his travel. That's probably why his buddy Jim is in trouble."

"And what if he doesn't?" asked Sally.

"Hmmm," I murmured as I walked out of the kitchen. Just let them think about that one, I thought, smiling inside.

After Sally left, Mother ran the dishwasher and went on up to her bedroom. When I got to my room, I had the urge to try calling Ted again. What was he up to? Where was he really having Thanksgiving today? This time I tried calling his landline, and he answered.

"Happy Thanksgiving!" I said, truly happy to hear his voice.

"Well, same to you," Ted answered in an equally happy tone.

"Did you end up going with your parents to Dover?" I couldn't help asking.

"No, I didn't." Without further explanation he said, "How did your dinner go?"

"Oh, great. We just finished the last of the clean up, so I'm pretty beat."

"You were nice to call," he said slowly. "Maybe I'll see you this week."

I was getting the impression he didn't want to extend the conversation. I said, "Sure, that'll be fine."

"Don't eat too much more turkey!" he said out of character.

"Right, you the same and I'll see you this week." With that, no love you, no time arrangements, and no questions about what the day was really like. I wondered if someone was in his apartment. He didn't seem like his old self. This new behavior was now making me mad. It now seemed to be a game. A game I probably started, and would have to end.

CHAPTER 15

Mornings were always slow after holidays. I told Sally not to come in and consider it part of the holiday. She was thrilled and thanked me again for one of the best Thanksgivings she ever had.

I was tempted to stop at a garage sale I passed on the way to the shop, but my mind was not focused on finding a bargain right now. The lack of shop activity allowed me to do some paperwork and place orders. There were no deliveries, so Kevin showed up and then left. Some of the shops didn't even open, although a few holiday visitors strolled slowly up and down the street. Many stopped to admire the fall flowers in my window boxes, but no one really shopped.

The day passed quickly enough and before I noticed, it was 5:30. I reminded myself it was Friday and I had no plans for the evening. There was no doubt in my mind Ted was trying to send a message, and I was now beginning to feel stubborn and like not responding to him at all.

If I hadn't felt so glum, I would have considered walking down the street and having a quick bite to eat at the bar at Charley's. I would surely see folks I knew.

I was coming around the corner from the design room when I heard someone enter.

"Hey, Anne, here I am," Sam announced.

"You found me!" I couldn't help grinning. He walked in the door, turning around in the shop to see it all.

"This is a beautiful and charming place. I always liked this little building when I drove by. The front windows are certainly perfect for your floral displays. Show me around, why don't you? I don't think I've ever actually been in a flower shop; I've just always called them."

"You need our number to put in your phone or tape on your desk." I couldn't stop smiling as I handed him my business card.

"I think I do need your number, but not just to order flowers." He was flirting with me! Hmmm.

But I pretended I didn't hear him. "Come this way." I showed him the large design room, which was still pretty messy from an arrangement I had just created for the Flemming funeral. My office was decent at least, and he was quite impressed with the very large refrigeration unit we kept full of floral arrangements.

"This is very nice, Anne." He nodded his sincerity. "How much time do you spend here?"

"Just about every day and many nights. I try to keep the payroll down, which means wearing many hats. I manage financially, but that's because I live at home. I don't have to worry about fixing meals, cleaning my house, and all that. I do my own laundry, but Mother has me very spoiled. I am great company for her as well as a comfort since my dad passed. Every time I think about getting my own place, guilt about leaving her alone surfaces and I can't think clearly anymore." I paused, looked at him, and then said, "Why am I telling you all this?"

"I think there is much more to tell, so do you have time for a drink?" He smiled.

"Well, I should be here another half hour, according to my shop hours, but yes, it's been dead most of the day, so I can do that! Just let me refrigerate this bouquet."

"I like that great little bar that sits down by the creek and large water mill. The name escapes me, but do you know where I mean?" he asked.

"Yes, it's the Water Mill. It's really nice in the summer when you can sit out on the patio and hear the water trickle down the creek. The inside bar is pretty small, but cozy."

"I'll meet you there when you're ready, if that's okay?"

"Great, it'll give me time to finish here and freshen up." I hoped I didn't sound too anxious.

Out the door he went and with that I went in the backroom and did a happy dance that I hadn't done for some time.

I could not believe what I just agreed to do. I thought to myself that this guy was smooth, and I probably was the easiest mark he had ever run across. Why was I feeling so brave about opening up to an almost complete stranger I had just met a day ago? I was suddenly feeling free, as if there was no Ted in my life, and I could make a few rash decisions, even if they appeared—or actually were—foolish. My heart told me it was time to explore. I was a grown-up, right? Sometimes, living at home, I questioned what feeling grown up was.

I locked the door before someone came in and ran to re-do my makeup. The phone rang, and I refused to answer. Right now I didn't want to talk to anyone, not a customer, family member, or friend. I closed my ears and grabbed the spray perfume that

I only reached for on special occasions. The smell perked up my femininity.

As I got in my car I realized adrenalin was rushing all through me. I felt like a high school girl!

The Water Mill was a dark, secluded bar that I had only been to once or twice. You had to go down the stairs to a basement level. I reminded myself to play it cool, because I didn't know anything about Sam. He was probably just buying me a drink to thank us for inviting him over for Thanksgiving.

I walked in, hoping I would see him right away. A guitar player was entertaining the filled tables of people and the few sitting at the bar. A sudden hello came right behind me.

"I see you made it," Sam said, standing close enough that I could feel his breath. "I just got here myself. I dropped off some dry cleaning. I was hoping to beat you here. Let's sit over there."

It was a small, round table with a wide, cream candle, already lit. This neighborhood bar was a romantic setting, no doubt. I could only imagine the secret affairs that might be conducted here. Outside, the pretty landscaped patio was twice as big as the inside bar.

I took off my coat and looked around to see if I recognized anyone. We ordered our drinks. It was my usual glass of merlot for me and a single malt scotch for Sam. After a quick clink of our glasses and a toast of cheers, he jumped into a subject I wasn't prepared to address.

"Julia says that you are dating a local accountant here in town."

I was surprised and hesitated before answering. "I'm not sure about that anymore. We've been going through a lot, and frankly, I think he may be seeing someone else."

Sam waited for me to explain further. When I sipped my merlot instead, he said, "If you don't want to talk about it, I understand. It's just that I was surprised that you were free to have a drink tonight. Friday nights are date nights for most single folks, right? Julia said this guy you date was out of town for Thanksgiving, which is why he wasn't at your house."

"Actually, he wasn't out of town. As I said, I don't know where it's going. I think he has a difficult time sharing our time together with my business."

"I understand completely," Sam said. "That's why it's hard for me to have a relationship with my travel schedule. Every woman I get to know eventually resents it. I won't be doing this forever, so I've steered clear of commitments."

"So is this how the story evolved about traveling salesmen?" I joked. "You just have a girl in every port?" Sam laughed.

Just then a tap on the shoulder made me turn around to see Mr. Alexander, the owner of Taylor-Alexander Insurance Company, located just blocks from my shop.

"Oh, hi there!" I said. He was with his wife, I think, but since I wasn't sure, I didn't encourage conversation. He knew Ted, which made me uncomfortable, and was probably hoping for an introduction. I turned away to focus on Sam instead, which was not hard to do.

Time was starting to pass very quickly. Sam was so easy to talk to; I had to stop myself from sharing more than I was comfortable with. We laughed, told stories, and I admitted reluctantly to myself that I was having a great time. Ted and I had stopped flirting with each other for some time now. I wasn't even sure I remembered how to flirt! It felt so good to have someone listen to each and every word I said. I loved the way he looked into my eyes when I talked. There had been many things I had hesitated to tell Ted about because they were too much a part of my world and not his.

The third drink came, and I told Sam that I had not said anything to Mother about going anywhere. I sometimes called her, but I had a feeling she was assuming I went out with Ted after work as I did on so many Friday nights. I didn't want to say that I should have really called my mother or for sure Sam would think I was too young, but there you go—I just had.

I had so many questions to ask him; I wanted to put my mind at rest about what kind of guy he was.

"Sam, I'm going to ask you something you may not want to answer, but because I care deeply for my Aunt Julia, I'm going to ask."

"What's that?" he said putting down his drink. "Shoot away."

"Promise you will not share this with Uncle Jim?" I pleaded.

"Wow, this must be important to you!" he said, picking up his drink, as if he might need it to hear the question.

"It is," I said, looking him straight in the eye. "Please be honest, or don't answer at all, okay?"

"Got it," he said, with a serious look.

"Is Uncle Jim seeing someone else?" I tried to get a reading on his face, because I thought that might tell me more than his answer. There was silence, as I knew there would be.

"I can't answer that question, Anne."

"You can't, or you won't?"

"Jim is a likable guy." He started to explain, then paused. "He's good at what he does, because he is a people person. I do know the ladies like him. I don't mean that as a bad thing, because I know a lot of guys like that kind of attention. Most guys who are having affairs are pretty good at it. They have no intention of giving up their wife and family, so they try to keep it neat and tidy. I can tell you honestly that Jim has not shared anything of that nature with me."

A moment of silence passed as I absorbed what he had said.

"Does Julia think he is?" he asked.

"Yes, and she seems to have evidence, according to her," I said sadly.

"She sure hides it pretty well," Sam said. "I didn't pick up on anything she said. Jim is crazy about Sarah, and I don't think he would do anything foolish to hurt their marriage. I guess guys don't look for things like that around other guys. We always have a lot from work to talk about, even when we play golf."

"Okay, subject closed." I finished my glass of wine. "I don't want to put you in an uncomfortable situation and I appreciate what you have shared. I'm relieved you could tell me what you did and nothing worse."

With that serious conversation, we called it a night. I'm sure I gave him plenty to think about.

"I'll walk you to your car," Sam said. That he did as we walked in silence. He gave me a hug and a kiss on the cheek as I reached for my car keys.

"I'd like to give you a call, if that's okay," he said as he closed my car door.

"I'd like that very much!" I gave him my best smile.

CHAPTER 16

Saturday morning came pretty fast. I had a great night's sleep with pretty pleasant dreams. When I was truly awake, I made a mental note again that I had not heard from Ted. I was pretty convinced that Wendy had indeed moved into his life or he would be at my doorstep.

I actually had made it easy for him to transition into what he was thinking about doing. I wasn't sure how it would all end, but having a good time with Sam last night made me realize Ted was no longer as important in my life. I couldn't help going over every detail of the night's event, as if I had had my first date ever. I forced myself to get moving, thinking of all the day's activities ahead of me, which included the floral piece I left unfinished last night.

Mother was away at the grocery store when I had to leave the house, so explaining to her who I was with last night didn't happen. Driving to the shop, I was preparing how I would handle

Sue, who would have news from home to tell me about. It was going to be interesting to see how she would take to the news of not knowing who her real mother and father were. I wondered if she would even share the information. I decided not to bring up the subject. I also wasn't sure if I would confide in her about my drink with Sam.

It was a cold, brisk, sunny day, and I had enough energy to turn the shop upside down. I was turning over the open sign when Sue walked in. "Welcome home, my dear!" I said.

"Yeah, right."

"How was Thanksgiving?" I ignored her somber mood. "We missed you very much. Aunt Julia and Uncle Ted brought a guest, and I invited Sally to join us, so it was very nice. We almost called you after dinner to talk to all of you, but we got busy, and it didn't happen. So, how was your visit?"

"I'll get right to the point before anyone comes in," Sue said. "I doubt if it's any secret to you that it was very informative." She put her purse under the counter. "It was pretty upsetting to Mom and Dad, but I insisted we get everything out in the open about my childhood. I am adopted. Sue Davis, your cousin, was adopted! How did I not figure this out sooner? At first I was furious with all of you for keeping this from me, but then a day later I realized it wasn't your fault." She was on a roll so I stayed quiet.

"Can you believe how this feels at this stage in my life, finding out that I don't know who my parents really are? I am determined to find out who this family member is that gave me away. Mom and Dad tried to discourage me from going there, but I'm going to find out. It shouldn't be hard. I can't wait to talk to Aunt Marie. I hope she will be open and honest if she knows something."

I remained silent until she was finished. I turned the sign around to say closed until Sue and I finished our conversation.

"Sue, your parents could not have loved you more." I gave her a little hug. "I hope you weren't too hard on them. They just could not bring themselves to tell you, and frankly; we all forgot you were adopted. Was it when you were one year old or so, like I heard?"

"Yeah, there's one photo I found of me when I was about eight months old, but I'm alone, propped in a corner of a couch somewhere. My parents wouldn't comment about the photo, acting kind of dumb, which aggravates me. I know they love me, Anne, but part of me really has hard feelings that they didn't tell me. How would you feel?"

"I think I would feel, well, half empty." I really did feel sympathetic. "You want to be grateful, and you do love them, but when you don't know your roots, there's part of you who is missing!"

"Thank you, Anne, that's exactly how I feel." She pretended to get busy with the work at hand.

"We all love you, Sue. You have to accept our love and go on with life. If you want to find your roots, go for it. Will you be okay if you learn it's not a pretty story?"

"Yes," she said. "I've thought about it. I know it won't be pretty, or it wouldn't have happened, but I still want to know."

I gave her another hug as Mrs. Wilhelm knocked on our door to see if we were open. We dropped the subject and went our separate ways in answering the phone and gathering flowers for orders.

It was nearly 5:00 before I realized we were so busy we hadn't taken time for lunch. "I'm starved," I claimed. "Those pretzels of yours just didn't cut it. Why don't you come over for dinner? I'm sure we have lots of leftover turkey and Mother would love to see you."

"Thanks, Anne, but I just got home. I have to go pick up Muffin from my neighbors, and I'm really beat."

"We're quilting Tuesday night, so I hope you can make that. Bring Muffin with you. She won't want you leaving her again so soon. By the way, that thimble of yours is still sitting at your quilting spot, no matter where we put it."

"No way!"

"Yes way. We decided that you're going to have to fake it and use it or it won't go away!"

"You're all nuts over there!" She was laughing as she went out the door.

CHAPTER 17

On Tuesday snow was blowing off and on all day. The shop was quiet except for the howling of the wind. Our phone was also more silent than usual. The town of Colebridge seemed to be nesting and was beginning to look like a scene on a Christmas card. I loved this little town, my street, and all the people in it. Many have told me that for the size of this town, I have a lot of loyal customers. I guess there is a real personal touch when I get to send flowers for the joys and sorrows and special occasions of each of our town's households. They knew I had my hands on their delivery so my reputation was at stake. The busy Christmas season was upon us, so the lull was a welcome touch.

Mother called to say she had cancelled her bridge club meeting for that afternoon because of the weather. She had put a pot of vegetable soup on the stove, thinking it was just the right touch for the winter air. We weren't sure who would or would not be showing up for quilting that evening, especially with the snow starting to stick, but I was certainly up for it. It was the perfect thing to be doing on a cold winter's night, plus I was anxious to catch up with everyone's life. I knew there would be drama from Sue with her news, and I was eager to ask Aunt Julia about Sam.

I closed the shop early. The bricks on the historic street were icing up and I could see looking north and south out my door that the street had closed down due to Mother Nature. The forecast was bleak for the next day, but in Missouri, the weather can change on a dime.

The aroma of something warm and yummy awaited me when I walked in the door. I hurried to change clothes and then ran down to the basement to turn on the lights and the gas fireplace. This was the perfect setting for a cozy quilting bee if ever there was one. I glanced over to confirm that the thimble was indeed in front of Sue's quilting spot. How could this continue to be such a mystery? Should we be more concerned?

I heard the door open and some chatter of chills and brrrs. To my surprise, it was Aunt Julia and Aunt Marie together. I went upstairs to join them and take their coats. Aunt Julia was a dear to pick up Aunt Marie so she wouldn't have to drive in the bad weather.

"Has anyone heard from Sue?" asked Aunt Marie.

"I think she will be here, although she may be not thrilled with the road conditions. I should warn you that everyone came clean this weekend when she went home. She knows about her adoption, but that's all they told her, which is puzzling her," I said.

As everyone accepted a glass of wine from Mother, we stayed upstairs by the fireplace in the den to warm up a little.

"I don't think they can legally tell her about who the parents are," said Aunt Marie. "Years ago, there were strict rules about adoption, not like today, where so much is open. If they signed an agreement to not disclose the parents, they have to uphold the law."

"Well, I can tell you right now, she is not going to give up looking for her birth parents," I said. "Does anyone here know who her parents are?"

Everyone but Aunt Marie shook her head. "I know they were telling some that it was a young unwed mother who had ties to the family," she said. "Remember, unwed mothers didn't flaunt their pregnancies like they do today."

"You're right about that," I said. "I can't believe the young schoolgirls I see that walk around pregnant these days."

"Okay, ladies, follow me," Mother said as she went to the basement. "Go ahead, bring your wine; we're going to need it to keep warm. We'll have our soup and coffee later."

"Where's the thimble?" asked Aunt Julia.

"Right where we knew it would be," said Mother pointing to its spot at Sue's place.

"I told Sue today at the shop that she was going to have to use it, even if she faked it, to get rid of it," I teased.

Everyone laughed and then took their places. "I think I'm making more consistent stitches, don't you think so, Aunt Marie?"

"Yes, you really have gotten better each and every time, Anne," she said. "You are a natural, which proves how artistic you are— just like your flower arranging."

We quilted for about a half an hour before I decided to call Sue to see if she would be coming.

"Oh, okay." I hung up the wall phone. "She's on Third Street and should be here shortly. She said it is slow going on the roads."

"I'll go ahead upstairs and get the soup bowls ready so we can eat when she gets here," said Mother.

Sue rang the bell shortly afterwards, and her body and little Muffin in her arms were covered in white flakes.

"Why am I doing this?" she asked. "I can't believe you got us all here, Aunt Sylvia! I almost headed home, but pictured all of you with hot soup and merlot so my car headed right here! It was too good to pass up. I passed a lot of stranded folks out there. I parked on the street, so if a snow plow comes by, I'm done for."

"Leave your wet things here by the fireplace and I'll have your wine all ready. The soup is really hot, about to be served," announced Mother. "We have hot homemade rolls from Marie, so I hope you're hungry. We waited till you got here, so we've been quilting about a half hour or so. Julia picked up Marie, so she couldn't refuse the offer."

Everyone downstairs greeted Sue with an extra hearty welcome for braving the weather. They were also telling her how much they missed her at the Thanksgiving table. Aunt Julia was the first to ask about Uncle Ken and Aunt Joyce.

"They all said to tell you hello," Sue said.

As she took her place at the quilting frame, she saw the thimble that we knew belonged to Grandmother Davis. "Anne said this was waiting for me, just like before. Should I be flattered or scared about this, I wonder?"

"Please, please try it on and pretend you will attempt to make a few stitches," I begged, putting it in her hand.

Everyone looked and stopped their stitching to witness a request that appeared to be answered. When Sue put it on her finger, it fit perfectly. She asked Aunt Marie if it was the proper finger.

Aunt Marie said everyone had their preference, but the middle finger that she chose generally was the one. "How strange that you have the perfect fit. Mother had fairly large fingers I think, and I knew I never could wear it. I think it was meant for you, Sue!"

With that, Sue tried to manage a few stitches. "This is so weird," she complained. "I can't imagine getting used to this."

"Everyone feels that way at first," consoled Aunt Marie. "When I was seven or eight years old, I remember we had a very tiny thimble that I could wear, so I did. I loved it and felt like all the grown-ups sitting there. I sure wish I still had that today. I don't know who it belonged to."

"You mean you were always a good quilter from little on?" I dared to ask.

"Not at first. I was the only one of my friends who really had an interest. The others played under the frame, constantly giggling. As I got to be closer to my teenage years, I remember bits and pieces of the quilters' conversations. That was where I first heard the word 'menstruation' said out loud. I didn't know what it meant, but from the way they whispered it, I knew it must have meant something bad or mysterious."

Everyone was chuckling as she continued. "They would always talk about other people from church, and it didn't take long before I figured out what the word 'divorce' meant."

We all added to that comment, and then began having short conversations with whoever was sitting next to us as we quilted on.

"Soup is on!" Mother called from upstairs. She had set up trays in the den around the fire. Everyone eagerly helped themselves from the kitchen. There were the famous hot rolls and the promise of warm berry cobbler for later.

"You are the best cook in the whole world," Sue smiled as she found her place to sit.

"Yes she is. If I didn't run around all day long at work, I would weigh tons more from eating Mother's cooking. She always knows just what would be perfect for the occasion. Many afternoons after school, I came home to fresh-baked cookies, and I'm still treated like that today. Sally loves it when that happens, because they find their way back to the shop."

"Try to make that happen on Saturdays," Sue said to Mother.

The phone rang, and Mother went to answer it in the kitchen. "Anne, it's for you."

My first thought was that it might be Sally or Kevin asking what time to come in the next day, considering the weather. Then I thought of Ted, and how he hadn't yet made any attempt to reach me. Who could it be at this hour?

"Oh, hi, Sam!" What a nice surprise!

He knew he caught me unexpectedly and asked if it was an inconvenient time. "I thought this actually might be a good night to catch you at home, with the weather and all." His voice was deep and appealing. Hmmm.

"You got that right. The quilters braved the weather, and are here tonight. Can you believe it?! Mother made soup, which was the hook to get them here, and we are enjoying it as we speak."

"Oh, sorry, I don't want to interrupt your dinner."

"Its okay, I have to let it cool a bit anyway. Can you smell it from there?"

"I think I do." I could hear the smile in his voice. "Well, I'll make this brief, but I am going to be in town this weekend, and wondered if you wanted to have dinner Saturday night?" Before I could answer, he added that he thought I was easy to talk to and that he felt as if he had known me for some time.

"Sure, I'd love to," happily poured from my lips. "Can we do a later dinner, like 8:00? I don't always get away from the shop right at 5:00, so it would give me some time to come home and change."

"Perfect, 8:00 it is. I'll let you go. I hope everyone is careful going home, because the snow is really coming down hard right now. You may have to provide some PJ's for a sleepover."

I laughed at the thought and hung up the phone with a wide smile on my face. I wondered if anyone would see me if I did my happy dance. Instead, I sat on the kitchen stool for a second to digest the fact that I now had an official date with Sam Dickson. We both took the bait, and wanted more. Was I available to date someone other than Ted? Had Ted and I broken up? What had just happened here? Why did I respond so quickly, like it was the natural thing to do? What was I going to tell Mother and the rest?

As I thought about our conversation, his suggestion hit home about the pajamas. When I looked out the window to a real blizzard, I knew good and well that no one had any business being on those roads. Maybe I wouldn't have to tell the others who was on the phone. My mind now was on the blizzard conditions and what to do next.

When I walked in the den, Mother reminded me that I better re-warm my soup. "I have an announcement to make," I stated firmly.

"What about? asked Sue, taking a roll out of her mouth.

"You are all invited to an all-night pajama party right here at the Brown's residence." It was truly another Kodak moment to see the looks on their faces.

"I was just on the phone with someone who told me how brutal the weather is out there. If you want to see for yourself, look out the window!"

Mother immediately jumped up to look out the bay window in the den, and she could hardly see the street. "I'll turn on the Weather Channel and see what's in the forecast," she said turning on the TV. Everyone began to stir and mutter concerns.

"I think it's a great idea to just camp out. We have plenty of robes to get comfy in and between the couches in here and Sue and I on the floor, we'll huddle around this fire, drink all the wine and coffee we want, tell ghost stories, and not worry about a thing till tomorrow when the roads will be clear." My enthusiasm was contagious. Each one of us looked like a little kid just given permission to play in the rain.

"What a great idea, Anne," Mother exclaimed.

Everyone responded in excitement all at once declaring what circumstances they might have to sort out.

"Julia, you are the only one that has to call home," Mother said. "I'm sure Jim doesn't want you driving in this weather. Are we all on board?" She and Aunt Marie giggled and said they were.

Sue was concerned about getting into work, but then she knew there would be many calling in about the bad weather. "I don't think I have ever gone to a pajama party," she giggled.

"Well, it's quite fun, and it's never too late to have a little fun and excitement," I said as I started rearranging the room. "Even if the electricity goes out, the gas fireplace will keep us warm. Mother, what about hot chocolate later?"

Aunt Julia called home, not expecting to wake up Uncle Jim. She said she wasn't sure whether he really understood what she said about her plans, but that he would figure it out in the morning when she wouldn't be there. "I'll call in the morning and make sure Sarah knows whether they have school or not." When she hung up she said, "Let's get back to the quilt, and Sylvia, that cobbler will taste pretty good with that hot chocolate later."

"You all head back downstairs while Anne and I arrange the den with bedding and robes," Mother said. She couldn't wait to ask me who was on the phone, as the others went downstairs. "It was Sam Dickson," I said as calmly as I could.

"I didn't recognize the voice." Mother rearranged the couch pillows. "So what did he want?" From the look on her face, I don't think she had a clue because she didn't know about our little drink after work.

"He wanted to know if he could take me to dinner this weekend," I said in a low voice so no one would hear. I thought for a minute she was going to throw one of the pillows or chairs at me.

"What about Ted?" She was clearly astonished.

"I'll fill you in later, but now we have to get back downstairs," I said bluntly. She reluctantly accepted my answer and we arranged the room so invitingly and comfy with all the blankets, robes, and pillows that I wanted to put on my pajamas right away and pull up the covers.

CHAPTER 18

W e have created a love nest upstairs," I announced. "I almost dove under the covers without you all! I brought more wine, and you don't have to worry about drinking and driving!"

No one refused, so I made the rounds refilling the glasses. With that done, I settled into my quilting spot, commenting that I hoped I could still quilt in a straight line.

After we exhausted the topic of the horrid weather, we quilted in silence until Mother said, "I think we should play a little game of true confessions to keep us entertained tonight."

"What's that all about Sylvia?" asked Aunt Marie. "Like we did in high school at slumber parties?"

"Like what?" asked Sue.

"You'll see," said Mother. "Anne, you start by telling us about the phone call you just got, and then we'll keep going around the quilting frame. Inquiring minds want to know!"

There were giggles and curious remarks about not knowing what Mother was getting to. I stared at her warily. Of course she wanted me to start since I was on her mind. I had had too much wine to be mad at her, so I gave in to the request.

"Okay, I get it. I promised her I would tell her about the phone call, so here goes. It was Sam Dickson. Aunt Julia, did you know that he was going to call me?"

"No, for what?" She was all innocence.

"He has asked me to have dinner Saturday night," I said calmly.

"He did what!?" Aunt Julia exclaimed.

I waited for more reactions before I explained because I knew they would be coming. Sure enough…

"What about Ted for heaven's sake?" asked Sue. "Did you break up? Who is Sam Dickson? Did I leave town for only a couple of days and all the players changed?"

"Oh, Anne, what are you thinking?" asked Aunt Marie. "He seems a bit older than you; am I right, Julia?

"She has a lot of explaining to do," said Mother in her mothering voice.

"Hello, hello, before this goes further, who is Sam Dickson?" Sue interrupted, impatient with all the inquiries.

"We brought Sam with us to Thanksgiving dinner here at Sylvia's because he has no family here in Colebridge," responded Aunt Julia.

"Hold on everyone," I said as I clinked my glass for attention with my thimble. "Take another swallow of wine. It's not a big deal. I'll start by telling you that Ted and I have been in trouble for some time. I'm pretty sure he has started seeing Wendy Lorenz, and I think it's entirely all my fault. I'm not ready for a wedding, as you all know."

"Well, that's no reason to start seeing someone else," said Sue.

"Ted and I seem to want different things in our lives right now. I won't say much more than that except that it's pretty much over. I know I should feel sad about it, but I guess I've felt it coming for a long time."

"So let's go back to this Sam guy," Sue begged. "What do we actually know about him?"

"I can answer that, Sue." Aunt Julia said. "Sam is a single guy Jim works with. He has a bright future, so I hear. He plays golf with Jim, and he speaks quite highly of him. He's originally from Ohio, although I think his family lives in Chicago now. He was alone on Thanksgiving and we invited him to come with us to Sylvia's. He enjoyed it very much and commented on what a warm, loving family we had, loved the food, and obviously centered in on the youngest hostess that day."

This comment had to be digested before Aunt Marie spoke up.

"He was very nice, and well mannered, but didn't he know about Ted?" Aunt Marie asked.

"I told him," I jumped in to say.

Aunt Julia continued, "He did comment how nice she was when we were leaving, but I had no idea he was thinking anything other than being hospitable."

"He probably wasn't, Aunt Julia. He came by to see the shop the next day, which he told me he was going to do that evening at dinner. It happened to be near closing time and he asked if I wanted to get a drink. I didn't think much about it, so I agreed. After all, it was a Friday night, I didn't have a date with Ted, and it seemed pretty innocent. Sam is very nice, and we seem to have some things in common, but that's as far as it goes. It's no big deal, you guys!"

"Well, how old is he, Anne?" Sue wanted more information.

"I'm not really sure. Do you know, Aunt Julia?"

"Not for sure, but in his thirties, thirty-six or thirty-seven, I would guess," Aunt Julia thought.

"That's not a big deal for me, and hey, we're not exactly a couple—he just wants to have dinner." Why was I starting to feel defensive? "He is really nice and has his own life and interests, just like me."

"So, are you going to tell Ted?" Mother asked. "How can you handle this so lightly? He will not be happy!"

"Yes, yes, I will likely tell him—if he tells me about Wendy!"

"I loved Ted," said Aunt Marie with affection in her voice.

"You and me both," Mother agreed. "I bet Ted is not seeing this Wendy. I bet it's your imagination."

It wasn't my imagination that saw them together in the bookstore or she and her sister nosing around my shop, I thought, but didn't say. "Okay, enough is enough. We have exhausted this topic. Who wants to confess next? I want to move on. I'll keep you all informed, and remind you all that I am a grown woman, so not to worry."

"I'll go next," said Sue. "I want to confess that I now know that I was adopted at the age of one!" The room went quiet.

"Keep going," Aunt Julia finally broke the silence.

"There's nothing like being the last to know among your family members, but hey, nobody's business, right?" Sue still seemed a little peeved. "I had an interesting visit Thanksgiving. Frankly, the baby quilt discussion I had with all of you and then the realization of no baby book in my life had me putting two and two together. I guess I have to thank all of you. I understand why those of you who knew did not want to say anything, I really do."

"Are you being sincere, Sue?" I asked. "I didn't know until Mother recently told me, so please don't feel there was a conspiracy."

"Oh, Sue, it wasn't our place to tell you that kind of information," said Aunt Marie. "I'm glad you understand."

"Ken and Joyce loved you as one of their own," said Mother. "You were so darling, and they were so proud."

"Okay, I have no complaints, I guess," said Sue sadly. "I just wish everyone early on would have been honest about who my parents really are. Would any of you tell me if you knew? Does anyone here know?"

"No, we don't, Sue," said Mother trying to comfort her. "I think we know there was a distant relative involved, but we don't know who. Am I right everyone?"

"Yes, that's correct," said Aunt Marie.

"Then I will continue my mission to find out." Sue went back to her quilting.

"I think you should, if that's what you want," said Aunt Julia. "We will all support you and help in any way we can, right, you all?"

"Do you want to keep quilting after we do this roll or should we go upstairs and have my scrumptious cobbler?" asked Mother.

"Let's keep going while you warm it up," I suggested. "I think I'm ready for coffee as well or my head will be quite large tomorrow from all this wine."

"Don't let the next confession take place till we all get upstairs," said Mother as she went up to prepare dessert. We all laughed like schoolgirls.

After a bit Mother called for us to join her. We felt pretty good about getting another turn finished on the quilt. There was no doubt we were all beginning to get the hang of the quilting routine. The quilt was coming alive before our eyes as more stitches appeared. Isabella had a quilt sign in her shop that said "A quilt is not a quilt until it's quilted!" We all gave our verbal approvals and then trooped up the stairs looking forward to some more food.

"This was such a great idea, Anne," Aunt Marie said giving me a little squeeze. "Let it snow, let it snow, let it snow!"

"Come in by the fire. I have everything here on the coffee table," invited Mother.

First we all went over to the window to peer out at the falling snow.

"Oh my, it's getting up near the mailbox." Sue's excitement rippled through all of us. "How deep do you think it is? It's really beautiful. Look over at the your neighbor's pine tree."

"How will we all ever get out of this in the morning?" Aunt Julia asked.

"Can we stay for days, Aunt Sylvia?" Sue joked.

We laughed and found our nesting places among the cushily arranged pillows. Some grabbed a robe, took off their shoes, sweaters, and extra clothing to make them more comfortable. I was happy to be in my favorite robe with my furry red slippers. We laughed as we took in all the silly wardrobe combinations. The room was colorful with afghans, old quilts, and robes from Mother's closet I hadn't seen in years. I thought this would be a hilarious Kodak moment to remember.

The first bites were taken from the cobbler and everyone was praising Mother for her choice of comfort food. Their appreciation and her love for entertaining could not have pleased her more on this unique occasion. Hot chocolate and coffee aromas filled the room as everyone filled and refilled their cups.

"It's my turn to confess," said Aunt Marie. "Are you ready?"

"This ought to be good," said Aunt Julia. "Let's hear it, big sister, and try to keep it clean."

We laughed more than usual, for the wine had had its effect on all of us.

"I have had a date," Aunt Marie stated. You could hear everyone's breathing, for there was no other sound. The noshing had totally subsided.

"Be still my heart," Sue was patting her heart with her hand. "You, my sweet older Aunt, had a date and I can't tell you when I last had one! This is depressing!" She grinned.

"Marie, you didn't tell me!" Mother was clearly surprised. "Please give us more information! We need details, my dear sister."

"Well, I go the senior center to play cards most Thursdays, and my partner is Joe Wilhelm, who retired from the A&P, remember?" She started to blush and stammer a bit, but then she continued.

"One day a couple of weeks ago, we got to talking about being widowed, and what was difficult about it all. He said he really never got used to eating alone. He was happily married for many years. He said he had no interest in looking for another wife, but that he found it really lonely when he would come home from his days of activity, pick up a bit of food, situate himself in front of the TV, then fall asleep shortly after. I told him I understood, because I had many of those nights myself. He said he loved good food and that he and his wife always treated themselves to nice restaurants, and that he really missed that."

We all were quiet, so Aunt Marie continued.

"He said he had heard good things about a new German restaurant over in South County, and wondered if I would like to join him for dinner there. It did not take me long to say yes. It did not occur to me that it qualified as a date, because hey, what the heck at my age? I told him I was raised with some good German food, and that it would be a real treat."

"So how did it go?" Mother was still in shock. "I can't believe you didn't tell me, Marie."

"Well, it wasn't a big deal, and I felt better about it all by just going and keeping it to myself," she said.

As I listened to Aunt Marie, I agreed with her choice to keep it to herself, and perhaps I should have kept Sam Dickson a secret for awhile. I found the conversation fascinating and enjoyed the interaction of the sisters. I could only imagine the stories they shared growing up.

"It went well," she continued. "The food there is wonderful; I highly recommend it. It's called Herman's."

"I don't care about the food, Marie," Aunt Julia interrupted. "How did it feel to be with him? Did you like him? Did he ask you out since? Did he give you a kiss?"

"Julia, for heaven's sake." Mother said sternly. "None of this is any of your business."

"Well, you're the one who asked for secret confessions," Aunt Julia huffed.

Aunt Marie broke up the fuss by answering sheepishly, "It was like being with an old friend, and there was nothing romantic about it unless you can count the little hug he gave me when I got out of the car."

"Did you ask him in?" Sue asked. We waited for an answer while Aunt Marie sipped her coffee.

"No, I wasn't ready for spending more time with him," she said. "He waited till I got in the house before he drove off. It was a great time, and I'm glad I went. I'll see him again Thursday at the center. If he is still friendly, I may ask him over for dinner sometime."

"Yea!" I shouted. We all clapped. "Good for you, Aunt Marie. You are a dear to be with and there's no reason you can't enjoy his company in any way you want. Does he have any man friends for my good-looking mother?"

A roar of laughter spread across the room. "Anne, you are up to no good," Mother smiled.

"I can't believe it's midnight already!" Aunt Julia looked at the grandfather clock in the corner. "I guess I have to go next, unless you're ready, Sylvia."

"No, you go, my dear."

"I've been thinking about this confession." Aunt Julia was thoughtful and then she hesitated. "I think what I want to tell you all is that I am in this very strange marriage. I know you all worry about me, but I want you to stop. I know Jim sees someone else but I don't care! He is really good to me in other ways and a great father to Sarah. It would break her heart to have us break up. My confession is I have a plan."

We all wondered where this explanation was going. Aunt Julia rearranged her position on the couch, and laid down her cobbler on the end table.

"Sarah will be getting older, and if I can handle it, I will hang onto this marriage till she goes away to college. Then I will move into second gear to have a life of my own."

For the first time all night, the quiet in the room was sad. Mother and Aunt Marie looked at each other mutely, dreading what Aunt Julia would say next. I decided to break the silence.

"Don't you want to try to save what you have, or bring back what you had?"

"No, Anne, I don't. I no longer respect him. I no longer find him attractive. And I happen to love it when he's gone and travels. I have a beautiful home and he leaves me alone most of the time. My plan gives me time to figure out things financially for the future."

"Does he really think you are so naive as to let this affair go on?" I moved to the floor from my chair.

"Yes, I think he does. Most men are stupid, plus he thinks I'm an airhead, irresponsible, and dumb. He reminds me of how my own mother felt about me."

"Stop this. Stop it right now," Mother was suddenly loud. "We are not going to go into that."

"Well, now you know," said Aunt Julia. "Please do not say anything, and don't treat Jim any differently than you do now. I've thought about this for some time, and I don't want you all to try to talk me out of it. I feel really calm and confident now that I have this plan. I will survive and it's better than things getting ugly."

Most of us shook our heads, not knowing what to say.

"Hey, Aunt Julia, I give you credit," said Sue. "Most women would make a big fuss, want to get even, and take the guy to the cleaners. Frankly, he doesn't deserve this kind of consideration if he really is being unfaithful!"

Mother then moved to the center of our nest, sat like an American Indian with her legs crossed, and said, "I better take my turn before you all fall asleep or get too drunk to remember what I say." It was hard to concentrate on what she might confess after hearing Aunt Julia's plan for the future.

She took a deep breath. I wondered what in the world it could be. "My confession is that I am thinking about taking a part-time job at Pointer's Main Street Book Store!" She was beaming.

Before anyone could say anything, she told us that her friend, Terry, who worked there, said there was a two-day-a-week job opening, and wondered if she would be interested.

"You know I kind of miss being around books. Being a librarian for so many years gets in your blood. I have lots of time to read, which is good, but I have the time to do more. Anne is almost never home, and I have to confess, I get kind of lonely."

I was not surprised at what she shared, so why did I feel this might be my fault? She liked Terry and often talked about how she envied her having a little job. She probably had had this on her mind for some time, and I wasn't around enough for her to share her thoughts with me.

"I think it's great, Mother." I leaned over to give her a hug. "I hope you can adjust to being on your feet, because retail can be hard."

"I know, and if I don't like it, I will quit. It's not the end of the world, but I would like to try it."

Another "Yea!" and we all clapped.

"Discount, discount," joked Sue. "Aunt Sylvia, I'm so proud of you. Go for it!"

"Wow, I don't think I can handle any more news," said Aunt Marie. "Let's have a toast to our confessions."

"Here's to all our new adventures!" I cheered.

Everyone grabbed her cup or glass and we all clinked to our toast of future happiness. We were tears and laughter in one big pile. Sue was hugging Mother, and Aunt Marie and Aunt Julia were snuggled close together. It was another one of those Kodak moments that I knew we would probably never forget!

"So much for hot chocolate, I'm getting us all bottles of water," I said, heading to the kitchen. "It will help the wine disappear, and kill any headaches tomorrow."

Sue was probably the most inebriated of all of us. She did not drink often other than a glass of wine now and then. It was as if she needed this evening badly. She wanted us to confirm she was indeed family, but wasn't sure what she should do next.

We grabbed our bottles of water, thinking our little game was over, when Sue stood up. She swayed a bit and I asked if she needed help. "I'm going to give you all something to think about before you go to sleep." She was tipsy for sure. "When I got back from home, I started researching an idea."

"Does this mean we have to be serious?" Aunt Julia teased. "It's pretty hard to do, because you are indeed under the influence."

"I know, I know," Sue laughed. She flopped herself on the quilt nearest the fireplace and started to be as serious as she possibly could despite her consumption. "If I don't tell you tonight, I may not have the nerve to do so later." This got everyone's attention.

"You have the floor, Sue," I said. "Go for it!"

"I am looking into adopting a child, a very young child. My good fortune with my parents makes me want to do the same for someone else. Before I get too old to qualify, I want to give it a shot y'all."

Once again, silence overtook us for a moment.

"Okay, Sue, you win the prize for the best secret and nightly news. Good for you!" I said. "If you could qualify, it would be awesome! You would make a wonderful mother."

"They do this now; there doesn't have to be a dad," Mother said, like she was telling us all for the first time about such news. "We didn't hear you say a baby, right?"

"That's right. Ideally, I want a little girl who has been passed up by other folks. I wouldn't mind a little Korean or Vietnamese girl. Little girls are not wanted in so many foreign countries, and I would just love to have one of them. I'm not getting any younger, and I want my own family. I can't wait for Mr. Right to come along, for it may never happen."

"This is a bombshell," Aunt Marie's mixed feelings evident in her tone. "Have you said anything to your mom and dad?"

"No, I haven't."

"It would be so wonderful to have a child in the family. It doesn't look like Anne is going to be a mommy anytime soon!" Mother said.

"You're right, Mother, and thanks for the pressure. Continue, Sue; this is most interesting."

"You know, these things take a long time, and I still don't know if I will ever qualify, but I want to be a mother, and I want to try!" A loud "Yea!" and clapping and hugs were again in order. Aunt Marie was the only one still holding back any excessive joy, but she still showed support.

As we settled down for good, the warm fireplace was just the heat we needed. I could have gone to sleep in my own bedroom, but Mother and I decided we would all stay cuddled together in the same room. The only light was a nearby lamp in the hall so everyone could find the bathroom. The scene was set for those who could shut their eyes for a few hours of sleep. Sue and I snuggled up in our sleeping bags and giggled like we were ten years old again.

"Do you think Mother is with us now like she seems to be when we are quilting?" whispered Aunt Marie to Aunt Julia.

"Do you want us all to have nightmares?" asked Aunt Julia.

The light suddenly went out in the fireplace as well as the hall lamp. We all stopped talking and shared the silence of the darkness.

"Is the whole neighborhood out?" Aunt Marie asked in a whisper.

"Okay, now we know Mom is here," said Aunt Julia.

"Calm down, we can all still see a bit," said Mother, making her way to the front window. "I'll get matches and see if the lights are out anywhere else."

"Well, the others have some lights, although it looks like most everyone is asleep," Mother said.

"Check the kitchen and other rooms, maybe it's the breaker," I said, not wanting to leave my warm sleeping bag.

Mother came back saying the electricity was working, and that the lights were fine in the other rooms.

"It must be a circuit," I said.

"No, it's a message," said Sue. "This is too weird."

"It's our message to get some sleep, and we don't need the light for that," Mother said. "I'll light this candle, which we can take to the bathroom, so it shouldn't be a problem."

The only one really bothered seemed to be Aunt Julia. "I feel her here, what about all of you?" she asked.

We all knew the answer, but did not respond.

"Go to sleep Julia," Mother said.

CHAPTER 19

I was awakened by the smell of good coffee, a piercing light from the side window, and shoveling noise from outside our house. I got up slowly, feeling a bit hungover with a dull headache. Then remembering when, where, and how I got here on the floor, I grabbed my robe and quietly went into the kitchen. Mother was nowhere around. I went straight to the smell of the coffee pot. Aunt Julia was the next to follow, rubbing her eyes as she sneaked into the kitchen, also trying to keep quiet.

"Oh, that coffee smells so good," she whispered as she reached for one of the empty mugs sitting on the counter. "I need to call home and find out if Sarah has school."

"I can't imagine they would," I said, filling her mug. "What time does Jim go to work?"

"He's pretty flexible," Aunt Julia answered. She took her cell phone and coffee and went into the hallway to make her call.

I figured out that Mr. Carter from next door was the one shoveling. He was always so good to us, but he should not be doing this heavy shoveling at his age. I bet he wondered about all the cars out front. His only fault was good and bad. On the bad side, he was a nosy neighbor who had to know everyone's business and loved to gossip about it. The good news was that he would be the first to discover if a stranger appeared to do harm in our neighborhood. The stir of footsteps, the coffee aroma, and the crackling of snow outside woke Aunt Marie and Sue.

"Good morning, everyone!" I called as cheerfully as I could.

No one seemed to be very chipper. Sue made a quick run to the bathroom. Somehow I knew she would be the one to suffer most from our overindulgence last night. Mother came from her bedroom already dressed. I figured she wasn't comfortable on the couch so she had gone to her room sometime last night.

"No school," said Aunt Julia with relief. "Sarah is still asleep and Jim was going to work at home for the morning till the roads were clear."

"Did he mind your overnight stay?" I asked out of curiosity.

"Guess not, he must have gotten the message; not a word was said about it. He probably enjoyed it!" she said sarcastically.

Sue came into the kitchen looking like a bomb was going off in her head. "I don't feel so good," she mumbled as she ran her fingers through her mussed hair. "I think if I drink this coffee something may not stay down."

"You are in no shape to go to work, so you better call in before it gets too late," I handed her my cell phone.

She slumped in a chair. "Let me just sit here a minute to gather my body parts and think what words to say."

Mother and Aunt Marie started fussing around the kitchen to put out some breads, fruits, and yogurt. They were the undoubted "mother hens" of this group.

"I am proud of us," I said as we gathered in the kitchen. "We had an unforgettable night! We got a lot of quilting done, got some weight off our chests, and experienced a long overdue pajama party."

"Well, I liked the quilting part." Aunt Julia took a bite of coffee cake. "I hope what was said last night stays here and doesn't go out the door."

"What's said in the basement stays in the basement!" said Mother. "That's where we store everything else." We all laughed and agreed that it would be a great idea.

The phone rang and it was Sally wondering if she had to try to come to work. "No, I don't think so," I said. "I'm going to have the calls forwarded to me here at home, at least for the morning. I don't think anyone is going to stir in the whole town for some time. Stay home and stay warm."

Sue made her phone call to work, and she felt comfortable with their response. It sounded like only half of the staff had shown up. She let Muffin out the back door for a quick relief. When she scampered back into the warm kitchen, Sue headed straight to the couch to lie down.

"Okay, everyone is taken care of, so let's relax with our coffee," Mother said. "Who knows, if we revive ourselves, we can go back to the quilting frame."

We just looked at her. It was obvious that the very thought of quilting was the last thing on our minds at this early hour. By now the nesting spots in the den were a good place for all to retreat with cups of coffee in hand. The fireplace was going strong, and suddenly the light in the hall went on by itself. We had already forgotten that they mysteriously went off during our pajama party.

"Mother is waking up I guess," Aunt Julia said.

CHAPTER 20

Aunt Julia and Aunt Marie were the first to leave from our snow-buried house. Mr. Carter made sure he had a shoveled path to the street in order for everyone to get to their cars. He didn't ask any questions as he watched them go to their cars; he knew about our quilting activity. The sun was shining brightly on the snow crystals, which would help melt things a bit, but the cold wind was brutal when I shut the door behind them.

Sue's car was blocked in heavily with snow, which the street crew caused when they plowed the road. Forced to stay with us for part of the day until things improved, she was happy to stay on the couch with her coffee and Muffin.

Mother and I did go back to the quilting frame. I stayed in my robe and we carried our mugs of coffee down the stairs. We were like little girls waking up to a called-off school day, enjoying the free hours that nature had given us. As we made a few more stitches, we recalled how wonderful it was to share and be together the night before.

"I'm afraid this quilt is going to be done sooner than we thought," Mother said. "We'd better think of another quilt to replace this one, because I will miss everyone's visits."

"I'm still pondering the flower quilt for my shop, Mother, so who knows? I'll stop in at Isabella's to see if it is something that is not too hard to do."

The phone rang, which startled both of us. I grabbed the wall phone quickly, hoping not to wake Sue. I couldn't believe my ears, but it was Ted.

"Hello over there, are you all okay?" His voice seemed to be like family.

"Sure, buried in snow like everyone else. We had a group here quilting last night. They all stayed over, which was quite fun. Sue is still here; her car is blocked in from the snowplow. We'll try to shovel it out this afternoon."

"Do you want me to come over and do that?" he asked, like the dependable guy that he was.

"Oh, no, I'm sure the roads are still bad, and she's in no hurry to leave. She called in sick today, so thanks, but we'll be fine." I think he was actually disappointed that we did not need his services.

"So how are other things with you?" He clearly wanted to continue the conversation.

"Fine," I said evenly. "We had a nice Thanksgiving. How about you?"

"Yeah, good," he said, without saying where he went.

"Did you get my message on that day?" I wanted to relieve some of my guilt about not inviting him.

"Yes, I did," he said without any apology about not calling back. Then he asked, "So, are we still a twosome?"

His directness shocked me. I certainly wasn't ready for this heavy subject so early in the morning. After a long pause, though, I said, "It doesn't appear that way, does it?"

"Do you want to talk about it over a drink tonight?"

"I suppose it would be a good idea." I felt like I owed him that much. "I'm not going to open the shop today. Do you want to pick me up at my house?"

"Sure, how about 5:30?"

"See you then," I said, hanging up the phone.

Mother kept trying to get some kind of response out of me. What I was going to say to him, she wondered.

I wasn't at all sure myself, but it was not going to be a warm and fuzzy meeting. What, if anything, had he heard about Sam? I knew I wanted to end things for two reasons. I didn't want to be dumped for Wendy, which might already have happened, and the number two reason was Sam. Sam awoke my femininity in a way Ted didn't, and I really liked being with him. I didn't care if the relationship went anywhere, but I did want to explore and find out what opportunities there might be for me.

Sue overheard part of our conversation as she came down the stairs to join us. She warned me about saying too much and destroying what I might want back someday. I kept my conversation light and showed little concern around Mother and Sue. No one wanted me to be cruel to Ted, and neither did I. I sensed they felt that I was making a big mistake to let wonderful-in-their-eyes Ted go for this Sam guy that none of them knew very well.

About 3:00, Sue and I ventured outside with snow shovels. She had recovered from her evening and was back to life. We laughed as we threw a few snowballs at each other. I felt ten years old again as Mother watched me fall back to make a snow angel. She gasped and waved at me from inside the window like she did when I was a small child.

We soon realized how out of shape we were when we tried lifting shovel after shovel of snow. We had to catch our breath every few minutes but we kept on going. Mr. Carter came out of his house to rescue us, but we rushed him back inside since he had cleared the entire driveway for us.

Soaking wet and a few pounds lighter, we called it a day. Sue's car was free from the avalanche of snow along the street, so after we went in to share a cup of hot chocolate, she was able to go on her way.

CHAPTER 21

Ted was always right on time. When I saw him pull up, I was ready with my coat on so he wouldn't have to park by the snow-filled curb. I was impressed with how clean his car was coming from his garage. He must have stayed in the entire evening. A somber greeting of how cold it was greeted me as I got in the car.

"Is Charley's okay?" he asked, getting our awkward conversation started.

"Oh sure," I shivered from the cold air. I thought to myself how fitting that we would end our long relationship at a place where we had spent so much time.

We continued to make small talk about the snow. For the first time I felt ill at ease with Ted. He couldn't help but be his nice self, but something told me he was going to break up with me and not the other way around.

Charley's was very quiet and empty because of the weather, so we walked to a high table for two that was toward the corner of the restaurant. A waiter we knew recognized us and asked if we wanted our usual drinks. They appeared like clockwork. Why was this comfortable response unsettling for me all of a sudden? I waited for Ted to start our conversation.

"So the quilt still isn't finished, I take it," he said, trying to soften our purpose in meeting.

"We're getting close," I answered, trying not to look directly at him. "I think all of us dread when that time comes because we've enjoyed our visits, plus having a purpose to our madness, so to speak."

"You all sure surprised me," Ted said.

"Hey, Anne," a voice called over my shoulder. It was Uncle Jim and Sam—of all people. I jumped when Uncle Jim touched my shoulder to greet me.

"Oh, hi, you guys!" I couldn't have been more surprised.

"Uncle Jim, you know Ted. Sam Dickson, I'd like you to meet Ted Collins."

"How ya doing?" Ted reached for Sam's hand.

"Sam works with Uncle Jim," I explained, wanting to get away and fast from this uncomfortable meeting.

"How's that quilt coming along?" Sam asked.

"Close, very close to getting done." I wondered what Sam was really thinking. I could tell Ted was not comfortable with that question. I'm sure he wanted to know how this guy would know about the basement quilt.

"We're just back from a sales meeting, so we stopped by to get a drink," said Uncle Jim.

"Well, sounds like fun," I said, not wanting to know more. "Good of you to say hello."

They both walked toward the bar area. Ted pretended to be distracted with giving an order for shrimp cocktail to our waitress. I had to take a deep breath to appear normal, and commented that the shrimp sounded like a good idea. I knew Sam and Ted would eventually meet in this small town, but I had not expected it just yet.

"I take it you've met Sam before?" Ted's tone indicated he wanted to know more.

"Yes, he came over for Thanksgiving." I watched his forehead wrinkle in dismay. "He was going to be alone, so Aunt Julia and Uncle Jim invited him. He's a really nice guy."

"Is he single?" Ted asked.

"Yes, actually he is."

"So, Anne, where are we anyway?"

I took a second or two before I responded. I knew this was the time to be honest and get to the point.

"I see us sitting here at this table, but I'm afraid there isn't much more than just respect and friendship between us; at least for me." He looked as shocked and hurt as if I punched him in the stomach.

"So when did this happen, do you think?" I heard anger in his voice.

Okay, here goes, I said to myself. "It probably happened months ago, but for me everything changed when Wendy showed up."

"What do you mean by that?" Now he sounded confused.

"Why don't you just admit that she has come back into your life, and that you allowed it because I wasn't there for you?" I said with accusation. "I frankly don't want to know the details. I admit I don't have the time that you deserve and she does."

Before I changed my mind or lost my nerve, I kept going. "I think we need to go our separate ways, as we have been doing lately." He didn't say anything, so I added, "And let's spare each other from any drama and not say things that may just hurt one another."

"Man, oh man, you have it all figured out." His voice was rising. "Aren't you something! You have no idea how difficult it has been for me to figure you out, but I'm not stupid. Yes, Wendy sensed our relationship was not going well, and yes, I have been talking to her, but I don't think she's the answer to what I want. We are not a couple, if that's what you think." His face was getting more and more flushed with anger.

"Well, I have a confession to make." Now or never, Anne, I steeled myself. "I have someone as well I have been talking to, and frankly, I'm enjoying it. I, too, am not sure whether this guy is what I want or what I will ever want in the future. I just don't want to feel bad anymore about trying to be me. You make me feel guilty when I focus on the importance of the shop. I know that's not fair to you because you deserve more than that. And I'm not fooled into thinking that the shop will or should ever be my whole life, but for now, it is." I paused. "I guess we just got stale and lazy. I take my share of the blame." I could tell by Ted's reaction that he had not heard a word I had said after I mentioned that I had someone.

"Do I know this guy you're talking about?" He looked like I better come up with a good answer.

"You just met him." The look on Ted's face was one I will never forget.

There was silence, and then he asked, "Sam? This Sam guy I just met?"

"Yes," I said with practically a whisper. "Don't be asking me about it. Let's just leave it there."

A mean squint was now forming around his eyes. It was too late to go back now so I told myself to keep going and get it all over with.

"I say we have a toast to our friendship, and leave it with that,"

I said as calmly as I could with a thudding heart. "Who knows what will happen in the future? A new year is coming soon. Maybe some time will help us figure things out."

"You think it's all that simple? I can't believe I'm hearing this from you after all we've been through together." This was not going too well.

"I didn't say this would be easy. Ted, I've given this a lot of thought, and it was painful. I don't want us to destroy what respect and fondness we do have for each other." The more I said, the unhappier he looked.

"Oh really, Anne? How does that work?" He was really angry now. I kept my head down, wondering what would happen next. Just then the waitress came over to see if we needed anything. I was grateful for the interruption, but he wasn't.

Ted was silent for a second, shaking his head in disbelief and then rudely asked her for the check. It made me sad to affect him this way. Clearly he must not have had any idea that things would go like this. He took my coat and dropped it over my shoulders. In silence we went to the parking lot to get in the car.

The smoldering silence continued until we arrived in front of my house. He finally spoke.

"I don't think you have thought this all out, Anne. I am sorting this through myself, but I can tell you this. You are very special. I have always loved you. Our timing is probably not in tune right now, but be careful of this guy. He appears to be much older than you, and perhaps he's like Jim, who I know can be a womanizer. Do you know anything about his background?"

I interrupted so he couldn't continue his sermon.

"Thanks, Ted." I wrapped my scarf around my neck in preparation for leaving the car as soon as I could. "I understand what you're saying, but I am a smart woman and I can figure this out for myself. I am very sorry if I hurt you, but let's just end this evening for now."

I didn't look back at him as I left the car, slamming the door a bit harder than usual. I wondered how in the world I was able to do that, leave him there without a hug or kiss like I usually did, but somehow it seemed like the right thing to do. I didn't want to send mixed messages. I learned a long time ago that for me there was very little middle ground. I was pretty determined once I made up my mind about something, and I very seldom remember looking back with regret at one of those decisions.

Being Ted, he waited to drive away until I was safely in the house.

CHAPTER 22

———◦◦◦———

The chill in the room made me turn on the fireplace in the den. Mother was dozing on the couch in front of the TV. I quietly went into the kitchen to grab some cheese and crackers for my dinner. I also poured myself a glass of wine, which I knew would take the edge off of any guilty pangs that might haunt me. As I came out of the kitchen with my wine and snack, I looked at the stairs to the basement.

I went down the stairs as if I would find love and support from my family waiting for me at the bottom, but there wasn't anyone there. I turned on the floor lamp that was placed over the spot where I always sat to quilt and sat down. I took a good swallow of wine, laid my cheese and crackers on the side table, and stared at the quilt in front of me.

I looked across where Sue always sat to quilt, and sure enough, there was Grandmother's thimble, waiting for her to put on her finger. It usually brought a smile to my face, but not tonight. As

I stared down at this beautiful quilt, I looked at my stitches that improved each and every time I sat to quilt.

I thought about what a memory we had made for Aunt Julia. What if she had not brought us the quilt top to quilt? I so appreciated everyone so much more now.

They all gave me the confidence to find my own way. If it meant sorrow like tonight, fine, I could handle it. I knew I would have the love and support of family, even if they thought the world of Ted. If it meant I would never marry, that would be okay, too. If I worked 24-7 at my shop, no one in my family would complain.

I kept re-hearing in my mind all the cheering and clapping we shared as our confessions were revealed just the night before. Unconditional love at its best, I thought.

Suddenly, all the lights went on in the room, including the fireplace we enjoyed so many nights. I jumped and looked around to see if it was Mother joining me.

There was no one there. I called out, "Mother, is that you?"

Silence.

No one but me was in the room.

No one except the spirit of Grandma Davis, that is. I knew darn well it was her. She didn't want me to feel alone.

I finally said, "I know, Grandma, thanks for being here." We all were getting used to her presence. Oh God, did she know what I had just done with Ted? And did she approve?

I suddenly filled up with tears to the point of bawling aloud and laid my head on the quilt. I felt someone was listening even though the room was vacant. I felt a warmth around me like I had never felt before. I couldn't remember the last time I had cried, and I was really crying now. I couldn't stop the tears that had been held up since who knows when, and I didn't care who heard me.

I was crying for Ted, Sue, Aunt Julia, Aunt Marie, myself, and even the loneliness that my own Mother was experiencing. I lay crying till sleepiness took over, with my head lying right on the quilt. The wine and the sadness of a relationship ending with someone were taking their toll. I soon fell into a confused dream.

I suddenly awoke with Mother calling my name. I jumped in amazement; I actually had fallen into a deep sleep. The lights were dark, the fireplace turned off, and the only thing lit was the floor lamp that I had turned on. Who had turned off the lights and fireplace that had comforted me just minutes ago?

"I'm here," I called up the stairs. "I'll be up in a minute."

I looked down and could not believe my eyes. I had smeared lipstick in a couple of places on the quilt and it was damp with my tears! There was black mascara in a place or two. What was I thinking? Was I really that upset? Did I have too much to drink? And why was I too upset to get myself up to bed?

I was going to be in big, big trouble, especially if none of these stains came out. What was I to do? Should I try to get them all out with water?

I didn't want Mother to wonder what I was doing and come down the stairs. I really didn't know where to start, so I did nothing. I was so tired. I was emotionally and physically drained from head to toe. Right now I didn't care about anything. I just wanted to get up to my bed. I told myself I would come down early before work and look at it the quilt in broad daylight.

I came up the stairs and, of course, Mother had questions about when I had gotten home.

"I didn't want to wake you." I rubbed my eyes. "I went down to quilt awhile to relax. I am so tired now. I just want to get up to bed. I'll fill you in on everything in the morning."

Thank goodness she was distracted by something in the kitchen and didn't look at my face smeared with makeup colors that were no longer where they were supposed to be. I had to look terrible, so I quickly ran up the stairs before she could see me.

I flopped across my bed, leaving on every stitch of clothing. It felt so good to be in my safe place. I didn't care in what condition I or my clothes would be in the morning. Right now, it was all about sleeping in the darkness of nowhere.

The morning came way too quickly. I rolled over to see myself in a wrinkled ball of cotton. Realization then set in about the night before.

I jumped out of bed, pulled off all my clothes and quickly turned on the hot water in the shower, hoping to cleanse all sadness from the night before. Drying off, I looked in the mirror to see puffy, red eyes. Seeing my pathetic look made me want to cry all over again.

Oh, yes, the quilt! I suddenly remembered the messy, soiled quilt that I had to address before I went to work. Where would I start? Hopefully Mother had not been in the basement.

I finished dressing and applied heavy eye makeup and quietly went into the kitchen. Mother was in her bedroom, so I grabbed a clean, dry rag and dish soap and hurried down the stairs to the basement.

I turned the light on and looked where I had made the mess the night before.

I looked and looked at the place I had been quilting. No stains.

I frantically looked up and down the quilt thinking I must have been sitting in a different spot because the soiled area on the quilt was not there.

I turned on more lights. Still, there was no evidence of makeup or tear stains.

Then I thought that the quilt must have been rolled, but who would have done that? Mother would not have been able to do it herself and I was the last to be here in the basement, I thought to myself. Was I dreaming? Was I really that drunk?

Mother came down the stairs in confusion, wondering what I was doing in the basement at this early morning hour. "Anne, what are you looking for? You're not going to quilt this morning are you?"

I pulled out my chair and sat down in silence. Did the soiled spots dry and disappear? Was I losing my mind? I knew I would have to say something to her.

"I am so puzzled, Mother. I came down here last night to quilt, just to unwind. I had a rough night with Ted. Basically, we broke up."

"What!?"

"I can't discuss that right now, but everything is fine. It was pretty mutual. It will all work out one way or another, so don't worry. When I got home, I had a lot on my mind, so I came down here to quilt, thinking it would help clear my head. I got pretty tired after quilting awhile, then had a few tears thinking it all over, and laid my head down on the quilt."

"You did what!?"

"I know, I know. I was tired and mostly sad for Ted. So what I'm trying to tell you is that I got lipstick and mascara on the quilt by mistake. I was too tired to take care of it last night, so I came down here this morning to take care of it, and I can't find it."

"Oh, my gosh, we have got to find it and try to get it out!" Mother fussed, looking all over the quilt. "Aunt Julia will kill you, or even worse, both of us!"

We both started looking where I usually sat. Mother turned on more lights. My few quilting stitches from last night were there, but the quilt was as clean as if I had never been there.

"Mother, I have to tell you that I felt Grandmother with me last night," I confessed. "All the lights and the fireplace went on by themselves! Honestly, it was like she was here and had her arms around me. It was very comforting, and I wasn't the least bit scared."

"Are you very sure you made the stains?" She was still examining the quilt up close.

"Yes! I was pretty upset about it. Had I not been crying, the makeup stains wouldn't be there—just the tears."

"Why didn't you let me know you were here?" She touched my shoulders with love. "As much as I hate to say it, I think you will probably regret what you did to Ted, as well as anything you did to Aunt Julia's quilt."

I shot her a look that said stop talking. We both gave the quilt another once-over inspection, to no avail.

"I don't see any stains, Anne. I didn't roll the quilt or remove any stains. This is where we were all quilting the last time. I guess we know who took care of the mess, don't we?"

We looked at each other and nodded in unison.

"Oh, my word, what does all this mean? First the stitches come out and then Grandmother's thimble appears, if that isn't weird enough! Thank goodness the stains all disappeared. We have to keep this quiet and not tell the others," I begged.

Bewildered, we went upstairs to have coffee in silence.

"I promise to tell you more about Ted tonight, Mother, but now I have to get to work." I put on my coat. "I'm running late as it is. Isn't today the day you go talk to the bookstore about that job?"

"Yes, this afternoon. I'm pretty excited about it. I hope I don't say or do anything dumb! I'm so glad you don't mind, Anne."

"Oh, aren't you something." I kissed her on her forehead. "I'm so proud of you! Call me at the shop or stop by afterwards to let me know how it went."

CHAPTER 23

Sally was busy finishing our Christmas decorations throughout the shop. She was especially good at doing the windows, which was more of a pain for me. She had added more lights than the year before. Everything was looking more festive than ever.

This was my favorite time of year and a very profitable one for my shop. I had added a line of vintage reproduction floral containers for the season and they were already getting noticed.

I could tell from little comments that Sally was curious about Ted and I but there was no time to talk. The phone was busy, people were coming in, and there were arrangements to be finished before the noon delivery run.

Kevin, who was punctual and dependable with our deliveries, was also helping to get us organized, which he did pretty often. He was a clean-cut young man without much direction and seemed to be happy in our creative environment. Sally would try to prod him about his perhaps being gay, but he would not go for the bait. He knew us well enough to know that it would not matter to us one bit.

My cell phone was ringing; it was Mother saying she was hired to work one Saturday a month and every Tuesday and Thursday! "That sounds great! So when do you start?"

"Next week, because of the Christmas rush." She was so excited.

"Christmas rush," I answered with familiarity. "I should have hired you! It's pretty crazy right now, so I'll see you at dinner. Hey, even better, let's meet up for dinner out somewhere and celebrate your new job."

"I'm all for that," she quickly agreed. We decided to meet at Donna's Tea Room at 7:00 because it was her favorite place to go for dinner.

Sally overheard our conversation and said if we didn't mind, she would love to join us. "Sure, the more the merrier to make her feel confident and energetic to tackle the work world again. I may call her sisters and Sue if I can find some time."

"Your mother mentioned at Thanksgiving dinner that she missed being around books, so this doesn't surprise me. Good for her!" Sally really was a nice person.

Kevin came over to me after answering the phone, and asked, "Is there another Anne Brown living here in Colebridge?"

"Not to my knowledge. Why?"

"Because some guy by the name of Sam Dickson just ordered a dozen long stem red roses for an Anne Brown."

Sally and I burst out laughing.

"It's for me," I exclaimed! "Oh, my goodness, how cool is that? I know this guy, and I must say, this is a first! I wonder if he knows that there is another florist in town?"

"Well, that would be nervy," said Sally. "Why would he want to give them any business?"

I told Kevin that if we had roses to spare I would receive them, but not to bother if we were running short.

"You better keep this customer happy and do what he wants," Sally wisecracked.

"I hear you. Then they'd better be the best Colebridge has to offer!"

I was pretty impressed with this kind of treatment. I think Ted might have brought me flowers once or twice, but they didn't come from me. Was this a good thing, that Sam seemed to be pretty aggressive? I felt like a very, very young girl in the movies trying to react to her first kiss. It was hard to concentrate the rest of the day. I wouldn't be seeing Sam till tomorrow night, but I had to admit I was anxious, and curious as to what the evening would be like.

After we had a quick bite of leftover pizza that Sally brought for our lunch, I decided to take a few minutes to call the others to see if anyone could join us for dinner at the tea room. Aunt Julia had to go to Sarah's school, so she couldn't come, but Aunt Marie and Sue were totally up for the last minute call to celebrate.

"Here are your roses, Miss Brown," Kevin said, as he handed them to me with a big grin.

I actually blushed and held them close. "Leave them here, right here on my desk," I instructed. "I practically live here and there's no point in taking them home. Don't sell them, Sally!"

"You always say, a sale is a sale, so don't tell me that!" she teased as she admired them.

Everyone got to the tea room around the same time. Our moods were chipper and we were anxious to hear all about Mother's new job. It was good to see her happy and excited. She was pleased when I showed up with a small bouquet of mixed flowers. I told her it was part of our celebration.

"I ran into Ted at the bookstore." She looked for a reaction from me. "He seemed to be in a hurry, so he just said hello. Not like Ted's usual behavior, I thought."

I realized I was going to be hearing many comments as people ran into Ted. I'm sure I would somehow be made out to be the bad guy, as everyone, yes, everyone but me, loved Ted.

"Well, since most of you are here, you may as well know Ted and I are no longer a couple." I tried to be heard over the busy chatter.

"Does this mean that you're going to date Sam Dickson?" Sue's question was bold and she knew it.

"I do have a dinner date with him tomorrow night, and I'm pretty excited about it. I don't know if that really means we're dating, but it does mean that Anne Brown is now available!"

I guessed Mother and I both had something to look forward to!

CHAPTER 24

My busy day at the shop Saturday didn't give me much time to think about what might lie ahead for the evening. I wanted to get home early enough to freshen up and change clothes. Aunt Julia called the shop around 4:00 to share that she knew about my date.

"How do you feel about that?" I asked her.

"You're a big girl, and I hear nothing but good things about Sam. It is pretty interesting to have Jim's spin on your going out with him."

"What do you mean?"

"When I start to discuss it, he brushes it off like he doesn't want to encourage the relationship. I know Jim way too well, and this is how he acts when he doesn't want to share any more information or even wants to hide something."

"I can see him being hesitant because I am family, and if anything goes wrong, he may feel responsible."

"Good point. Just go and enjoy, and just so you know, I had a gut feeling Ted would never entirely win your heart for you to make that marriage commitment. Marie is pretty upset about you messing up a good thing with Ted, though. She and your mom really liked him."

"I know, I know. We just need some space, and frankly, I think he was going to break up with me until I turned the tables on him with what I wanted. I bet he has a hot date with Wendy Lorenz tonight. He didn't deny a relationship with her, so that said a lot!"

"We are all coming over Sunday afternoon to quilt, so be prepared to give an account of your evening with Sam. Well," she laughed, "at least the parts you want us to know. Sam is a smooth guy and hasn't dated a lot of girls. He always seems to be a gentleman and not present himself as a womanizer, if you know what I mean."

"Do you sense he wants to settle down a bit like he was suggesting when he said he wanted to travel less?"

"I'm not sure." She was thoughtful. "You know the travel scene does get old, and he's not getting any younger. I bet you'll have a better sense of that after tonight."

When I got home to change, Mother was preparing a small dinner for herself. "Think of me and my salad and chicken soup when you chow down on your lobster tail tonight," she teased. I laughed and asked if she was trying to hint that we take her along.

Basic black was always my standby outfit with some cool, updated jewelry. I seldom took time to shop. The retail side of me said it was better to sell than to buy!

When I looked in the mirror, I had a bit of cleavage showing that made me feel sexier than the usual outfits that I wore with Ted. I decided to wear my swing coat with a velvet scarf and call myself hot! I wanted my blonde hair to look a bit different as well so Sam wouldn't think I just dodged in front of the mirror at work and called it a day. I was a big fan of Jil Sander cologne and I planned to test its effectiveness with Sam. Yep, I looked hot, I said to myself as I took one last look and rubbed my red lips together.

I didn't hear the doorbell, but I heard Mother calling me. She probably was watching out the window and didn't give Sam a chance to ring it. I was ready, and came down to greet this mysterious fellow I was anxious to get to know.

"Pretty nice, Miss Brown," Sam said with a smile. "Your mother and I were just discussing her new job."

"How did you know about that?"

"Julia mentioned it to Jim and Jim mentioned it to me. It's a small town, remember, and I see Jim every day at work. I was telling your mother I that know a few folks here."

He helped me on with my coat. "I thought we'd drive across the river and go to a great steak house over there called Mavericks. Have you heard of it?"

"I think Aunt Julia mentioned that she had been there."

"Yes, Jim likes it, so she probably has been there."

Sam's black car appeared to be so new and shiny that he might have just driven it off a dealer's lot. I sunk into the seat next to him and wondered how long a drive it would be. I wondered if he really liked the place or just wanted to get out of Colebridge. Maybe he was hesitant to be seen with me. Maybe he just wanted to stretch out the evening? Either way, it felt good getting out of downtown where most of my social life occurred. I wouldn't be running into Ted most likely and that helped me relax.

"I hope you don't mind taking the extra time to try out this place." He sure had a great smile and white teeth.

"I'm looking forward to it." I smiled back and it took no effort at all. "With my schedule, I go to the same places over and over.

Colebridge is blessed with some good restaurants, but this is a great idea."

"Great," he said as he patted me on the hand.

"I owe you a big thank you, before I forget. I love the roses, and need to thank you for making me smile, and for helping me have a successful retail day at the shop! Kevin, my delivery boy, really gave me a rough time about it."

Sam laughed, and then I told him how rare it was that I got flowers because people felt I was around them all day long. "I knew you'd get a kick out of it. Besides, I like supporting small businesses that have attractive owners such as yourself."

The forty-five-minute drive to Mavericks went like it was five minutes, with all the conversation. We went in with Sam doing all the gentlemanly duties like opening doors. The owner happened to be near the door when we arrived, and Sam introduced Colin Maverick to me like they were longtime friends. Colin, I learned, was the third generation to run their family's two restaurants in the region.

The place was very elegant. I was thinking a steak house might be more on the primitive, casual décor line, but instead it was white-tablecloth with rich, deep, earth colors splashed with just the right touches like palm trees and plenty of plants. The lighting was romantic and light music filled the air.

"I'm very taken with some of these plants. I've never seen some of these varieties."

"I thought you would notice that," Sam smiled. My goodness we smiled a lot together. "I like to come here in the winter because it's like a breath of spring."

Our table was rather private with a view from a nearby window that looked out onto the beautifully lit patio. There was still a bit of snow on the ground, which glistened in the lights. It was like being in a dreamy painting. Yes, the whole scene was set. I was happy to be with Sam. It was like having my first real date.

I had my usual merlot and Sam asked what kind of single malt scotch they had. He made his choice and we studied the menu. Sam ordered the crab cakes for starters, as he recalled them being so good. For my entrée, I chose salmon with a fancy-named dill sauce and Sam ordered a veal dish with asparagus. He shared with me some of the things he liked to cook. This impressed me a great deal, because I knew he traveled a lot and probably had an expensive palate for quality food.

"I eat in restaurants most of the time, so when I can throw something together for myself at home, I am thrilled to do so."

"Well, need I say why cooking isn't in my world with a good cook in the house, and always getting home at all hours?" Suddenly I felt as if I was always making excuses.

"Do you like your arrangement at home or is it just easier?"

"I ask myself that question now and then, and I always come up with the same answer. Right now in my life, it's not only easier, but the food is certainly better than anything I could cook. And it has been great for Mother since my dad died. I am gone so much, but it is still comforting to her that I do come home. She never pries, other than normal inquiries. She can read me pretty well and she knows when I've had a bad day and prefer to be left alone. I am so thrilled she will be working at the bookstore. I just hope being on her feet will not be a problem."

"I'm the only child, so I can easily envision the house being mine someday," I continued. "I grew up there and love the neighborhood. Would I remodel, yes, and certainly make it my own, but there is no hurry. There is a time and a place, and life can change on a dime."

"Wow, this is all pretty revealing." Sam looked very seriously into my eyes. "You have thought a lot about this. You seem to prioritize things in your life, which many people do not. I also give you much credit for considering your mother's needs."

"What about your family, Sam?"

"My family is all in the Chicago area," he said. "Both my mom and dad are still around, but Dad is in poor health. He's had more than one cancer. It's hard on Mom sometimes to take care of him. My sister, Elaine, lives nearby and I don't know what I would do without her being there. I'm close to Elaine and try to help her in any way I can. My other sister, Pat, lives in Tulsa and I think I told you she is the one who is a quilter."

"Please be helpful to Elaine, because it always seems to fall on the daughter's shoulders."

"I like Colebridge very much and would like to continue to live here," Sam said.

With that break in our conversation, we made a toast, tipping our glasses to our families and to a great evening.

His eyes were so penetrating that I could hardly look at him. I loved the sound of his voice. He had the presence and sound of someone in control and I found it very reassuring and comfortable. I wondered if he could tell that I was pleased with what I saw and heard.

When our entrées arrived, Sam finally asked about Ted. "So this relationship with Ted Collins is over?" He took his first bite.

I gave him a look of surprise and was hesitant to answer. Could I think, eat, and talk at the same time about such a sensitive topic? I was hoping to dodge the subject since I had explained to him about Ted when we had a drink together.

"Yes. I told you before he's a very nice guy but he wanted more than I could give."

"I'll remember that!" He laughed. "Does he know about me, by chance?"

"Oh, yes. Hey, not to worry, he quickly hooked up with an old girlfriend, so all is well."

"Then that is my good fortune." He touched my hand as I took a sip of wine.

With that said, the subject was dropped. Another drink was ordered and Sam remarked that Christmas music was now in the air, no matter where he went.

"Yes, we've had it playing in the shop since Thanksgiving, but Sam, I can't say I really get tired of it. I have loved Christmas all my life. Will you be going to Chicago for Christmas?"

"Yes, I'll have to show up for a short span of time, I just don't know exactly what days. I worry it may be the last Christmas for my dad."

I was touched by everything he said, especially when he talked about his family.

"Have you ever been seriously involved with anyone?" I felt brave asking this.

"No official engagement, however I did have a heartbreaker a few years ago. I am thankful now that it did not go further, but it was what it was. She had a couple of children and a very involved former husband, so had it continued, there would have been problems."

I laughed and said, "So far I have avoided that!"

"How do you feel about having kids in general?" Wow, he doesn't beat around the bush, I thought.

"It's hard to know my own desires when I want to strangle most of the kids that come into the shop!" I responded safely with humor, I hoped.

"I bet you have many stories to tell about being in retail."

"Yes, indeed. I've tried to journal now and then because there is a book waiting to be written."

"So, you write?"

"Yes, when I have time, so that means not often. I enjoy it very much, though. I journaled for many years growing up, and I occasionally write poetry because it fills short periods of time. I try to write a weekly store newsletter for my customers. If I am not on schedule with it, they actually e-mail me out of concern. My e-mail list has grown quickly in a short span of time. It's my best means of advertising. Being around beautiful flowers and growing things is wonderful inspiration. I give garden tips, floral arranging advice, and occasionally some etiquette about sending flowers. I also give them reminders about any street events that may be going on. And there are always many questions, of course, that I need to respond to."

He was really paying attention to me, so I continued. "I also feel the written word is the best legacy to leave. The thought of someone reading my words twenty or thirty years from now is pretty awesome. There are one or more books in me. I just haven't decided when that will ever fit in my life."

Sam was listening to every word, and the time was flying. "You mustn't give up on that dream, Anne." He was serious. And thoughtful. And interested. In me! Hmmm.

After our amazing meal, Sam ordered a chocolate cheesecake dessert but I was totally full and feeling my third glass of wine. When I started to yawn, Sam took it as a hint, and asked for our check.

"I must remember that you had a very hard day at work today, and I didn't." And sympathetic. And courteous. Hmmm.

We walked out into the cold air, which made me feel refreshed and alive. Sam had his arm around me as we walked to his car. I was feeling very vital and very content. When we got in the car, Sam told me to shut my eyes if I was tired because we had that forty-five minute drive home. The warmness of his presence and the merlot made me want to curl up next to him, but I resisted.

I didn't blink an eye as I hung onto every word he said. We continued to have nice conversation, and he would take my hand and squeeze it now and then.

When we arrived at my home, he said he better not come in because of the hour and my sleepy composure. He than pulled me close and planted a most delicious kiss on my lips. I kissed him back more passionately, which was almost unknown to me. I told myself that I must have kissed someone back like this before, but it wasn't Ted. My relaxed mood and the smell of this man was heaven right now. Could this moment just stay in place for awhile?

"You are very special person, Anne," he softly whispered. "I want to see and feel more of you if you'll let me. I haven't been this relaxed with someone in a long time. I feel as if I have known you forever." He hugged me very closely, and I told him the feelings were mutual.

I ran my fingers across his cheek, as if he were a prize possession that I cherished. "I don't want this evening to end."

"You'll rethink that tomorrow morning," he laughed. "Don't you have the gang coming over to quilt?"

"Yes, we do."

"I only want you to say good things about me, you hear?" He smiled that wonderful smile.

"I'll give them the clean, edited version of my thoughts." I smiled right back.

Sam opened the car door and walked me to the house door to give me another hug and kiss that flowed through my body and lifted me into the house and all the way up to my room.

CHAPTER 25

I should have joined Mother for church the next day, but instead I rolled over and was thankful I didn't have to jump out of bed at the crack of dawn to open the shop. She was very respectful of not waking me; she knew I seldom ever slept late because of my work schedule.

I laid there with a dream-like feeling that was so good that I wasn't sure it would still be there when I fully woke. I hugged my pillow and wished it were Sam. The smell of his cologne was still on the hand that had brushed against his cheek.

How could I have this high school crush at my age—and his age?

How could I have these kinds of feelings having just come out of another relationship?

Then I told myself to slow down and not make a fool out of myself. How would I be able to hide my feelings about Sam with the quilting crew today? Should I hide them?

Then I remembered that Aunt Julia warned me that he was a pretty smooth guy. Should I take that to mean a bad thing, or a compliment?

No wonder I fell for him. I was pretty naive with my love life. Before Ted, there were not many men in my life who made much of an impression. Maybe that's why I fell in love with having my own business.

Ted was charming, had a good career, and he was very good-looking. He was safe, and everyone liked him, so okay, I did well, as they say. But I never did have the initial feeling with Ted that I had—was having!—with Sam.

Perhaps writing about all this in my journal would make sense of it, even though words could not describe the evening I had just shared with an amazing guy.

I wished I had time to journal these new and exciting feelings before they vanished into reality.

By the time Mother returned from church, I was showered, dressed in my jeans and sweatshirt, and had two cups of coffee working in my favor.

"Good morning." She was all cheer as she came in the front door. "Things were pretty quiet up there, so I didn't try to wake you. I didn't hear you come in, so should I assume you had a nice time?"

"Yes, yes I did," I answered with a big smile. What is it with this guy and smiling? "The restaurant was so elegant, Mother, you would have loved it. I had salmon, which was so delicious. Sam was such a gentleman. We talked and talked and talked. We both said that we felt we had known each other for a long time. I sensed that when I met him Thanksgiving Day!"

Instead of responding to my enthusiasm, she got busy in the kitchen pulling out bowls and ingredients before she even put on her apron.

"Would you help me whip up some of this cookie batter, Anne? My arthritis is acting up. I think warm cookies would be nice this afternoon."

"Oh, sure." I jumped off the counter stool. I had to get off my cloud and be helpful. Mother always knew what would be pleasing to everyone, and it usually revolved around food. I could sense she had words of warning for me, but knew I was no longer sixteen and that she better move on to a different subject. I started mixing the batter as she went upstairs to change clothes. I wondered why she didn't say she was glad I had a good time? It was like she put up a closed sign on the discussion.

Sam called around noon to see if I had a good night's sleep. I thought it was a nice touch, and frankly, it was his style. Nice words were exchanged. Why is it so important to women to have a guy call the next day? I guess we need to know the feelings and sweet nothings really mean something.

I then went down to the basement to prepare for our quilting. There was Sue's thimble in place where it always was. I was hoping she would get used to it and choose to use it and take it home. It was obvious that Grandmother wanted her to have it. Did Sue have any idea that when Grandmother made her mind up about something, it was the end of the discussion? Maybe her dad never relayed such opinions to her about his mother.

I took my chair, and noticed that my quilt book was placed in front of my chair. I didn't remember leaving it there, but perhaps Mother had been looking at it. I sat down and thought I'd take a look myself, as I had not taken the time to do that yet. Others seemed to have enjoyed it more than me.

I decided to look for quilts with flowers and there it was. The opened page had a very charming quilt with nine blocks of flowers that were surrounded by a border resembling a picket fence. How cool this is, I thought. I knew it wasn't an accident that this quilt was shown to me. I loved it, and there weren't a lot of pieces to it. It was a size that would be perfect for one of the walls in my shop.

I felt I should thank Grandmother Davis out loud, as if she would be expecting my thanks. I decided then I would take the book to Isabella's and ask her to help me pick out the fabric. What I did say out loud was, "Are you going to help me with that, too, Grandma?" If I had gotten an answer, I'd have been shaking in my boots if I had had them on!

"Did you say something?" Mother was coming down the stairs.

"Yes, I did. I was just thanking Grandma Davis for having my quilt book open to a flower quilt that she knew I would like."

"Well, now, we're giving her a little too much credit, don't you think?"

"Nope. I haven't touched the book. It was sitting here open at my place where I quilt." I pointed to the quilt I liked. "Now, if you did this, speak up."

Mother shook her head as she sat down at her place. "I haven't seen the book since the day Ted brought it here." She laughed. "I think Julia has enjoyed it more than anyone."

The doorbell rang, and down the stairs came Aunt Julia and Aunt Marie, who had driven over together and let themselves in the unlocked front door. "Sue had to run an errand, so she'll be along in a few minutes," said Aunt Julia.

"I smell baking, like homemade cookies, am I right Sylvia?" Aunt Marie draped their coats on the back of the recliner.

"Are you really ready for some now?" Mother asked. "The coffee is ready as well, so I'll just bring it all down and everyone can help themselves."

"I made some lemon bars to share so we'll have a sugar high," said Aunt Julia.

"I let myself in, the door was unlocked," announced Sue as she came down the stairs. "I locked it back; don't worry Aunt Sylvia."

"Thanks, Sue, I didn't realize it was unlocked till Julia and Marie arrived. Now that we're all here, Anne might want to share with you Grandma's latest communication."

"It's not a big deal, you all, but still inexplicable." I told them every detail about finding the open book at my place. Once again we shared looks that made everyone feel a little crazy. The truly crazy part was that no one thought it was stupid or that I was imagining things. It was like a "so what?" reaction, only not quite.

"So, the message here is I am going to Isabella's to get what I need to make this flower quilt."

"Let's all go." Aunt Julia sat up with excitement. "I want to make a simple quilt for Sarah out of lavender prints. I'm going to miss not having anything to work on when this quilt is finished."

"I need to start a friendship quilt," said Mother. "I was mostly thinking of my bridge group, book club, and of course, all of you. I remember seeing one at our church auction, and I kept wondering how in the world any family member could let go of something so personal. No doubt Mother will have to advise me how to proceed."

Oddly enough, we all let her reference to the unexplained basement quilt occurrences slide by.

"I've been thinking," said Sue with a pause. "I want to make a baby quilt. It needs to be the size of a large crib quilt, and a quilt that I could start working on without knowing what sex my baby would be."

"Oh, what a great idea." I clapped happily. "So you are definitely going to pursue an adoption like you said?"

"Yep, I've had one preliminary interview, and another one is scheduled for next week. It won't be easy, but it felt so right when I was talking to the agency person about my reasons to be a mother.

In that conversation, I kept leaning towards an international child who is having trouble being adopted. I don't think I, as a single mom, could handle a special needs child, but one that has been passed by because of her age or color seems doable."

"This is major information!" said Mother. "Have you still kept this from your parents?"

"I've told them a little, but not the details. They basically think it's wonderful, but warned me of many complications."

"They say the devil's in the details." Aunt Marie quilted steadily on.

"Tell us more," said Mother, as she passed around the cookies.

"Don't get crumbs on my quilt," warned Aunt Julia.

Sue was truly the center of conversation for a change, and it felt good. We chatted about what age child it would be fun to have, and whether she should consider a boy or girl. We even talked about names, which created a lot of laughs. The more we talked, the more excited Sue became, but she still wouldn't use Grandma's thimble.

CHAPTER 26

Aunt Julia asked me how many days till Christmas and how the shop was doing.

"We look really good and festive and it's keeping me hopping. This is the busy season, so we hope to break last year's record. Main Street becomes so magical at Christmas. I love the hustle and bustle of the shoppers and then of course all the carolers and other Christmas characters that roam the street during the season. It's the place to be doing business in Colebridge during the holidays, that's for sure."

Then she said, "We'd all love to know how last night went if you'll share that with us."

I blushed inside, hoping it would not show on the outside. "I can't believe we've gone this long without me being interrogated," I laughed. "I had an amazing time. We went to Mavericks, Aunt Julia. I understand you've been there with Uncle Jim?"

"No, I haven't," she said. "I've just heard good things about it. Jim said he has been there on business. Well, I guess we really don't know that to be a fact, but I do know it's very expensive, so I guess Sam wanted to impress you."

"Well, he did, and I hope he calls me again."

"I am so pleased with his family values and how he worries about his parents. He's also close to his one sister. Have you met her?"

"No, I haven't. You are right, though. He is quite fond of her and feels badly that she has the day-to-day duties of his parents' care. I must warn you, it is hard to have a relationship with someone who travels like he does."

"Can he be trusted, Aunt Julia?"

"In what way are you referring?" The room fell silent as though E. F. Hutton had just spoken. Oh, please, let this be an answer I want to hear.

"Well, I just mean do you know him to be faithful with whom he is dating?"

"I just assumed that Sam dated, but he hasn't brought his dates around Jim and me. I know what you're thinking, Anne. You're concerned that he and Jim might have the same practices."

"Oh, my, I guess I didn't think what I was saying. I'm sorry. I didn't mean to…"

"You have every right to ask that question," Aunt Julia stopped my embarrassment. "I think you are smart to do so. I'll ask Jim more about him."

"I'm afraid she's smitten," said Mother. I blushed and then assured them all I would be careful.

"Ouch!!" Sue yelped. She had stuck herself with her needle. "Oh no, I've got blood on the quilt!"

Mother jumped up to get a cold, wet towel.

"No, wait Sylvia," Aunt Marie said. "Remember it's your own saliva that takes out the blood."

Sue was still bleeding so she grabbed a tissue. We all stood up to see what could be done. Mother came down the stairs with a wet rag, but again was warned to wait till Sue tried her own saliva. "Okay, okay," she said. "Here I go; I'll give it a try."

She tried and tried, dabbing it with her own saliva, before she started to have some luck. "I'm so sorry, Aunt Julia." Sue was close to tears.

"It's going to be fine, I can tell," Aunt Julia assured her.

"Now let me wipe it with this." Mother used the rag. The blood was on a white section of the quilt, so it really showed up like a wound that begged to go away.

"There, I think it'll dry fine," she said, bringing closure to the subject.

"I'm done." Sue stood up. "I need to go home. I don't want it to start bleeding again."

"I have a band-aid here, Sue, just relax." Mother put it on her finger. It was just like Mother to always make everything okay. She was the one, the one in the middle of Aunt Julia and Aunt Marie, who didn't get attention but would always be on hand to serve both of her sisters. She was the caregiver of all of us, it seemed.

"We should all probably call it a day." Aunt Marie stood up and stretched. "I'm pretty much done with this section, and I'm feeling pretty tired."

"If you want to go, just say so, Marie. I have to help Sarah with homework sometime today, so it's fine with me." Aunt Julia also stood and went for their coats.

"We'll let this dry and then by next time, we can roll again," Mother said. "It's almost done."

"Marie said she would show me how to bind the quilt," Aunt Julia added with excitement. "I have enough of this blue fabric, which I think will look nice as a binding, don't you agree?"

"Yes, I do," I said. "I think it'll look great. What would we do without Aunt Marie?"

We all went up the stairs and started to say our good-byes.

"Be sure to let us know what happens on your next adoption appointment." I gave Sue a hug. "I'll see you next weekend, if not before."

"I hope you feel better, Marie." Mother helped her to the door. "Call me tomorrow."

"Keep me informed about Sam." I hugged Aunt Julia.

"I will. I'll have to have the two of you over for dinner, if you would you like that."

"I would, but you better clear it with Uncle Jim and Sam first." Here came another big smile.

"I still can't believe bringing Sam with us to Thanksgiving dinner turned into this." Aunt Julia laughed.

"I'm sure glad you did!" I kissed her on the cheek good-bye.

CHAPTER 27

———∞∞∞———

My week was going to be crazy at the shop. Besides daily business tasks that were coming due, it seemed it was this week I had to make some decisions in my personal schedule with shopping and events. I told myself to get a grip as I had gotten through this many times before. The holidays were coming faster than I remembered. Or was it because I was more distracted this year?

Mother asked if I thought I could help put the tree up at home, but I wasn't sure when. Why, oh why, did I talk her into buying the biggest tree our living room could possibly handle? It was gorgeous, but a big task to say the least. She always depended on me to do anything that required decorating, so I brought this task on myself.

We hadn't talked about our plans for the holiday, however, I was sure we "basement quilters" would have our own special way of celebrating.

This year would have a different spin for me personally since I no longer had Ted in my life. The anticipation of having Sam around excited me more than Christmas itself.

Christmas was always a big deal growing up, and I always looked forward to decorating with live greenery, poinsettias, and lots of candles. Having my own floral shop gave me opportunities to express Christmas décor in my own way and the whole Main Street historic section knew it. Everyone would place their live greenery order with me and then they would pick it up to decorate their own shops.

The "Christmas Traditions" events started right after Thanksgiving. An active committee did a marvelous job in planning things from concerts to "Breakfast with Santa." My contribution would be to provide any decorations they would need, since I could not donate much time.

My first order of business today, however, would be to send something to Sam's loft to thank him for a wonderful evening. I found out he liked plants from our conversation at the restaurant, so a plant seemed like a clever idea. I thought it should look like a holiday piece since he likely did not do much decorating of his own.

Was it a bit aggressive, I asked myself? Yes, it probably was, unless you were a flower shop owner. I signed the card, "Accept this seasonal token of my appreciation for such a great evening – Anne." I re-read it three times, thinking it might be a bit formal but better that than too cutesy!

Around 5:00 when I was finishing up corsages for an anniversary party, Sue called and asked if I could join the others on Wednesday for a trip to Isabella's Quilt Shop. "We want to go on our lunch hour, Anne. Do you think you can take a break?"

"Yes, especially since I know ahead of time. I'll need more time than an hour, so I'll drive separately, in case I can get free." When I hung up, I was pleased we really were going to move forward on making the quilts we had talked about.

Mother called shortly after to tell me she was taking Aunt Marie to the doctor. She still wasn't feeling well, and her doctor wanted her to have an EKG and a blood test. "I worry about her, since our mother died from a heart attack," Mother said.

"Tell Aunt Marie we hope she feels better. Sue called, and we all are on board for the quilt shop visit on Wednesday."

Later, just as I was getting ready to leave the shop, my cell phone rang. It was Sam, saying he found the arrangement sitting at his door when he returned home.

"You're not going to make any money in that business if you give away your inventory." I heard his smile over the phone. "It's perfect for the season! Thanks so much!"

"It's good PR, don't you think?"

"It's working, it's working." He paused. "I'm going out of town for a few days, but I hope you'll save Saturday night for me. I may be home Friday, but to play safe with your schedule, can I count on seeing you Saturday night?"

"Sure, I think that would be great." I hope I sounded calmer than I felt.

"Think about what you'd like to do, like a concert, dinner, shopping, bar hop, movie, or whatever."

"I say we do them all if you're up to it!" Could he hear me smile?

"You could probably handle that, but remember I'm an older guy and may not be able to keep up with you!"

I laughed. "I'll be thinking about it, and looking forward to it."

When I hung up the phone, I wondered how I was going to be patient until Saturday. Anne, Anne, Anne. Was this all happening too fast?

CHAPTER 28

⟨⟨⟨⟩⟩⟩

"Anne, this pattern is beautiful." Isabella admired my choice when I showed her my quilt book.

"Do you think I can do this as a beginner?"

"I think you can, but as you go along, I may have to give you some pointers. That is, unless you know someone who would be there to help you."

"I found a quilt kit here that has everything in it, so maybe that's perfect for me." Sue held it up for us all to see. It was a darling animal quilt with few pieces. We commented that the design and colors would be perfect for a boy or girl, and the size could easily be made twin quilt size by adding a border.

I knew Sue was getting more and more excited about an adoption because her last appointment was encouraging. She had beefed up her chances at the agency by telling them she would take a boy or girl up to the age of five. We all noticed a more positive, mature Sue than we had ever seen before. She was doing some painting in her apartment and seemed to be more open to all of us. We had a good time teasing her, and told her no matter what her outcome may be about her chances, there were other agencies.

"How are you feeling, Aunt Marie?" I moved closer to her at the cutting counter. "What did the doctor have to say?"

"Oh, my blood pressure has been up, so he increased my medication and told me to get out and walk more. I knew what he would say, of course, but I do feel fine today. What do you think of these?"

Marie was attracted to some pre-stamped quilt blocks. "I shouldn't buy these until I finish the others." She put them back on the shelf. "I love roses, and almost bought these the last time, but got the baskets instead. Do you like these, Anne?" She picked them up again.

"I do, but I like embroidery all in one color instead of lots of colors, but that's just me."

"I never knew any other way," she said. "That's the way I was taught. What color do you see these in?"

"What's your favorite color?" I asked her. "What color is your bedroom?"

"I really don't need a quilt for myself. I have quilts from Mother I still haven't used. How about if I make this for you, Anne? You'll have your own place someday, and since I am your godmother, I would like to do that."

"Oh, Aunt Marie, that's not necessary, but I would love anything you made. I love red, I think you know that, so do you think you could make all those roses red? Would you get tired of stitching in the same color?"

"Not if it pleased you, Anne."

"It would be beautiful in red. Here is just the shade I love." Isabella joined us, taking the embroidery thread skein I had chosen out of my hands.

"This color is referred to as Turkey Red. It's a deeper red like the red they used to make the older red and white quilts. I have several of those I've picked up at estate sales."

"How interesting! I love using red at the shop. Red vases, antique buttons, and ribbons, so this quilt would be a delight to me."

"Sold," Aunt Marie smiled at me as she handed her merchandise to the sales clerk helping Isabella.

The others heard our conversation and it all felt like a celebration.

Mother jumped from one kind of fabric to another. "I probably shouldn't start anything, since I now have this job." She put yet another fabric bolt back on the shelf.

I suggested she pick up something small and quick. "Here's a darling table runner kit, Mother. This would look great in several places in our home during the holidays. It's all cut out, so you just have to sit down and sew."

"It is very pretty, isn't it?" She took a closer look.

Isabella reminded all of us that the shop had classes, and that she would help us in any way she could. She saw the sales adding up as we made piles of our anticipated projects.

"What time is it?" Sue checked her watch. "Oh! I have to get back to work."

"I decided I'm taking off the rest of the afternoon because we are going to put up a Christmas tree!" I didn't want to lose the festive shopping trip atmosphere."

"Oh, Anne, that would be great," Mother said. She was as surprised as I was by my announcement and indeed delighted. Most of the orders at the shop were done, and Sally and Kevin could handle the walk-ins, I decided, as I called them on my cell.

We arrived home, kicked off our shoes, threw our quilting supplies on the kitchen table, and went to the basement to retrieve the huge artificial tree we bought last year. It was hidden pretty far back in the closet. It was in pieces and I managed to get it all up to the living room by myself in several trips. We were so pleased that we had paid extra for the pre-lit model. Not having a man in the house to do some of these technical chores, we tried to make things as easy as possible.

We assembled it and placed it in just the right spot in our formal living room. Mother started putting the boxes of ornaments on the floor around the eight-foot spectacle. "It's very beautiful, but oh, I miss the smell of the cedar trees of my childhood." She sat down for a moment.

"I loved that, too, Mother, but this is what the two of us need in our lives right now. I'll hang some live greenery from our mantle and front door, which will give us just the smell we need." I kept opening boxes.

"You're right, Anne, I just get so sentimental seeing these ornaments. Your dad would tease me every year how overboard I went with Christmas. I could tell he loved watching me do so, however."

"Next year, maybe Sue will bring a little one with her to Christmas dinner. Won't that be fun! Sue said her parents may come here this year. Do you think that's realistic?"

"It might be if I call and invite them!" Mother looked as if a light bulb had gone off. "They turned me down last year, remember? Sue may not want to be away in case something happens with her adoption process. It's been at least a year since I saw Ken. He's always so busy, but he needs to see his sisters. You never know how long we will all be here."

How sad to think of anything happening to any of my family. As we placed the ornaments on the tree, I encouraged her to call him that evening. Deciding to leave off a box of unattractive old ornaments, it didn't take long before we had a gorgeous tree to admire. The tree was a swirl of gold and white elegance. We celebrated with a cup of hot chocolate, which was another tradition, I so remember.

The home phone on the end table rang, and I picked it up to hear Sam's voice.

"Hey, what are you up to?" He sounded serious. "I called the shop and they said you took the afternoon off. I almost dropped the phone in disbelief, so are you okay?"

"Yes, of course," I laughed. "We went shopping and then I decided this was a good day to help Mother with the Christmas tree." I was cheeriness personified. "It is simply beautiful! We just finished, and I was just about to place the star at the top. I hope I don't fall off the ladder."

"Well, you should be a pro at that by now."

"Aren't you supposed to be working as well?"

"I just left a meeting, and don't have anything else scheduled for the rest of the evening. You were on my mind, so I wanted you to know I was thinking of you hard at work at the shop."

"Well, this has been a lot of work and if you were here, we would have put you to some good use."

"Then I'll let you go so you can get back to work, and if you want, call me later tonight. By the way, it's snowing here, so I'm heading to the hotel to stay in the rest of the evening."

"Sounds like a good idea." I started to envision him in a hotel room but banished the thought. "Stay safe, and have a drink in the hotel on me!"

"How did you know they even have a lounge?" There was that smile again.

"Good night, Sam." I was grinning as I hung up.

It was not a pleasant thought picturing him in some lounge where he could meet someone. He was so approachable for any stranger and his politeness would be appealing for most people. I told myself to put it out of my mind. He would not appreciate a jealous girlfriend he had just started to date.

"Have you started your Christmas shopping?" Mother asked as I stacked the empty boxes for the basement.

"No, but I have a list. I think there will be a lot of gift cards this year. How about you?"

"Well, I happen to get a pretty good discount at my new job, you know, so I think books will be in order. What do you think?"

"I think that would be great. I'll start making my reading list!"

After placing Christmas wreaths on the two front doors and the back kitchen door, we decided to call it a night on decorating. We munched on fruit, cheese, and crackers, and then I went to my room, anticipating an early visit with my favorite cotton knit pajamas. I brushed my teeth and turned on the TV on the chest of drawers. I kept thinking about Sam. Would it be too forward or anxious to call him back? My instincts told me to leave him alone. We had a short, nice conversation earlier, and I didn't want to say too much or appear too anxious for his attention.

I did give some thought as to what I wanted to do on Saturday evening. There was a Christmas concert at Colebridge Hall on the university campus that sounded wonderful. I wanted to take every advantage of the Christmas season if my schedule allowed. I knew Mother would enjoy it as well, but I didn't think I should suggest her coming with us. There were so many social things that required a couple; Mother always complained about it. For a while there I always had Ted if I needed a partner.

Ted, what about Ted? I wondered who he might be with right now.

CHAPTER 29

Friday morning was staring me in the face, and I still had not heard from Sam. Was I again doing to Sam what I did to Ted so often? I didn't call him back, protecting myself from being needy. When I got to the shop, I decided to call him on his cell. I knew the concert tickets would be a good idea. He didn't answer so I left a happy, fun message that I had an idea for Saturday and was looking forward to seeing him.

Sally came in with a list of grievances. I learned early on to give her time to unload, and once she did she was good to go for the day. She had financial problems, and I had considered various ways that I could help her. She was a huge help to me and really a nice person. It dawned on me some time ago that I might want to make her manager someday so I could take more time to travel to flower and gift shows, as well as promote the store more than I had been doing.

It was now noon and traffic in the shop had slowed down, but we still had a funeral order we were trying to finish. I used to immediately check to see who they were for just in case I knew the deceased or their family. As time went on though, it became less important how quickly I knew. Many folks turned out to be my mother's age, so I would share obituaries with her on occasion.

Sue walked in on her lunch hour, and said she had another appointment next week with the adoption agency. She said she had put me down for one of the references, and wanted to warn me that they might be calling me soon.

"Oh, that's great, I will coat you with all the sugar I have. Are they giving you any information that gives you a clue on when this could happen?"

"I'm certain they don't do that, plus they haven't told me that I definitely qualify." She explained that many adoptive parents have been accepted who were single just like her, so she felt encouraged.

"Well, we're going to think positive!" I kept working as we talked. "I went to pick up a pizza last night at Cusumano's and guess who I saw sipping wine and enjoying pasta?"

"I give, who?"

"It was Ted and Wendy. Ted acted like he didn't see me, but I know he did."

I wanted the wind out of her gossip sails. "This is not news to me Sue." I wrapped a stem perhaps a bit too tightly. "Your seeing them together just proves there really was something going on. I guess when I saw them at the bookstore the relationship had already started. I'm happy for him, but I wish he had been more honest about it." Another stem suffered my ministrations. "He wanted to make me feel that I was the bad guy in breaking us up. I wonder how I would feel right now if I didn't have Sam to think about?"

"You are really fond of Sam, aren't you?" Sue turned my head so I had to look at her instead of my work. Sue really cares about me, I thought.

"I am, and it feels good to say it."

It was 3:00 and Sam finally called. He sounded in a good mood.

"Well, my sweet, what's on the agenda for tomorrow night besides giving you a squeeze?" Wow, he sounded lusty and vigorous.

"I thought we could go to the Christmas concert at Colebridge Hall."

"That sounds fine, so can we get tickets there?"

"Yes, and I'm happy to make it my treat. I love Christmas, and I usually go with family, so it will be really nice going with you!"

"Does your mother typically go with you?"

"Sometimes." Where was this going?

"You're welcome to invite her to join us if you like. I've been trying to think of some way to thank her for that wonderful Thanksgiving dinner. I insist on you letting me pay for those tickets; so if you'd like to ask her, it's fine with me."

"She would be thrilled." Nice guy! I thought, as I pictured the three of us together. "I'll find out what she's doing, and thanks so much for thinking of her." We chatted for a few more minutes and then hung up, agreeing we would meet up Saturday.

Just as I thought, he was the type to include family and see the value of having them in your life. Was he too good to be true? Did this mean I would be spending the Christmas season with him? Did it mean we were, indeed, becoming a couple? I was picturing how we must look together. He had dark hair, I had blonde. He had sharp brown eyes, I had soft blue. He was tall and I was not. He was big boned, and I was thin boned. I guess opposites attract, I told myself with a smile.

I couldn't wait to call Aunt Julia to tell her we were going to the concert and that Sam suggested we ask Mother to join us. "Do you think I should ask her, or was he just being polite?"

"Ask her; she'd love it. He may as well get used to your lifestyle and your family. I have our house pretty much decorated now, so maybe next week you and Sam can come to dinner." She sounded excited. "I've got to be thinking about what do for Jim's birthday as well, darn it!" Her excitement faded.

"Do you think Uncle Jim will feel okay about the dinner?" I was hesitant because of the tension between them.

"I really don't care what he thinks. It's the holidays, and I want to have my family around. Sam loves my cooking. Hey, we're still on for quilting Sunday afternoon, right?"

"I think so. We may have that quilt finished for Christmas, Aunt Julia. Wouldn't that make a terrific gift to you, and from us, by the way!"

"Oh, indeed!" Her gratitude shone through her voice.

When I came down the stairs the next morning, Mother was preparing a cake to take to a friend whose husband had died and her mood was sad. "Funeral food" they call it. It was the common practice to take food to a family dealing with grief.

To cheer her up, I told her I had talked to Sam and he wanted her to join us for the Christmas concert that evening. She was delighted and commented about the sweetness of the suggestion.

"But I think I'm going to pass," she said. "I'm going over to Marie's. She is either depressed or there is something still not good with her health. If she is up to it, I thought we'd go eat somewhere, but if she's not, which she claims, I'll go over after dinner with a dessert."

"Oh, gee, I hate to hear that, Mother. She felt good at the quilt shop the other day! I wish she had other family, like her own children."

"It's meant a lot to her for us all to be together. She feels she's been very helpful with her quilting."

"I hope she feels up to coming over tomorrow."

"I do, too."

"You're being a wonderful sister, you know," I said as I hugged her.

CHAPTER 30

I rushed home after work leaving Sue to finish checking out for the day. I often wished I had Sue there every day. She was dependable and loved the change from her regular job. I even hoped a single, male customer might walk in one day who would capture her attention.

I stewed over what to wear to impress Sam. I wanted to look sexy, yet together and sophisticated for the concert. I needed to go shopping. I had not really updated my wardrobe for some time. Somehow my appearance took on a whole new meaning with Sam in my life. I bet he was always a good dresser, I thought. I made the best choices I could with what I had, adding a red belt I had never worn before. I gave myself a quick once-over in the full-length mirror, and got myself downstairs to wait for him.

He was a little late, but not enough to concern me. When he came to the door, he looked absolutely great with a red scarf around his neck. "You look like you're ready for the holidays!" I wanted to kiss him on the cheek, but didn't.

"I have some red on, too, so we look pretty festive!"

"Is your mother joining us?" He sounded as if he really did want her to go.

"No, she had other plans, but she said to tell you thank you. They have a matinee performance, which she hopes to go to, so you are stuck with just me. Me, and the hundreds of others who'll be there."

Smiling (again!), he helped me with my coat, told me I smelled good, and off we went.

Our seats turned out to be pretty good and Sam said so. I was getting a lot of double-take looks when people saw me with this guy who wasn't Ted. I held onto his arm like he was indeed my guy, at least for now. The concert was beautiful as well as entertaining. We held hands most of the time. During the intermission, I introduced him to various folks including other business owners from the street. I was pretty sure we wouldn't be running into Ted and Wendy. I had dragged him to the concert one year and he hinted I might want to take Mother next time instead.

Coming out of the concert hall, I told Sam that Aunt Julia wanted to have us over for dinner soon. "She said the house was all decorated and Uncle Jim has a birthday coming up, so perhaps she would schedule it around that time."

"That would be great. She is an awesome cook."

"Are you comfortable when you go over there?"

"Yeah, aren't you?"

"I'm not around Uncle Jim that much and they seem to have some problems, so it makes me a little uncomfortable. I always wonder how much he thinks I know about their marriage."

"Yeah, Jim likes to have a good time for sure, and he does comment now and then about Julia not always approving of things, but I don't take him too seriously."

"Do you think he really loves my Aunt Julia?" We were walking briskly in the cold.

"What kind of question is that?" Sam stopped abruptly.

"I just want to hear it from a man and his close friend, I guess."

"I don't know that I am an authority on such things, but he's never talked about divorce or leaving her."

"Okay, subject dropped," I knew I had gone too far and deep.

As we got in the car, Sam suggested we go across the river to the Capitol Hotel, which had a nice lounge with a piano bar.

"Sounds great." I wanted to be accommodating to cover my gaff. "I didn't know they had a piano bar. They actually have ordered flowers from us on occasion. They have a nice place for lunch there, but I don't remember the name."

"Some of our clients stay there when they come into town. Colebridge doesn't really have much in fine lodging. It's a nice quiet place to talk without distractions."

"So were you okay with us going to the concert?"

"Oh, sure! I like Christmas but it takes a feminine touch to bring it all to reality. My mother and sisters love it as well, and they do a lot of entertaining around the holidays."

"I really never thought of holidays being more of a woman thing, but I guess for all the frills and details, the woman does almost have to take over." Was this a good thing or not, I wondered.

When we arrived in the dark, warm lounge, the gas-lit fireplace got my attention. Sam asked if we could have the table nearby. The place was quiet, which Sam said happened on the weekends. Their busy times were mostly during the week with business people. When we got our drinks, Sam lifted his glass to toast.

"Here's to spending the holidays with the sweetest girl I have ever met!" We laughed and clinked our glasses, me blushing warmly.

"My turn. Here's to the most handsome, sweetest man in my life right now." He grinned from ear to ear.

"You had to build me up by adding handsome, didn't you?"

"You are handsome." Was it the fire that was warming me up so? "I could hardly keep my eyes off you when you were over for dinner. I found it hard to believe you were single." Was this the wine talking?

"I guess that's what I found hard to believe when I met you. I thought to myself, what is this chick, or woman, I should say, doing still single and living here with her mother? I knew there had to be more to the story."

"Well, now you know that I have another focus and that I'm being kind to Mother and economically helpful to myself."

"Got it!" He laughed. "I was told there was a guy in your life, but I thought to myself he must not be hitting the mark if he couldn't take you away for his own. I guess what I mean is that he hadn't convinced you to have a place of your own, or one together."

"I never thought of it that way." This was an interesting twist, I thought.

"Okay, drink up." He looked serious. "The next subject is going to be a bit more personal. If you don't care to answer, it's okay."

He waited till I took another sip of wine and then pulled the one side of my hair behind my ear. I took another swallow, enjoying the moment before it might go away.

"Where did you have your private time together?" He was looking right at me. "Or should I come right out and say 'sex'? Was it usually his place or yours?"

"Sex? Did you say sex? What's that?" I laughed and nearly choked. I could tell he really wanted an answer. I coughed some more, took another sip of wine, and decided to go for the answer.

"Do I really have to answer that?" I said, playing coy. "That's pretty personal, and I'm surprised you don't have more imagination than what you're projecting."

He laughed and knew from my body language he might have gone too far.

"Okay, let's try another question." Oh, he was cute when he was meek.

"Hey, mister, just remember you'll have to answer the same questions that you ask me." I ran my finger across his chin.

Before he asked, he ordered another round of drinks. The piano music was soft and sexy, which made a delightful background for serious talk. I saw a few couples dancing in the small corner reserved for that and hoped he might talk less and ask me to dance at some point.

"Ready for one more attempt at something personal?"

I nodded, "Perhaps."

"Were you a virgin when you first had sex with Ted?"

I chuckled. "Okay, now I'm piecing together what you are wondering me to be." I took another sip of wine.

"I don't think so." I had him on the ropes for being too nosey, but I decided to let him off.

"No, I wasn't a virgin, and that's as far as you get to fish tonight, Mr. Sam. May I be so bold as to ask you to step to the dance floor before you ask me anything else? I find this music pretty romantic, how about you?"

"Forgive my curiosity and not noticing the wonderful opportunity to hold you in my arms! By all means, my dear, follow me."

I was going to ask a few questions of my own as we danced slowly, but the touch of his cheek and smell of his cologne kept me still. He kept quiet himself, holding me closer and closer. After the music stopped, we hesitated, looking into each other's eyes. Without need for further communication, we went back to the table. As I sat down, he kissed me on the forehead.

"Okay," he said. "Go ahead and ask me anything you want."

"Well, I asked Aunt Julia this question and she didn't know the answer. Who were you seeing before me, or should I say, who saw you last?"

Sam laughed. "Let's start with the fact that I have never been married," he said. "I almost got married, but she changed her mind, so now you know I am not perfect. That was a few years ago. I have dated some women off and on, but no one seriously since her."

"Who is she?" What a stupid question! Like I would actually know her.

"She lives in my hometown. She has since married. I moved on, so that was the end of that tune."

"Oh. I'm sorry it didn't work out. It sounds painful."

"She was divorced with two children. She was a knockout, no mistake, but there was baggage I wasn't sure I could handle."

"Do you mean the children?" I wondered how he felt about children.

"It wasn't so much the two kids; it was my traveling. Her children were cute and clever, but she seemed to be very needy, the more I got to know her. I figured it was a combination of things, like wanting a father for her children, and then more of my time than I could give. I said to myself that if it was this way just dating her, I could see a train wreck for whoever she would marry. Don't get me wrong, I want to have a family someday, but starting out with one was going to be difficult with her. Jim met her a few times back then, and he kept warning me about her need to protect me and occupy my time. Thank goodness she broke it off, and I'm glad she did. This is what is so refreshing about you, Anne. You have a life! You know what you want, which makes you very attractive to someone like me. With my schedule, I have to know that someone isn't counting the hours till I get home, and then I don't want to be interrogated as to where I was and what I was doing."

He sipped his drink. "Now, of course, I want to be missed. I want to look forward to coming home, even if it's to chores and listening to what a terrible day someone is having. I know that's life, but I want to hear interesting things from my partner about her life. I don't want to have to provide all the conversation and excitement in our relationship. You're an independent woman, despite living with your mother. You're being smart about your choices, and frankly, I admire your dedication to your mother."

"Wow! I'm speechless." I choked and sipped wine to recover. "This is all insightful. Thank you for sharing." I would have to go over all I had heard and digest every word at a later time.

It seemed the right time to leave, so Sam asked for the check. "Let's get out of here and enjoy some time alone."

I was ready to run away with this guy. He sure had a way of putting things in their proper place. When we got in the car, we were both shivering from the cold. He gave me a hug and a lovely kiss on the lips.

"I'm going to take you home, Anne, ask for a hot cup of tea, and then be on my way. I'm going to be around most of the week, so I promise I'll have you over to dinner this week. Take a look at your calendar. I'm anxious to fix you some serious food."

Home we went, and again before we got out of the car, he gave me another serious kiss. This kiss was bold and promised more in the future.

Mother was still up. She welcomed us at the door and invited Sam in with open arms.

"How is Aunt Marie?" Her solemn face concerned me.

"She didn't want to go out, so we had dinner in and watched a movie."

"The concert was great," said Sam. "I'm sorry you couldn't join us. I met a lot of new people tonight."

We both laughed, and I told Mother that I got a lot of second looks when they saw me with Sam.

"You make a great-looking couple. I'm glad you both enjoyed the evening." She was always so sweet. I just loved her.

I told Mother we were going to have some hot tea and that she should join us. "No, I'm dead tired, but thank you." She headed up the stairs.

Sam and I mostly made small talk. I took him in the living room to see the glorious big tree. As he admired our handiwork, he then took in all the family photos placed about the room. I explained who they were.

"You look like your father, Anne. The blonde hair and blue eyes certainly didn't come from your mother."

"He was a very tall and handsome man, if I say so myself. I really miss him. He would have been such a help in my business endeavor. He belonged to many civic groups and one year was 'Man of the Year' for the Chamber of Commerce."

"So what do you remember most about him?" Sam was so sincere in his interest about me. Hmmm.

"When I think of him, I think of both Mother and Dad because he adored her." I stared into the photo. "He would worry about her, and I don't remember ever seeing them quarrel. He always worked long hours, but I never felt neglected. I'm sure there were times Mother did, as most wives would. I was his little girl, and he treated me special that way till the day he died."

Sam could tell the topic had curbed my joyous mood, so he changed the subject.

"How's the quilt coming along?"

"Come downstairs and check for yourself."

He followed me into the basement. Just as I started to turn on the light, Sam took my hand and pulled it around him. His hold was firm, and one hand went up my neck to cradle my head for the perfect kiss. He then whispered that he loved my kisses and asked if we could see the quilt in the dark. I hugged him like I would never be able to hug him again. I then reached for the lamp.

"If you think I'm great, check out the quilt." I didn't want to leave his embrace. "We're almost done, so maybe the next time you see this it will be back home at the Bakers'."

"It's very nice, if my opinion means anything. I know it's a lot of work." He walked slowly around the frame.

"We've decided that we'll miss this quilt, so we all went to the quilt shop and decided what we each will make next, since we have the hang of this now. I found a very cool flower quilt perfect for the shop that I want to try to make. It looks a bit difficult now, but I'm determined to do it."

"I think you could put your mind to doing anything you want, Anne." He pulled me close for another kiss in the dimly lit basement. We then headed up the stairs like two teenagers who might be getting caught at something.

We sipped our tea in the living room for another half hour. Time just went so quickly when we were together. There was so much we still did not know about one another. Like everything in my life, there wasn't enough time.

Sam drank his last swallow, set down his cup and said, "Off I go, my dear Anne. We need our sleep. Save your thoughts till we meet again."

He left me with a wonderful evening to think about as I reluctantly saw him out the door. My mind was so preoccupied that I didn't remember getting undressed and placing myself between the sheets. Now that I knew about his prior love, would I fit in or not?

CHAPTER 31

———⊂∞⊃———

S ue and Muffin were the first to arrive Sunday afternoon. I
had been to church with Mother, and then we stopped at the
bakery to get delicacies for the afternoon quilting. Nick's Bakery
had the most delicious cookies and chocolate truffles. They were
just across from my flower shop, so it was a frequent weakness of
mine and others who shopped in the area. Nick Notto's family
was such a blessing to our street and community. The large Italian
family all worked in the bakery for many generations. Nick's
darling two daughters were soon to be in charge when Nick
retired. No matter what charity event you attended, there was
something good to eat donated by Nick's Bakery.

"Aunt Julia is bringing Aunt Marie." Sue put her coat on the
coat rack.

"Is she feeling okay?" I asked.

"Nothing was said, so I guess so. I'll go on down and start
quilting, I guess. They should be here any minute. They were going

to drop off Sarah at the mall, and Uncle Jim was going to pick her up."

"Oh yes, the mall," I quipped as we both settled in at our places. "What would the social scene be without the mall? Speaking of the mall, I need to do some serious clothes shopping one of these days. I need to update, too, a bit, perhaps from one of those cute boutiques I hear others mention. Do you know which ones are hot, Sue?"

"You're asking me, me the one who has to wear a boring suit to work everyday?" She laughed. "You need to take Sarah with you."

"You know, that's not a bad idea!" I wished I had thought of it sooner.

"So…Sam has got you thinking?"

"Yes, he does have me thinking—about a lot of things."

Five minutes later, Mother, Aunt Marie, and Aunt Julia joined us downstairs.

"We are going to finish this quilt today, you all!" Aunt Julia announced. "We cannot roll it again, so if we get this border and corner done, we can celebrate. I thought ahead, and have champagne in the car! I also brought my camera."

She started taking close-up photos of the quilt and then a photo of each person quilting.

"I'll take your picture Aunt Julia." I got out of my chair. "I'll take one of the three sisters on one side quilting and then you take one of Sue and me on the other side. I'm also going to take a photo of Grandmother's thimble sitting there in front of Sue, in case it disappears on us."

Each picture was one of pride in what they had accomplished. Everyone laughed and joked about our unseen guest. What if she showed up in the photos, I wondered? We then sat down to get some serious quilting done.

"I read all the directions to the flower quilt." I broke the silence.

"I get all the cutting part, but hand appliqué is going to be a big-time challenge for me."

"You should have gotten a precut quilt kit like I got, Anne," said Sue. "I need to be looking for a sewing machine—something really cheap. Did you see the price tags on some of those machines at Isabella's? I'll never be able to afford one of those. I could buy a new car with that kind of money!"

We laughed and wished her well.

"Just take mine," offered Aunt Marie. "It's not that old, and I don't plan on using it for some time. I'm enjoying the embroidery for now."

"Wow, Aunt Marie! I'll be happy to buy it from you."

"No indeed, Sue. You are family, and I can't think of a better place for it. It's only several years old, and has pretty many features on it. You may be sewing little dresses and who knows what in the very near future."

"That would be so cool! I'll take you up on it." Sue jumped out of her chair to hug Aunt Marie. "Thanks so much!"

"You saw Sam last night, didn't you?" Aunt Julia looked at me across the quilt.

"Yes, we went to the concert at Colebridge Hall, and it was great. He hadn't been there before. Oh! I ran the idea by him about coming over to your place for dinner, and he seemed pretty glad to do it."

"Perfect, it'll be a more comfortable way of celebrating Jim's birthday. I'll get with Jim and we'll set a date."

"We had a lot of good conversation last night," I announced to everyone. "Aunt Julia, is he as wonderful as he seems to be? I keep waiting for the shoe to drop." Before anyone could answer I said, "Well, you know if it does, it does. I'm a big girl and so far I have no regrets."

"I know no secrets about him, Anne." Aunt Julia stopped quilting. "Now, keep in mind—would my husband share everything with me? No, probably not. But, Anne, he thinks you are wonderful, and if Sam was an insincere guy with a seedy past, Jim would not encourage you to keep on seeing him."

"That's a good point," Mother chimed in.

"I am so excited about sharing the holidays with him."

"Speaking of Christmas," said Mother, "you're all invited here Christmas Eve, like last year. This gives you Christmas morning with your families."

"I think Sam is going home to his folks, but maybe he'll share some time in both places." I wondered if this would really happen.

"What if he asks you to meet his parents?" Aunt Marie remained cautious about Sam, I could tell.

"I think I'd like to go as long as I don't leave Mother for too long." I realized I, too, was not quilting.

"Hey, we're all getting a little too far ahead of ourselves, aren't we? This is moving fast!" Sue shook her head in dismay.

"Enough about me." I picked up my needle. "Sue, do you have a plan B, C, and D if the agency gives you discouraging news?"

"Yes, I do." The new, more mature Sue was prepared. "There are many agencies. I have lists of them, and with all the tragedies around the world, everyone says it's possible for sure, if you can just be patient."

"I love your attitude," I said. "I want to go Christmas shopping for this new little person."

Everyone chuckled.

"Wouldn't it be great fun if this happened before Christmas so we could buy extra presents?" Mother spoke for us all.

"It probably won't happen by then, but I may have enough information to be really hopeful," Sue said. "If I am approved, they could easily have a child identified for me by then. That would be cool enough, and give me time to plan. I've talked to other parents and generally this is how it happens: They are given a photo with the sex and age. Sometimes there is a name, and sometimes not. I don't think I can really give the child a name until I see him or her."

"That makes sense," I agreed. "We have a lot of love waiting for him or her."

"Sarah needs to have a baby-sitting job," Aunt Julia added.

"Sue has to ask us first, right Mother?" She was on her way upstairs to make coffee but yelled back that I was right.

The phone rang and mother answered it from the kitchen. When she came back to the basement, she carried all the treats from the bakery on Grandmother's silver tray. The smell of freshly brewed hazelnut coffee followed her down the stairs as well.

"You are to call Sam after everyone goes home," she said, grinning at me. I smiled (again!) and then listened to all the kidding from the others. They threatened to stay all evening!

"Hold on, Sylvia," said Aunt Julia. "If we can get this little section quilted, we can be done!"

"My finger is so sore, you all finish that row." Sue got up from her seat. "You should put in the very last stitch, Aunt Julia."

"I'll have the camera ready," I promised. Mother held up pouring the coffee until we could finish.

Ten minutes later we all were as quiet as mice as we watched Aunt Julia put the last stitch in the quilt. With that last stitch, yells of celebration broke out. This Kodak moment was important in so many ways!

"Can you believe this!?" Aunt Julia shouted toward the ceiling. "Mother, are you watching!?"

"Congratulations to all!" exclaimed Mother. "We did it, and

we couldn't have done it without the effort of Julia and the help of Marie."

Aunt Julia had tears of joy in her eyes. This was indeed a big moment for her and we all knew it. We hugged each other over and over to celebrate our great accomplishment.

"Well, let's spread it out, and open it up." Aunt Julia quivered with excitement. We unpinned and unrolled the quilt so Sue and Mother could hold it out, open for all to see.

"Did we miss anything?" I looked at each row of fans in the quilt.

"It is so beautiful." Aunt Marie had such love in her eyes. "Look how it has come alive from the stitching. I'm glad you didn't skimp on the amount of quilting."

"Stand by the quilt, Aunt Julia." I took a picture of her standing in front of the quilt. Sue went to pick up Muffin who was just as excited to see what had just occurred.

Then she had us all stand in front of the quilt as she took a picture. Muffin kept still as Sue embraced her for the flash that was about to go off. We all somehow felt it was our quilt as well. The colorful quilted fans did come alive. It was a good choice for Aunt Julia. The gleam in her eyes was the sign of success she needed to experience.

"Okay, Marie, we need to get together sometime to get this binding on," Aunt Julia reminded her.

"Sure, just bring it over anytime, or I can stop by." The two of them folded up the quilt.

Everyone then dug in to taste the pastries and coffee. Aunt Marie had said early on that quilters love to eat as much as they love to quilt, and from observing this group, I had to agree with her.

"We'll save the champagne for another time," said Aunt

Julia. "I want you all to come see our tree, so I'll be calling you for another celebration. I'll have the quilt on the bed, how about that?"

With that, much chatter continued about Christmas plans and how wonderful the quilt looked. It was a Kodak moment none of us would ever forget.

CHAPTER 32

⎯⎯⎯∞⎯⎯⎯

Mother and I were still patting each other on the back with our recent success as we followed the others out the door. Aunt Marie and Aunt Julia were walking to the driveway where Aunt Julia's car was parked when I saw her turn to Aunt Marie with a frightened look of concern.

In just seconds, Aunt Marie fell to the ground, grabbing her chest. We ran to her, concerned and alarmed. It was real; we knew it was her heart. I got there first and stooped to hear her whisper, "My arm, my arm."

"Sue!" I tried not to panic but I yelled anyway. "Call 911 right now!" I turned back to Aunt Marie. "Do you have any pills with you to take?"

"No, but get me an aspirin," she whispered. She was having trouble breathing. She was pale like I have never seen her. I tried not to think how serious this could be. She turned her head to the right and we lay her on her side on the sidewalk.

"Aunt Julia, run get an aspirin and water," I shouted. So much for staying calm. I wasn't going to leave Aunt Marie, and from the look on Mother's face, she was in no condition to be part of this emergency. Sue said an ambulance was on the way.

"Calm down, calm down and take deep breaths if you can," I said, as much to myself as to Aunt Marie. "Help is on the way. Have you had this pain all day?"

"I had some sensations in my arm this afternoon but thought it would go away." She wanted to move. Mother and I now held her sitting up, Sue hovering nearby. Aunt Marie's face was going whiter and a light sweat appeared on her forehead.

Aunt Julia returned with the aspirin and water, looking as if she was about to faint. "I'll go with her in the ambulance," she announced. "You follow with your mother. Sue has Muffin and will follow in her car to the hospital." Good plan, I thought.

Aunt Marie started to cry. "I'm so sorry to spoil a perfect day."

I hugged her lightly and said we should say a little prayer that everything would turn out fine. Mother was just as frightened as her sister and lacked the right words to say. They were close sisters, no doubt. I wondered if Mother knew Aunt Marie had a serious heart situation and hadn't said anything to all of us. What if this was my mother right now? Way too many thoughts were going through my mind, chief among them, why was the ambulance taking so long?

Finally! It arrived with sirens blaring louder than I had ever heard. Every neighbor within blocks—not just Mr. Carter—came out of their house to see what the commotion was all about. Many of them knew my aunt because of her frequent visits to our house and because Colebridge was a small, close community.

The paramedics were quick, efficient, and kind. A very young man knew just what to do and say to Aunt Marie. She listened intently as they assured her everything would be all right.

Aunt Julia stayed with her, holding her hand as they both disappeared into the foreboding white vehicle. "Sue, please call Jim on your way to the hospital and tell him what's happening."

I told Mother to stay with me. Sue and Muffin were already in her car and she was dialing Uncle Jim. We closed the door to the house and followed the ambulance in my car. I couldn't believe this was happening. We were in tears.

"Say a prayer," I said to Mother. It was my way of asking for emergency help for a situation out of my control. Certainly none of us were useful just now. My tears had dried but Mother was sobbing.

"It will be okay." I held her hand extra tight. Did I believe my own words?

"I should have made her go to the doctor yesterday when she didn't feel well," Mother lamented. "It's too soon, God, please don't take her."

Although Sue never had any serious medical situations to deal with in her life, she had immediately followed the ambulance to the hospital. From what I could tell, she maintained her control and didn't weep. I would bet she thought everything would be all right.

Thankfully, we lived just a few miles from St. Joseph's Hospital. Mother and I quickly parked in the emergency lot, not saying a word to each other. When we arrived in the emergency waiting room, we were told to stay in a certain room while they gave Aunt Marie tests.

Aunt Julia, in tears, came running to meet us.

"How is she?" My voice broke.

"She was quiet and exhausted." She shook her head in sadness. We found seats and held each others' hands. Sue arrived and joined our fearful huddle. Each one of us was praying in her own way with her personal God. Words were no longer appropriate until someone could tell us something.

There was another couple in the room as well who were worried about a bad accident involving their child. They, too, were crying and not making too much sense. They wanted to be with him but it sounded like an emergency surgery was going to happen, which kept them here till they had further news. This place was a room where life met death on a regular basis. It was a terrible place to be unless you had to be there. Thank goodness the medical staff was doing something!

My cell phone went off. I jumped out of my seat and went into the hall to see who it was. It was Sam. I weakened and answered, breaking into a frantic sob.

"Oh, Sam! I'm at the emergency room. It's Aunt Marie. She was leaving our house and had a heart attack. The ambulance just got her here, and Mother and I followed in the car." I gripped the phone like it was a lifeline and tried not to bawl.

"Honey, oh, honey, I'm so sorry. Do you want me to come there and be with you?" His voice was steady and calming.

"No, no," I said, thinking yes, yes. I almost sobbed out loud at just the thought of him being so kind. I was wiping my runny nose as fast as I could to keep up but managed to catch my breath and told him that we had been having such a great day.

"We finished the quilt and were celebrating our accomplishment. It was so wonderful! And now this. Please say a prayer for her, Sam."

"I will, I will," he assured me. "Has someone called Jim? What about her brother?" Wow. He was thinking more calmly about my family than I was at a time like this.

"We don't want to call Uncle Ken till we hear from the doctor. Sue called Uncle Jim, but he couldn't come right away, for some reason." I thought a bit. "Oh, yes. He was going to try to call Sarah on her cell, and pick her up from the mall before he came here."

"You sure you don't want me to come over?" he asked again.

"No, thanks, but I'll call you back as soon as the doctors come out and tell us something."

"Please do call right away, Anne." What a sweet man. He really understood that we were crazy with worry. Would Sam pray? I hadn't asked him about his religion. I hoped he was sincere.

Uncle Jim and Sarah arrived and I could see they both were quite concerned. Sarah was too young to have dealt with any serious emergency, so she was in tears and kept hugging her mother as though it were she about to die. Uncle Jim, to his credit, was trying to console both of them.

About thirty minutes later I asked the nurse to check for any results. This was too long and we were all anxious. Was no news good news or bad news?

"She is getting an EKG right now, but I think she was stabilizing before they took her down to the room," the nurse said. This was some degree of encouragement and gave us a little hope.

"I'll get you all some coffee," Uncle Jim said, wanting to be of help. "She's in good hands, and it sounds like she may be okay. Sarah, you come with me." Aunt Julia broke down in tears again, and started blaming herself for not noticing that her sister's health was serious.

"Darn it," Mother said, pacing back and forth. "We all have bad hearts in this family and die way too young." I thought there was no doubt that we all felt Grandmother's presence in the room, just as in the basement. Was my grandmother waiting for her daughter Marie to be with her?

I tried to calm myself, because Aunt Marie was being taken care of and, after all, was still with us. Aunt Marie was like a second mother to me. She was always there, and, of course, since she did not have any children, she pretty much adopted me in every way. She often reminded me how proud she was to be my godmother. She also made me feel like she was there for Mother when I could not be.

A long thirty minutes later a Dr. Massey came in the room. "Are you Marie Wilson's family?" His tone was gentle.

"Yes," all of us answered in unison. Mother and I stood up, arms around each other.

"Marie is doing fine right now. She had a pretty damaging heart attack, I'm afraid. We need to keep her here. You can go in two at a time to see her, if you like. She's very frightened, so please console her and tell her people have heart attacks all the time, and with therapy and exercise, they do fine and live a good while longer. I told her she may need more exercise. People who live alone neglect themselves. There's no one there to see to it that instructions are followed." With that said, he walked out of the room with his clipboard in hand.

Mother and Aunt Julia were the first to go in her room. Sue, Uncle Jim, Sarah, and I waited outside the room in silence. They were only allowed ten minutes to visit with her, but it seemed like hours. When they returned, they were sad and worried.

"She looks terrible." Aunt Julia shook her head in dismay. "She isn't saying very much. She looks so very tired, which is why they don't want us in there. She needs to rest. She's not up to conversation and I certainly can see why."

Uncle Jim and Sarah decided they would not go in, but would try visiting the next day. I wanted to see her for myself, and told the others that I would be brief.

I walked in on a frightening scene; Aunt Marie was on oxygen. I wasn't prepared for that. I went over to hold her hand and smiled at her, wanting to be brave and give her the impression all would be well. She gave me a wan smile.

"You certainly made a grand exit from our house," I teased. She smiled a little bigger.

"We are here for you and we love you, Aunt Marie." I put my face near her cheek, and she shook her head and rolled her eyes like she couldn't believe what just happened. She grabbed my arm and squeezed it like she was trying to tell me something.

"Please think positive, will you?" I asked. "You can do this. Will you be strong?" She nodded her head yes.

I couldn't believe how weak and tired she looked. I couldn't even imagine her being strong again. It was almost two hours ago when we were all cheering about finishing the quilt. She took my hand and put it next to her cheek. She really couldn't talk, so I told her we would be here with her as she rested.

"The doctor said you should be just fine, so don't pull any more surprises, okay?" I gave her the most encouraging smile I could muster. "We need you!"

I kissed her cheek as I left the room and headed straight to my mother's arms outside the door and spilled the tears that I held back in front of Aunt Marie.

"It could be you in there, Mother!" I cried. "What would I do without you? How will she recover from this? The attack must have been a so painful, to wipe her out like this. This has to really scare her!"

The doctor and nurse attending her said we should all go home. They assured us they would call if there were any changes. "She is quite stable and resting well, which needs to happen after something like this," the nurse said.

We all looked at each other, not knowing what to do. I didn't think I could convince Mother to leave; she was taking this badly. It was so extra sad because there wasn't a husband, son, or daughter to say that they would stay with her no matter what.

"I'm not going to leave her," she said, sitting back down in the comfy chair in the waiting room.

Jim encouraged us to go get some rest. In a way, it was nice having a man there to tell us what to do. He was absorbing our grief and really did want to be helpful and consoling. When I saw what toll it was taking on Mother, I agreed that we all needed to regroup from the shock. She continued to hold her head in her hands, as though she was still expecting the worst. We finally agreed with Uncle Jim's guidance, that we plan to come back to the hospital first thing in the morning. I convinced Mother that her sister would be sleeping now, and we needed to refresh ourselves for what might be ahead.

We drove in silence back to our home. Mother and I went in the house and collapsed at the kitchen table. There were messages on the phone, but neither one of us wanted to talk. I thought if I made some tea it would help, like in the movies.

"Do you think she will be okay, Mother?"

"It took more than one heart attack to kill our mother," she said sadly. I laid my head down on the table wanting it to all go away.

Mother went into the den and called her brother Ken, even though Sue had been talking to her parents. They told her they were going to try and come to Colebridge, despite how well Aunt Marie was doing. They would try to get away the next morning. The conversation was short and solemn.

Mother said she was so drained, she thought she could sleep okay. She took a glass of water from the sink and headed to her bedroom.

She had nothing more to say, and frankly, I was out of words myself. My heart ached for her because I knew how scared she was.

I went on up to bed. I noticed Sam had called again, but right then, I wanted to rest just like Aunt Marie.

Nothing, not anything, seemed important enough to think about right now but prayers for my loving aunt.

CHAPTER 33

There is nothing worse than not being able to sleep when you are so emotionally and physically tired. I was tempted to make a cup of tea, but did not want to disturb Mother. I kept going over everything in my mind, and when I finally dozed off, my nightmare was cluttered with flowers, unsatisfied customers, Aunt Marie calling me to help her as she laid in our driveway, and Sam on the phone trying to talk to me. Thank goodness Mother knocked at my door and said she was going to the hospital. It took me awhile to come back to reality. The reality was not any better than my dream.

"Just come to the hospital when you can, Anne," Mother said, peeking into my room. "I couldn't sleep, so I'm going on over to the hospital."

I looked at the clock and it was 6:00 a.m. I knew that despite a lack of decent rest, I needed to shower, dress, and make some arrangements for the shop. As I became awake, I thought to myself that it was good news we had not heard from the hospital.

Before I left the house, I called Sally to open the shop. We touched base on what had to be done. Somehow these trivial chores did not seem to matter. She was amazing in that she knew how to do all these things with me not having to tell her. I loved employees who are self-starters! She also knew how close I was to my aunt, so she understood my concern and told me not to worry about a thing. I wanted to be with the others who were hurting. My mind would not be functioning if I had to be away from the family right now.

After I had my first cup of coffee, I decided to call Sam. He deserved to have a response to his concern last night. He sounded drowsy. "Hey you. How is Marie, and how are you?"

"Hi, Sam. I'm sorry I didn't return your call. It was an exhausting night. We have no word this morning, so that must be good news. Mother just left for the hospital and I'm going in the next half hour. Sally is going to cover the shop till this afternoon."

"Can we have a bite of lunch at the hospital?" He was trying to find a way to be helpful to the situation and to me.

"I suppose, if you're sure you want to be exposed to all this. I didn't sleep well. I sure hope Aunt Marie got some rest."

"She probably did fine, or you would have heard. I want to be there to give you a hug and tell you everything is going to be fine."

"Well, it's a nice thought, but it's in the hands of the Almighty right now," I said with hope in my voice.

I hung up the phone feeling very lucky to have a guy like this care at all about what was happening. I had not known him for very long, and he didn't need this drama in his life. Was I falling in love? Was it love, or was it gratitude for the sympathy he was now offering?

It was a needy feeling right now, but Sam seemed so right, and so caring. I told myself there was no way he could be having the same feelings I had. He certainly had experienced some family crises with his dad, so, was he just being nice? I didn't want to read too much into his reaction. He'd been a bachelor for quite some time, and he certainly wasn't going to jump into a serious relationship with a small town gal like me. I had to make sure I kept this relationship in perspective.

It was a bright sunny day for winter, which gave me a sense of comfort that all might be well as I drove to the hospital, nearly going right by Aunt Marie's house. Aunt Julia called and said she would meet me at the hospital. I thought Uncle Ken and Aunt Joyce should be arriving soon if they left early that morning from Columbus. I wondered when the two of them had last seen Aunt Marie. I was so glad they would be here for Sue. They would be staying with her, I was sure. I hoped their visit would not frighten Aunt Marie into thinking we thought she may die.

I arrived at the ICU, where we had been the night before.

"I just called you!" Mother rushed to greet me at the door. "Something is going wrong! They made me leave the room and many of the staff came running in."

"How was she when you saw her this morning?" My concern level skyrocketed.

"She was sleeping when I got here, and when I tried to talk to her, she started gasping for air. Luckily, there was a nurse in there with me. She hurried me out and called a code of some kind." I was medically naive, but I knew calling a code was not a good thing.

Aunt Julia came in just then and saw by our faces that we had bad news. Mother told her the chain of events. When she said the word "code," to Aunt Julia, her face was stricken with horror, probably like mine. We were all too frightened to cry. We held onto each other and prayed in silence as we sat once again in the chairs of the unknown.

Sue was the next to arrive. She could tell by the way we were huddled together that it was probably not good news. She approached us in silence, like she was not going to believe anything bad. When Aunt Julia told her, Sue sobbed, "No, no, no!" and then we all broke down in tears that no one could contain.

It was just minutes when the doctor finally came out of the room. The look on his face was sad and serious.

"Oh no, please tell us she will be okay now," Mother cried out to him.

"I'm afraid we lost her," he said softly.

Did I hear him right? Did he say she died? Did I misunderstand something?

My mind became a blur; I wasn't able to digest his further information to us. He focused on Mother, telling her how the attack Marie had had this morning was very strong and quick. He said she went suddenly, and that it had been the third attack that finally got her. I was trying to read his lips and digest it all, but I could not believe it.

We grabbed each other in desperation, as we cried out to each other.

The doctor stayed with us as we sobbed in disbelief. He gave us a while to cry before he said, "Would you like to see her and say your good-byes? Is there anyone besides all of you we should be calling who is close to her?"

We looked at each other, knowing we were her closest family. Aunt Julia told him that her brother was on his way, and that what he saw was her closest family. Mother pulled away from me and headed to the corner where her sobs were deep and heartbreaking. Oh God, why did you take her?

The timing was unbelievable; just at that moment Uncle Ken and Aunt Joyce walked in the room. They each cried out, "What's wrong?" although they knew by the looks on our faces and our reactions that it was the worst news possible.

I never saw Uncle Ken react like he did. It was a response of complete shock.

"I kept praying ever since you called that I would be able to see my sister alive one more time." His voice was teary and shaky. "This is too much like what our mother went through when she died. I called Marie last week, and she assured me her heart was fine. When you called, the first thing I thought about praying for was that it be her last attack and not more to come."

I went over to console this very broken man who had fallen into his wife's open arms. Sue joined them in their circle of grief and I stepped back a little. It was Ken's sister, for heaven's sake. How would I feel? Aunt Joyce was shaken as well, but her attention went to her husband, who needed her very much.

We let Uncle Ken and Aunt Joyce go in first to see Aunt Marie. It was just heartbreaking to think they drove frantically all this way, worried they may not see her alive, and then they were right.

Uncle Jim and Sarah finally arrived in the room with hope in their eyes only to witness Aunt Julia crying so hard it was scary. The three of them hugged in a huddle. Uncle Jim was certainly affected as well, or maybe it was just the sight of all us in such grief.

After Aunt Julia took a deep breath and contained herself to a few sniffles, their family was the next to go in and say good-bye. Sarah grabbed her mother tight, laid her head on her chest, and cried deeply. Sarah would indeed remember this funeral at her age and she had been so very fond of our Aunt Marie.

Aunt Julia did not want to leave the room that her older sister laid in for the last time. Uncle Jim and Sarah had to practically drag her away. This cannot be happening, I thought, as I watched our family fall into such sorrow.

After the three of them walked back into the waiting room to collapse on the chairs, Mother and I held each other tightly as we went into the room where my aunt's spirit had just left this world.

The look on her face was peaceful, like she was taking a nap. Her gray hair with its few remaining black streaks lay softly on the pillow. We laid our heads on her body and cried. When I touched her hand it was already cool. I then realized that she truly was gone. Aunt Marie was on to a better place. I tried to comfort myself by thinking how lucky she was not to have to waste away in a nursing home somewhere. I had to remind myself that she had been so happy with all of us being together, just the day before.

It broke my heart to see my mother so distraught. She kept repeating her name—"Marie, Marie, I am so sorry." This was going to be very hard on Mother. There was nothing we could say to Aunt Marie now. She did know we all loved her, and we knew she seemed happy as she spent many hours with all of us working on the basement quilt.

"We need to leave, Mother." I put my arm around her shoulders. "She is no longer here, and she may be looking down on us. She would not want to make us sad."

We walked out the door together. It frightened me to see Mother so weak. What if that were her I would have to say good-bye to? Her, lying there?

We sat down to visit with the others about what the next step would be. I looked up to see Sam walking down the hall. I had forgotten all about meeting him there for lunch.

It didn't take much for him to see what had just happened. He walked towards me and held out his arms. Without saying a word, he held me tightly as I sobbed in his arms. We walked over to a corner of the room to sit. I saw his eyes tear up as well. I hated that he had to go through this with me.

I filled him in on the latest attack and the timing of her death. "We just came from her room to say good-bye." I wiped my eyes and nose.

"I don't know what to say, Anne. I do know she was a lucky lady to have such a close, caring family. How is your mother doing?" His words and tone were soft and loving.

"She is devastated and shocked. I'm worried about her. They were so close. I'm sure she wishes my dad were here. This has got to bring back memories of his death, as well. We were about to discuss the next step."

"Can I do anything at the shop or your house?"

"I really can't think now. Kevin is helping Sally today, but we'll have to take one day at a time. I'm afraid we'll be doing a lot of the flowers for her funeral."

Too many thoughts were stacking on top of one another, so I told myself to slow down and think through one thing at a time.

I told Sam that Aunt Marie used to teach school and knew many people here in town.

"There isn't much family since she didn't have children, so we'll have to do most everything," I mused.

Sam said I needed to be with the family, so he got up to leave. He told me to be strong and that he would call me later that night, or if I wanted to be left alone, I should just call him when I needed to. I agreed as I watched him approach the others in the room. Right now, I was torn whether to leave with him or go home with Mother. This told me something long term was cooking in my heart.

He went over to my mother, Aunt Julia, and Sue, and gave them each a hug of support. Seeing that moment of my mother and Sam embracing was almost more than I could emotionally bear.

It was decided that Mother, Aunt Julia, and Uncle Ken would go to the Barrister Funeral Home the next morning to make plans for the funeral.

None of us knew any details of her will. So much would all reveal itself in the days to come.

CHAPTER 34

The next two days were a blur.

I felt like I was going through the motions of life for many people. Sue helped us at the shop because flower arrangements were being ordered for Aunt Marie as well as for the funeral of a gentleman I knew from the Chamber of Commerce. He died suddenly, too, so there was a huge reaction to his death. Kevin had a friend of his assist with our deliveries so he could be helpful in the shop answering the phone.

Aunt Marie's will was easily found. It was as if she knew we would need to find it soon. It was lying on top of her writing desk along with the key to her safe deposit box. The thought of her thinking about the possibility of dying just broke my heart. What a brave woman she was!

She left no charity preference in her will, so flowers seemed to be the easy answer for many, or they donated to her church. She left her estate to be equally divided among her siblings. She had a wide variety of quilts, which she requested that Sarah, Sue, and I divide.

We were in no hurry to see them or to go to her place to begin the process of helping our parents break up her household.

The funeral plans were simple. Aunt Marie was active with her church, but the plans for the service were only for family, as she requested. It was just like her modest way of doing things. Her family was everything to her.

I thought to myself at this time how sad it would be to go through life without a husband or child to see me through at the end. Aunt Julia and Mother chose a familiar navy blue suit for their sister to wear at her funeral. Aunt Marie loved pearls as much as I, so they chose a set for her to wear that Mother had given her one year for Christmas. She would have been pleased, I think, on how she appeared. Since she wasn't sick before her death, she had a natural look about her that we all knew.

Mother and Aunt Julia discussed briefly burying Aunt Marie with their mother's thimble. It had been their intention with their mother's funeral, but then they could not locate the thimble. I suggested including one of her quilts, but Mother said her sister would not have wanted that. She said it would mean more to her to leave it for the living to enjoy.

Aunt Marie's funeral fell on a dark, dreary day. Snow threatened. It seemed appropriate for the sadness we all were feeling. The service was at 10:00 a.m., with burial following at the church cemetery.

The pastor, whom she had known for a very long time, spoke briefly, and then Uncle Ken gave a eulogy that spoke to her kindness and charity efforts in Colebridge.

Aunt Julia was next to speak and was very brave and calm. She shared the story of the basement quilt we were working on and the joy we had just shared finishing the quilt. This brought many tears from all of us.

Mother did not want to speak, so I stayed close to her for anything she might need. I watched Sarah, also sitting next to me, as this was all so new to her and somewhat scary for her.

Sam sat in the row behind me. I could feel his support not only for me, but for his good friend, Uncle Jim.

The grave-side ceremony in the cold and dreary air was short, and none of us looked back once we left the gravesite. It was hard to maneuver Mother away from the grave, as she hated leaving Aunt Marie alone in the cold. A luncheon back at our house was held for family and a few of Aunt Marie's friends. Uncle Ken arranged for some catering, and neighbors and others dropped off typical funeral food, like angel food cake and gelatin salads. I stayed mostly in the kitchen with Sue and Sarah, letting the sisters host the many folks who came by.

Flowers and plants were everywhere. We brought most of them home so they could be divided up among family and friends. I could tell most of them came from my shop. I was amazed my helpers had managed to assemble so many arrangements. I reminded myself to look at them closer later. One arrangement of beautiful white lilies was placed in the center of the dining room table. I asked Mother where they were from as there wasn't a card. I assumed they were delivered from my competitor's flower shop. Mother didn't know either, but she commented how they were her mother's favorite flower. I was too distraught to even think about any spirit connection.

Mother insisted I ask Sam to the luncheon, so he was there, too. He and Uncle Jim were quite helpful in the logistics of it all, parking cars and gathering chairs and tables that were needed. As I watched all the activity, moving food around from place to place,

I realized that I wasn't being much help. I mostly sat and reflected on all that had occurred. So many folks accepted our invitation, but most did not stay long, for which I was grateful.

I would catch Sam's eye every now and then, but I was so deep in thought that I had almost forgotten he was there. I did notice that Uncle Ken and Sam seemed to share a lot of conversation. There was no doubt that Sam was fitting in with a family that he had quickly come to know.

"I sense you're tired, but if you want to go get a drink or coffee, we can do that." He had walked closer to me so he could directly look me in the eye.

"You don't know how I wish I could do that, and there's no one I would rather do it with than you, but I'm afraid to leave Mother tonight." Just then she was sitting close to Aunt Julia.

"I understand. You do need to be here with her. I can tell this is going to be hard on her. Can I help put anything away?" I simply shook my head no.

I walked him to the door, where we were left alone to say good-bye. He hugged me tightly and gave me a very pleasant kiss on the mouth. It was the kind of kiss I wanted more of. I hung on to him, letting him know that I didn't want him to go.

"I want to see you tomorrow night if you can get away, because the next day I'll have to go out of town again for a couple of days," he said as he pulled away.

"I can do that," I promised. I needed to do this for myself, I told myself. I was wiped out from all of this, plus trying to keep the shop going at the same time.

"I think we should do something low key," he said. "I'll fix a nice light dinner and we'll enjoy some wine in front of my fireplace. It'll probably snow all day tomorrow from what I hear, so we'll be snug and warm."

"Oh, I can't wait." I kissed him on the neck.

Most everyone cleared out in the next half hour and it was very hard to say good-bye, as additional tears wanted to flow.

Once everyone was gone, Mother went straight up to her room. It was not like her not to fuss around the kitchen to clean up. I could tell she really was exhausted and wanted to be left alone. I went by her door and told her good night and that I loved her. There was no response. I couldn't imagine how she felt at this moment. I went to the kitchen to fill up the dishwasher and then set up the coffee pot for morning, which she usually took care of.

The next morning I wanted to continue sleeping, but when I looked out my window, it was snowing very heavily, which meant I had to think ahead about my flower shop. Sally sometimes had trouble getting out of her subdivision in bad weather, so I had to get going.

The snowy conditions reminded me of the night of the pajama party that we all so enjoyed just weeks before. Aunt Marie especially enjoyed being a part of a foolish, young get-together. I remembered her confessing to us that night that she had had a date with some guy named Joe from the senior center. I wondered if he came anywhere around through all this or if anyone told him about her death. I didn't know what he looked like. I reminded myself to check into that matter.

I showered and then dressed for a cold winter day. Mother sat at the breakfast table, staring at the paper without reading it as I came in the kitchen.

"Believe it or not, I slept like a log last night."

"I did the same," I said, as I kissed her cheek.

Mr. Carter was trying to clear the drive with the snowblower. He and Mrs. Carter had sent over a cherry pie for the luncheon that I needed to thank him for. Most of the neighbors had been with us as long as I could remember, so in times like these, we supported one another.

"I'll leave as soon as he's done with the driveway." I joined Mother for my first cup of coffee. "I may be at the shop alone today with this weather and I promised I would have dinner with Sam tonight. He will be going out of town again tomorrow. I feel like I owe him so much. He was a big help with everything."

"He was a big help, as was Jim." She began to unload the dishwasher.

"Will you be okay?"

"Sure I will, Anne. It will be good for you to be with Sam, and I have much to think about. Plus I have to start on all the thank-you notes. I think he likes you a lot, you know. He has a maturity about him that I like."

"Yes, that's a good description of him, isn't it," I agreed.

"I have to admit, I was sad to see Ted go out the window so easily, but Sam is just so pleasant and he fit in right away." She stopped working to look directly at me.

"I'm so glad you think he's okay, Mother, because I am really falling for this guy!"

"I can tell, Sweetie. You know your aunt thought he was quite a nice young man too, even though she hated to see you break up with Ted."

"I know that. I'm lucky to have a lot of support from everyone, no matter what happens. Are you sure you'll really be okay today, Mother?"

"Yes, you have lots to do, so don't think one more minute about me."

I finished a quick English muffin and went on my way thinking that Mother would be just fine. She had a way of not allowing me to worry about her.

CHAPTER 35

My phone was ringing as I unlocked the door to the snow-covered front door, and, just as I thought, it was Sally, unable to come in. I always parked in front of the shop when there was snow and ice, so I would not get stuck in our sloped parking lot. I checked shop messages and so far there wasn't much that was urgent. As I turned up the heat and flipped over the open sign, Kevin called and agreed he could make it in if I had deliveries.

"So far we are good and if anything is called in, I'll tell them that deliveries won't be made till tomorrow because of the weather."

Kevin asked about the how the family was doing. He had remembered Aunt Marie visiting our shop on many occasions.

"It hasn't sunk in for most of us, I think. This snowy day is giving everyone time to ponder what just happened."

After hanging up the phone, I fell into a daze like the day before. Was I thinking too much of myself to spend the evening with Sam after what just happened to my mother's sister? Did she need me more? Something tugged at my heart that said I needed attention, too. Mother seemed to be okay, and frankly, might prefer to be alone.

The shop was pretty much in disarray from the past week's business. The scraps of Aunt Marie's flowers and ribbons were sad reminders. Thank goodness her funeral was not on this snowy day. I thought of her underground in the cold surroundings covered with a blanket of snow. It all seemed cruel to me right now.

I got busy watering, which was my favorite mindless part of the job, and every now and then I thought about Sam. I felt a bit uneasy about going to his place for the first time, but that was to be expected. I had a good bottle of wine here at the shop that I could take with me tonight. I had a stash of stress-relieving wine kept in the backroom. Sally, Sue, and I helped ourselves many a night after the shop closed.

I heard the front door open and figured it must be someone who had to get flowers for a very important occasion. I came out to the front room to see Ted standing there.

"Oh my goodness! What are you doing out on a day like today?"

"I was in the neighborhood, and I just had to extend my condolences to you and your family over your Aunt Marie's death." He obviously felt awkward. "I would have come to the funeral, but it was closed except to family, which I understand."

"Well, that is sweet of you Ted," I said with sincerity. "It was a shock for all of us although she had been having some pains off and on."

"Are you doing okay?" His look was full of affection.

"I am." I knew he wanted to get personal, and I did not want to have that conversation.

"How are things going with you?" I continued to water.

"I'm trying to take some time off before the holidays because then tax season appears on my desk, as you know."

"The funeral had us going crazy with floral arrangements, so I'm hoping today will be quiet for me to catch up."

"Well, if you need anything, let me know."

I nodded and kept working to discourage a long conversation. I was touched by his concern, but somehow his appearance was an interruption in my future thoughts and it was making me anxious.

"I'll be getting a card off to your mother and Aunt Julia. I even wondered if I should have sent flowers."

"It's really not necessary," I quickly said without thinking.

"So no one misses me, is that what you're saying?" he joked.

"Ted, I have moved on as you have done. Your friendship will not be forgotten by anyone, including me. Sure, I think they would like hearing from you. I think Mother did get a card from your mom and dad, come to think of it."

With that said, he went out the door.

"Stay warm and safe." I don't know if he heard me; he didn't look back.

I didn't expect to have to deal with Ted today but I felt pretty good about how I handled things. His timing was kind of weird, with me seeing Sam tonight and all. I would tell the rest of the family about Ted's concern. He was a good man. How many times had I said that about our relationship?

Mother called to see how I was doing and if I had something to eat for lunch.

"Yes, I'm fine." I tried to sound cheerful. I always kept health bars, small cans of soup, and microwave popcorn on hand for hungry moments.

"And you?"

"There's still plenty of the funeral food left over, so I'll be fine." She sounded more like herself. "We'll be eating some of this for quite awhile. Has anyone been in the shop?"

"No, it's rather lonely, but Ted stopped by to see how we all were doing. He'll be sending you a card."

"How nice of him. I hope you were kind, like the daughter I raised."

I assured her I handled it well.

CHAPTER 36

—∞∞∞—

S am called about 4:30 and told me to leave my car at the shop; he would pick me up at 5:30. The time passed slowly without walk-in customers, and I was more than happy to see Sam.

"I don't need you getting out with your car." His 'hello' was becoming so welcome and familiar. "The weather is getting worse. Have you had any customers today?"

"Not many, but interesting ones I'll tell you about later." He's still interested in my work life! Hmmm.

I changed into a different outfit I'd brought with me. A heavy red sweater and black pants would be great with the current weather conditions. I reapplied my makeup and put on cologne. Somehow, that promised me a nice evening. It had a floral/lilac kind of scent that was fresh, but not like a flower shop owner's smell, I told myself. I put the wine in a nice gift bag that was given to me as a thank you from Mrs. Roberts, who had been grateful for some planting advice.

Just like clockwork, there he was jumping out of his car and in through the door I left open for him. After a quick hello kiss, I locked the shop door. Sam helped me with my coat and then to a nicely heated car. His car was all cleaned off from coming out of his garage. I had a feeling this guy was a neatnik in many ways. I felt odd dragging in the snow with my heeled boots.

"I think we did this wrong." I stomped the snow off my boots. "My car is already a mess from the snow, and yours was clean in the garage, and now it will be a mess."

Ignoring my comment with a smile, he gave me a quick peck on the cheek. With the advantage of the indoor parking garage, it was much more pleasant getting into his place. We took the elevator to his floor. It opened to a charming hallway with tasteful photos of Colebridge on the wall, which then opened to his place. Sam took my coat as he turned on additional lighting. He hung up my coat on an antique hall tree, as any good host would do as soon as we entered the expansive room.

It was just as I thought. His loft décor was warm in color and masculine in style. He had large windows overlooking the river and a northern portion of Main Street. The view was breathtaking with the Christmas lights and snow. I loved views. This location would be awesome in every season. Making a quick assessment of the room, I saw there were many plants placed about taking advantage of the light coming in the windows. They looked like a lot of work for a bachelor to take care of, so perhaps he really did love plants as he claimed. Hmmm.

"Sam, this is wonderful," I said, as I watched him turn on his gas fireplace. "You did a great job with decorating." On one all-brick wall he had hung impressive pieces of art. They were contemporary in style, as was most of his furniture. He then showed me into his office down the hall, which was small, fairly tidy, and again looked out to a great view. I was picturing how he would look sitting there in his sweats or shirtless with either trunks or briefs. Should I guess which? Hmmm.

"How do you get any work done in here with all this outdoor activity going on?" I stared out the window.

"I'm used to it." He pulled the blinds even further back. "I do a lot of work from here when I'm not traveling. The sun gets very bright and warm in here most mornings, so I like working here in the morning more than any other time."

"I have two bedrooms," he said as he led me out of the office. "Right now I use one for storage, but here is my resting place." He opened the door to a room dominated by a very large bed adorned with tapestry fabric that matched the window coverings.

I saw personal photos here and there. On first impression, I supposed they were family. I wanted to move out of the bedroom; I was feeling like I was somewhere I shouldn't be.

"You did say 'resting place,' didn't you?" I smiled.

"Yes, I did, and that was a poor choice of words."

"That's okay, I'm just kidding you." I turned to go out of his personal room. "I smell something wonderful. What is it?"

"You'll see." He took my hand. "Right now, I want to get you some merlot."

"I'm ready for that." As I looked around, it was obvious that this cool loft did not come cheap. Aunt Julia had implied that he made a nice salary and lived well.

We went into the kitchen, which was pretty small compared to the rest of the loft. It did look like it had every convenience needed for a guy who liked to cook. I saw a tidy shelf full of cookbooks, which appeared to be at his fingertips when needed. He uncorked the bottle of merlot. He poured a glass for both of us in charming stemmed crystal glasses.

"You are joining me with merlot?" I took my first sip.

"Yes, it seems warm and perfect for the two of us on this chilly night, don't you think?"

"Can I help you with anything?"

"No, not for now, anyway." He ordered, "You go sit down, and I'll bring us some shrimp to nibble on till this casserole is done."

I sank into one of the comfy cushions on one end of the couch. The fire was artificial, but very realistic in the very large fireplace. I had never seen one like this. Sam joined me with a tray of fresh shrimp cocktail and cheese-olive-cubes on toothpicks. He sat down very close to me, and fed me the first bite of shrimp.

"Yum," I said, smacking my lips like a kiss. "I saved my calories all day so I wouldn't miss a single dinner course from you. I had one health food bar, a soda, and some cashews."

"I don't want you to think of any problems tonight." Sam's smile was loving and he put his arm around me. Then he gave me a light kiss.

"Let's make a toast to us." He lifted his wine glass.

"Here's to us!" I smiled. So much smiling! We clinked our glasses, and I forgot about the rest of the world in his light embrace.

We caught each other up with our days as we kept our wine glasses full and nibbled on the shrimp.

Out of the blue I said, "Ted stopped by this morning." Wow. Where did that come from?

"And?" Sam looked at me over his wine glass.

"He felt bad about Aunt Marie, and since we didn't have a public service or viewing, he wanted me to know how sorry he was."

"Well, that was very considerate of him. Did he ask to see you or get personal in any way?

"No, not exactly." I made sure I chose the right words. "I think he was waiting to see where the conversation was going to go. He didn't stay long. I reminded him that we both had moved on and hoped to remain friends."

Sam said nothing as he got up from the couch. He went into the kitchen to bring out some of the food, which he placed on a lovely dining room table. The dishes were on straw mats that gave the settings a manly look. The centerpiece was made of animal figures with greenery for a jungle air. The dishes were understated stoneware. He had made a wonderful lettuce salad with his own homemade salad dressing. I didn't cook, so I had to be careful not to ask any stupid questions.

"Who taught you to cook like this?" We began eating our salad.

"I learned early on that if you want to eat healthy at all, you have to be in charge of what you eat. I eat out way too much with high calorie menus. My mom is a good cook, and I remember some of her combinations that I was fond of. She made me a small recipe box of some of my favorites when I went off to college, and I've really used it."

"Great idea!" This was interesting. "I'll make sure I have Mother do the same, or at least lets me steal her best cookbook. You are something! This is delicious! I eat so many quick things during the week just to get by, but on the weekends, she makes special things for me. I never think about cooking because I've never had to. I help do what needs to be done, but I don't think I've ever entertained with a meal at my house by myself. I know that sounds like I'm a spoiled child, but it's about my priorities. I make up for it by taking Mother to dinner as often as she'll let me."

He smiled. "I bet she loves that."

The bread was crunchy on the outside and soft on the inside. "Please don't tell me you baked this bread?"

"No, but it's a big secret where I get it." He grinned. "The baker knows what I like. I enjoy finding corner markets and good butchers to cut meat like I want it, too."

He then went to get a seafood casserole that smelled heavenly. He placed our servings on a bed of white rice. The dish was steaming hot. Before we dove into the first bite, I made another toast.

"Here's to the chef of the evening!" I leaned closer to him. "As with my mother's food, you can tell when love has been added to the recipe."

"Just what do you really, really think of this loving chef?" He knew what a leading question he asked.

"I guess I have to reserve that for the end of the meal in case I get poisoned or something." We laughed. His was deep, yet he sounded like an innocent little boy I was teasing.

"You know exactly what I was asking, don't you?" He put his hand on mine.

"Okay, I do, and as you may already know, I'm pretty direct and talkative, especially after a few glasses of wine." I put my hand now on top of his.

"I really, really like this chef. Besides being a great cook, he is everything I could imagine. Knowing a great chef is certainly a bonus, but he knows what I like in a relationship." I sipped some wine. "I reserve going further till I know the feelings are the same, but I have to admit, he is consuming my thoughts day and night. I'm falling hard and fast for a guy I haven't known for very long, but I know what I like. I run my business that way as well." I paused. "So what do you have to say to that?"

He looked at me like he had swallowed a mouthful and was about to choke.

"For someone who is so direct, you chose too many words that could have been summed up a lot easier."

"So, like how?"

There was silence and the look on his face was serious.

"How about 'I love you?'"

I could have fallen off my chair, especially from being light-headed to begin with.

I stared at him, hoping this wasn't a joke, and took a deep breath.

"Would you agree to those words, if I said them first?" he asked, still not cracking a smile.

I still stared in silence, my head tilted in disbelief. This was a huge step. Should I take a step forward or try to go backwards?

"I love you, Anne," he said softly. His words were heavenly. His eyes burrowed into mine. Holy cow. I wasn't expecting anything like this to happen this evening.

Waiting for me to say something and finally getting impatient, he said, "I think this is where you respond, 'Yes Sam, I am in love with you.'"

Okay, then. Hmmm. "I love you, too."

Still sitting at the table, he moved closer and kissed me to seal our confession.

"That wasn't so bad, was it?"

I blushed with affection and he grinned. It was now official: We loved each other. Would this be my best-ever Kodak moment?

"Now that we got that out of the way, how would you like some chocolate mousse, which I call 'passion des chocolats?'"

"Passion des chocolats!" I laughed. "I've never heard of such a thing!"

He walked from the kitchen to deliver two parfait glasses of chocolate mousse with whipped cream and chocolate shavings on top. I was again very impressed. He knew I loved chocolate in any form. It was a perfect light ending to a delicious meal.

"Are we keeping merlot with our dessert, or would you like some coffee, my dear?" he asked.

"Merlot it is, and thank goodness I'm not driving. I think merlot and chocolate are absolutely wonderful together. One of my favorite things!"

"Have you looked out the window lately?" he said as he walked away from the table. "Bring your dessert over here, where we can look out."

The view was stunning as the snow glistened against the window and on the street below. The perfectly positioned love seat was ideal for such a moment, making me wonder who else might have shared this very same kind of moment with him.

"It hasn't stopped snowing and we could be up to a couple of feet of snow by now." Sam's tone was serious. "I don't think you're going anywhere tonight."

I didn't answer, but he was right. Besides, I didn't want to leave. Now I couldn't leave even if I wanted to. He would be stuck with me. After I had nearly licked the glass clean of the last of the mousse, we got up from our seat, grabbed the few things to be refrigerated from the dining room table, and then Sam said to leave the rest for him in the morning. His insistence was effective because the merlot was arousing my interest in things other than kitchen duty.

He took hold of my hand and led me to the living room, where we each pulled a large stuffed pillow in front of the fire. The warmth of the wine and really good food had mellowed me, indeed. I hadn't noticed until now, but there was soft music playing in the background. It was like I was living a dream. It was a dream in which Sam Dickson had just told me he loved me.

"This seems to be one of those bachelor pads I keep reading about," I teased. "Do you just press some buttons and all these bells and whistles start happening to woo your girlfriends?"

"Just for you, my love." He pulled me closer to wrap me in his arms. "Did you hear me say 'just you, my love?'" He kissed me harder and much more passionately.

We laid back together in a comfortable arrangement on the floor. Why was this feeling so natural? Was it the wine, or was he really having this affect on me? The grown-up business part of me said be careful, but my heart and feminine side said to let go, enjoy, and take a chance.

"This is the moment I looked forward to all day." I sighed. "When you said we would enjoy wine by an open fire, this is just what I needed, Mr. Dickson."

We were quiet for a moment, taking in the fire, and the music, and each other. "Are we moving too quickly?" I realized both our hands wanted to caress more and more.

"Perhaps, if we were seventeen years old." Sam rested his head on his elbow. "We are adults, leading adult lives. We both have had our share of ups and downs. I think at our age we should be grateful that neither one of us has been married before. That is a strong point for me. How about you?"

"Yes it is, but I've never made it a rule." Was I light-headed or light-hearted?

"I suppose in the right relationship I could adjust to an ex-husband and perhaps some children, but I would rather not." He sounded as if he had given it lots of thought.

Having Sam this close for such an extended time was a new feeling for me. I liked the way he smelled as I snuggled near him. Did it remind me of a lotion that my dad used to wear to work every day? He had a confidence about him that made me feel very safe, despite the fact I was a very independent woman. Independent did not mean that I couldn't accept someone making a decision or two for me, especially when they love you. He said he loved me! Wow. This new man in my life really said that. I said it back to him. I couldn't remind myself of that often enough.

Sam went to get more wine and a couple of bottles of water for us. I noticed he had taken off his shoes and removed the sweater he was wearing over his white shirt.

"Warm, are you?" I was thinking the same thing myself about my own big sweater.

"Actually, I am getting a bit hot. How about you?" He joined me again on the floor.

"We can back up from the fire," I responded with some degree of difficulty.

"It's not the fire getting me hot." Sam moved close to me again.

The lights were off in the other rooms. I was really, really alone with this man. As much as I was enjoying each and every embrace, I kept wondering how many other women had experienced these same moves. I had to put it out of my mind, because I wanted to be exactly where I was at this given time.

"I think you left me for a minute," Sam said.

"Yes, how did you know?"

"I've been reading you pretty well so far, and it looks like I'm right again."

"I guess it's my cautious mind and over-protection of myself that interceded. I don't want this moment to end, yet I don't want to be another trophy in your bachelorhood."

"Wow, that's pretty strong." He backed off to lean against a nearby chair and took a sip of wine. "I sure hope I haven't been treating you that way," he said. "My feelings for you have been a surprise to me. There are so many facets to being attracted to you. You have aroused feelings of belonging and loving that I wasn't sure I had anymore. I, too, want to be protected from being hurt." He paused, but I sat still.

"You have to admit I took a risk coming into your life during and after Ted. You could easily decide to go back to him. I, too, want to be cautious. Until I get into a position of not traveling, I risk that someone might become impatient with my schedule. I entertain clients on occasion, and I have to be careful of someone becoming jealous and over-protective."

"All good points, Mr. Dickson." I positioned myself in front of him, on my knees, and pulled his face to mine for a kiss. "Don't you love surprises?"

"We have talked a lot tonight, haven't we?" His hands were on my bare back as he pulled me closer. We were now lying totally next to each other for the first time among the cushions on the floor. This is where I belonged and wanted every inch of my body to be. I molded right into him.

The rest of the evening seemed as natural and loving as I could ever remember. This was an evening I would never forget, no matter where I journeyed in my life. I had imagined this first intimate encounter over and over in my mind and now it had become real. There was no turning back. Only Sam could bring about in me these new feelings and desires I had never experienced before. How could I be thinking of such things—and doing them—when everyone around me was grieving? Was I not totally absorbed in grief just a day ago? Right now it was a painful blur turned into bliss, thanks to Sam.

I think Sam and I both were proud that our attraction for each other had not gone this far any sooner in our relationship. It was timely, natural, passionate, and so beautiful. I needed him; all of him. He needed me, and I gave all of me.

CHAPTER 37

I woke up the next morning in a room unfamiliar in the daylight. Sam wasn't next to me. He had awakened earlier to put on coffee, telling by the aroma filling the air. The sun shining off the white snow created a glare of light across the room. This was certainly a change from my usual wake-up routine. I stayed there, taking it all in. Every detail was now coming back about our passionate night together. Regrets were not there, only contentment.

At last I felt I was a grown-up woman at the age of twenty-nine. Ted had often suggested I stay over at his place and I would not even consider it, living under Mother's roof. Getting permission was no longer needed with what I felt for Sam. Perhaps I really wasn't even physically attracted to Ted.

Oh, dear, enough dreamland, I had a shop to attend to and I'm sure there would be a couple of curious souls wondering where I was. The shop would open in an hour so I needed to get on my way. Before I forced myself to roll over, I saw the man I loved.

"Good morning, my love," Sam smiled.

He came over to the side of the bed to kiss me. He was even sexier (was that possible?) in a heavy, white terry cloth robe. The urge to take him in my arms and bring him to my side was very tempting. Wouldn't it be great if right now, at this moment in time, I could just enjoy this very special encounter and let my heart as well as my body give in to what it begged me to do, instead of what I should do?

"I smell the coffee, but I just looked at my watch," I said.

"I can bring you breakfast in bed if you like," he offered. "I knew looking at your watch would put you in a spin, which is why I got up and opened the blinds. I'd like to keep you here a little bit longer, if you know what I mean, but right now, I feel pretty lucky to have captured you here on a snowy night."

I gave him a hug as I grabbed the extra blanket to put around me. "Take a shower if you like." He didn't take his eyes off of my body. "Do you want something to eat?"

"Coffee is fine." I moved to the end of the bed. "I'll just shower and dress if you don't mind. Has anyone called?"

"I think you're safe." He grinned. "I'll get you back to the shop as fast as you like as long as you promise to come back real soon."

"You won't be able to keep me away!" I closed the bathroom door. I couldn't believe I was nude, then dressing in Sam's bathroom. This was the room he, too, would be nude in each day. Were there frequent visitors to his shower, or was I, indeed, special? Oh boy, did I have plenty to think about in the days ahead.

As I joined him in the kitchen and drank coffee from a heavy brown mug, I looked at our love nest sprawled about the living room floor. The fire was gone but the view was just as breathtaking as the night before. I would always remember this scene.

It didn't take long for Sam to dress. We gathered our things in silence and felt the letdown of getting back to reality. We hugged again before heading to the garage.

Main Street looked absolutely gorgeous with all the trees and buildings under the white blanket of crystals sparkling in the bright sun. My cheerful shop radiated with live spring flowers in the windows instead of the coldness of the heavy snow piled along the curb. Sam pulled as close as he could and helped me out of the car. He caught hold of me and brought his face close to mine.

"No regrets, good thoughts?" He asked.

I nodded and kissed him on the forehead. We hugged each other tightly, agreed to talk later on the phone, and then I turned to get inside and out of the cold.

After I entered, I checked calls on my shop answering machine and found none, to my surprise. I had a pretty savvy mother; she knew I was with Sam and could put two and two together. It was nice to know I didn't have to explain to her or ask permission for my actions; however, I didn't want to worry her unnecessarily.

Sally, I'm sure, wanted to come in to work so she wouldn't miss two days' pay. I expected her since I hadn't heard from her. There was plenty to do, plus a merchant's meeting around noon if it hadn't been cancelled. I had been negligent about attending lately as there was always so much controversy. A cliquish few were always determined to be against everything, no matter what was being discussed. I guessed every organization had them. Many of the street merchants referred to them as "the party of no." It was hard, as past president, to ignore the damage this group might do, but I had to. I had learned that it was too easy to spend valuable time on the street's affairs and in turn neglect my own business.

Sam was going to be leaving town today if his flight wasn't cancelled, so I wouldn't be seeing him for a few days. I needed time to digest our actions and my feelings, so it was probably best to have a break. I had enough memories of our perfect evening to last a lifetime.

I called Mother before Sally came in. She understood that staying over with Sam was the safe thing to do with the weather. She didn't pursue further information, for now, anyway.

Sally made it to the shop on time. She didn't know where I had been so our conversation went right to our work. We had gotten a call that one of the local high school students had been killed in a car accident overnight, so it would mean a lot of calls would follow once the funeral plans were announced. These orders were always more difficult when it was a child or young person's funeral.

Sue came by on her lunch hour. The flights were clear for her parents to go home and she had just taken them to the airport. Seeing her drew me back into the reality of losing my aunt and being a grief-stricken family.

"Oh, I'm sorry I didn't say goodbye to them."

"I was glad for them to go, I hate to say. They were driving me crazy with adoption questions. They are so afraid I'll be getting into something I can't handle. I should have waited to tell them until I was approved for a child. Is your mother doing okay?"

"She will have a hard time with this, but she's a trooper, as you know." I thought of her alone at home. "Your dad sure got a lot more gray than when I saw him last."

"I thought the same thing. Well, I better get back to work. They've been wonderful about me taking off so much time. Your mother called and said we may all get together tomorrow night."

"Oh, I didn't know! That sounds fine. Sam is gone, and the streets should be better."

"Yeah, I want the latest on the Sam thing, but we'll catch up tomorrow night," Sue said as she went out the door. I knew they would not get the real story out of me, but I would give them enough to talk about. Getting the basement quilters together was probably a good idea, except Aunt Marie's absence would certainly make us sad.

It was hard to concentrate on the day's activities. My mind kept going back to being at the loft, high above Colebridge, with a hunk of a man who said he loved me. I will never forget the night as long as I live, I told myself. Several times Sally had to go out of her way to get my attention. I'm not sure she figured out my distraction. She may have thought Aunt Marie was still on my mind.

Gayle, from the stained glass shop, stopped by to air complaints about the merchant's meeting. "This was a heck of a way to start my day. You made a wise decision not to come. Many were long-winded again, and of course the 'no' people have decided that the craft festival is going to attract drunks and criminals if it stays open past 8:00 p.m." I watched her mouth move as she complained, nodding my head, but today they could have decided to pave over Main Street and I would have said, 'Whatever.' I had never felt so mellow and content. Nothing was going to rain on my parade.

I went home to smell Mother's hot and spicy chili. I came up behind her and gave her a kiss on the cheek. Cooking something had always been a cure for making things better, according to her.

"Chili is perfect for tonight." I looked in the pot. "How do you always know just which appetite buttons to push?" I gave her a quick hug, which always meant a lot to her. I remembered my father would do the same, giving her an unexpected surprise.

She turned around, beaming. "I'm just glad you're home safe and we can have dinner together."

"Let me go up and put my sweats on. Hey, I hear Sue and Aunt Julia are coming over tomorrow night."

"Yes, I was hoping you would be available. We may have leftover chili. I'll make some corn bread and Julia said she would bring brownies. I know it will be hard without Marie, but she would want us to be together when we need each other. Am I right in thinking that, Anne?"

I pretended I did not hear her and did not answer. The silence took care of the big hole that would be there the next time all of us would be together. I think what Mother was doing was getting us all on the bicycle again after we had just fallen off. Oh, Aunt Marie, you are missed. She so enjoyed our food and company.

We were nearly finished eating before Mother asked about Sam. "Things went well last night, I hope?"

"Oh, yeah." I wanted to answer her without giving too much information. "Sam is a wonderful person and quite a good cook." I described the meal, and his place with the large windows. "I had no idea these lofts were so upscale and had such views!"

"Mrs. Harmon lives in one of those lofts now."

"Oh, I didn't know that."

"She bought it after Edward died, and she loves it. She is on the second floor, I believe. She doesn't come to cards anymore, because there is a group that meets there, from what she said."

After a pause she said, "I hate to bring it up, but I need you to help me take things from Marie's house before we have a sale."

"Of course, Mother. How many quilts do you think she has?"

"I don't know, she never shared that, but hopefully you, Sarah, and Sue will agree on who takes what."

"Oh, sure, not to worry about that."

"I know she has some from Grandmother Davis because she was the oldest one of us."

"Oh, I hope we can decipher which ones they are." I felt

mischievous. "After our recent experiences with her, I don't want to do anything to upset her!"

"Don't be funny," Mother quipped.

My cell phone rang and I looked to see it was Sam. I went into the den to talk privately. He made the flight nicely and had just finished dinner as well. "I miss you," he said quietly.

"I miss you too. I was just telling Mother what a good cook you were and how lovely your loft was."

"Did you tell her what a good lover I was?"

"No, smarty, she was glad I was safe and did not drive home."

"She's a good mom, and she said the right thing." We laughed, and then he asked if I got all the snow off the car okay.

"Thank goodness Kevin took care of that for me when he cleaned off the delivery van."

"That's great. Sounds like he's a pretty good guy to have around. I have to tell you that it was hard to concentrate today, wondering what you were doing and thinking."

"Me, too. We started getting orders for a young student's funeral today, so I was kept pretty busy."

"Sorry to hear that. When is the funeral?" He's still interested in my work life even after sex. Hmmm.

"Two days from now, so tomorrow will be busy as well. The students are trying to be creative by giving something besides flowers, like balloons and interesting signage. When will you be home?"

"If all goes well, it should be in a couple of days. It's nice to have someone to come home to, I might add. Save some time for me, okay?"

"Absolutely."

"I'll let you go, and by the way, I still love you!" he said softly.

"I love you too, Sam," I said, as I hung up the phone.

How long was it since these words truly had meaning? I was experiencing my first real love. As crazy as I was about Charles Bradshaw in the eighth grade, it certainly wasn't like this. I hadn't thought anyone would replace Charles. My dates had always seemed to be blank pages and with Ted, it seemed to be an arrangement of what was just a nice relationship, not a feeling that made me crazy about him. My body never ached for his touch and I rarely thought of him when we were not together.

CHAPTER 38

decorative divider

I have to admit I was looking forward to the basement quilters coming back to the house. I didn't want to think our bond had ended with Aunt Marie's death. Aunt Julia had a sad look on her face as she came in the door. She said it was hard driving over here without stopping to pick up her sister. We agreed not to make this a pity party and just celebrate being together.

We sat in the kitchen and poured wine as we waited for Sue to come. I told Aunt Julia that things were going well with Sam and I.

"He should be home tomorrow." I sounded like a girl in love. "Do you still want us to come over Friday night for Uncle Jim's birthday?"

"Yes, of course! I invited Jim's sister and her husband, too. Jim never takes time to see her and they are such a nice couple. They've been married about ten years. They have a daughter, Patty, whom Sarah enjoys, so that will keep her busy."

Aunt Julia shifted gears. "Sylvia, have you been in the basement since Marie died?"

"No, and I don't think Anne has been either, right, Anne?"

"No." I tried to keep the sadness from my voice. "My fabric is down there, and I really want to get started on the flower quilt. Maybe you all can help me with that tonight."

Sue and Muffin finally arrived. "I'm really glad to be back where we left off." She hugged Aunt Julia and then Mother.

"Well, I hope you know I can't bear to look at my quilt right now," Aunt Julia said. "I didn't take it home because Marie was going to show me how to put the binding on. Now what?"

"Oh Julia, we can figure that out, or Isabella will show you, if you take it in to the quilt shop." Mother tried to comfort her.

"It's not the same." Aunt Julia was close to tears.

"I brought my quilt kit along." Sue was trying not to sniffle. "I've lost all my confidence now that I don't have Aunt Marie to rely on."

"Christmas is just two weeks away, and I was hoping the Christmas runner kit I bought would be finished this year, but I guess there's always next year." Mother's face was sad.

To lift the mood, she went to the stove and announced that the leftover chili was hot, so we filled our bowls and sat at the kitchen table. The corn bread was heavenly. I ate like a farmer, with two helpings of everything. Was it true that people in love have heftier appetites? The others kidded about how spoiled I was to have my own chef. Aunt Julia's brownies hit the spot as well. Mother did notice my helpings and seemed to be happy to watch me consume the calories.

Aunt Julia was filling us in on Sarah's first boyfriend. The boy down the street finally made his move and Aunt Julia and Uncle Jim were amused but cautious. Mother reminded Aunt Julia that when she was thirteen she had oodles of guys coming by the house.

"Remember when you sneaked out on a date without Mother

knowing?" Mother teased. Sue joined the ribbing and together they made Aunt Julia laugh, which was good to see. So it seemed we could manage to have a few laughs despite our grief.

Aunt Julia said she went to the senior center to find Aunt Marie's friend, Joe. "He was playing bingo, but I interrupted him and introduced myself," Aunt Julia said. He said she is indeed missed at the center and he was sad they could not have more dinner dates together."

"That was so sweet of you to do, Aunt Julia. Aunt Marie would have been grateful for your efforts. You just don't realize the lives that other people touch."

"We're getting many sympathy cards. How about you?" Mother began clearing the table. Aunt Julia and Sue agreed the response was pretty amazing, considering Aunt Marie did not have much family.

"Sure she does! She's with Grandma now." Sue had a strange smile on her face. We could have had a serious response to her comment, but instead we started to giggle at what that could mean in heavenly terms.

We finished cleaning up, leaving the kitchen presentable, and finally braved the basement without Aunt Marie. On the way down the stairs, I started tearing up as did the others.

It would never be the same coming down the stairs as before. Would we feel her presence like we did Grandmother's? Would this basement ever be a happy place again?

I turned on the first lamp and then the others. We each took one of the chairs, which were placed about the room. The absent quilting frame left a large hole in the center of the room. I went over to the table where we usually kept our treats for the evening and on the table was my quilt book. It was open, as if someone again had been looking at it.

"I thought I put this away after I chose my quilt, Mother."

"You did," she answered with certainty.

"Aunt Julia, come look at this." She came over to the opened page and there was an article entitled, "How to Put a Binding on a Quilt" staring at her in the face.

"I didn't do this, did you, Mother?"

"Heavens, no, I haven't been down here."

We all looked at each other. This was surreal. After a moment of silence, we shook our heads in disbelief. Then we started to smile.

"Thank you, Marie," Aunt Julia looked heavenward. Without saying more than I needed to, I knew it was Aunt Marie's way of helping Aunt Julia.

"We'll help you figure out the directions, Aunt Julia." Sue hugged her.

Next to the book was another surprise. "Do you remember Aunt Marie leaving her thimble here?" Aunt Julia asked. Silence prevailed as everyone thought for a moment.

"That's Marie's thimble," Mother said, examining it closely. "I would know it anywhere!"

"Well, maybe she just forgot it that day," Sue suggested.

"I don't think so, because I made sure everyone had all their things when we took the quilt out of the frame," Mother said. "I also remember cleaning off this table, for one thing. I don't think anything was on it when we went upstairs."

Aunt Julia started crying again, holding her head in her hands. It was like someone opened the floodgates, and we all started crying.

"This basement is haunted!" Sue wept.

"I'll never get anything right with Mother and now Marie will be on my tail!" cried Aunt Julia.

"Is this nuts?" I sniffled but kept control of myself. "Are we all crazy?" We tried to comfort each other, my heart going out especially to Aunt Julia, who started the basement quilt that we all had shared.

"Now, wait a minute everybody," Mother said with authority. "Stop this and calm down right now! Think about it. Nothing has happened with Mother or Marie that is mean, scary, or threatening. They both loved us very much. They felt our presence and love and the bonding that was going on down here. I say we embrace them, accept their comfort, and even their advice. Let's continue to remember them in the best way we can. I think that is why this place, this basement, has been so special."

"Well, I know I'm not uncomfortable being down here," said Sue. "You know, when you think about the very first thing that happened with the stitches being removed overnight, it didn't frighten us like it would have most people. I could have really freaked out over Grandmother's insistence on me wearing a thimble. I was actually amused by it, quite frankly."

"I haven't told you all about an experience I had down here one night." Now I was ready to share that sorrowful evening. "I was down here alone quilting and I got upset over something. I shed some tears. Actually, it was a lot of tears. Don't ask me what that was about because I'm not going to tell you. But it was late, I was tired, and I laid my head on the quilt without thinking. I kind of dozed off and then woke up suddenly a while later. I looked at the quilt, and there was mascara, lipstick, and makeup on the quilt."

"What!?" Aunt Julia was upset.

"I was so tired and stressed about what to do about the terrible thing I had just done, I decided to leave it alone and attempt to get it out the next morning."

"You did what?" Now she was mad.

"I went on to bed." All of the guilt I felt before resurfaced, and I couldn't look at her. "The next morning before work, I came down to remove the stains, and everything was perfectly clean, like I had not touched it!"

There was silence. "Really!" They waited for me to tell more, especially Aunt Julia.

"She's right," Mother said. "I came down with her and saw her astonished reaction. I was as mystified as she was."

"It was a miracle." I was convinced. Was Aunt Julia?

"Thank goodness, my dear Anne, or I would have killed you!"

"I really didn't think you all would believe me, and I didn't want you to know I had been that careless." I hoped confession would atone. "So, Aunt Julia, you have your mother to thank for cleaning that up. I was very grateful, and after that incident, I was a believer in spirits and the good that they can achieve. It has been a mess! Praise the Lord!"

"Are there any more stories you and Aunt Sylvia haven't told us about?" Sue sought to bring humor back into the room. Mother and I shook our heads, and then we all had to once again shake our heads in wonder.

"See why I didn't want to tell you, Aunt Julia? I say we open this bottle of wine, forget the coffee, and get back to our business of future quilts. Hand me the corkscrew you brought down with you, Mother, and I'll open this merlot."

"I didn't know we were going to have wine, Anne. We were drinking coffee with the brownies."

"Well, why did you bring it down, if you didn't want to drink it?" My curiosity was sparked.

"I didn't bring down any wine, did any of you?" Mother looked at her sister, then at Sue, then at me. Again, silence was in the air.

"It was here on the table by the book, and I thought you

brought it down, Mother." I sighed. "Okay then, someone would like us to have wine, so I'll get the glasses. If the glasses appear before I get back downstairs, let me know!"

They laughed and we all moved a step closer to accepting all the happenings of the spirits in the room.

After our glasses were filled, we held them high for a toast. "Here's to my houseguests, who are just like family!" Mother said.

"Excuse me, Mother," I said. "They are family!"

"Here, here!"

"We are altogether again," said Mother, tears of love and happiness in her eyes.

CHAPTER 39

Once we had a few swallows of the mysterious merlot from the table, we became more comfortable talking about our new projects. I laid out my fabrics, and got everyone's opinion on what fabric should be the strips around the blocks, which Isabella called the sashing. I picked out the easiest block to start with. I told myself I could do this.

Mother decided she would put off her Christmas runner and help me cut out some of my pieces for the flowers instead. She loved the variety of flowers in the quilt and it was indeed more exciting than her Christmas runner.

Sue was so excited about her crib quilt choice. It was bright and happy in multiple bright colors, which reflected the whole prospect of the adoption event. You would have thought her child was arriving very soon, given her enthusiasm.

"I'm going to take Aunt Marie's offer to have her sewing machine," she said. "I think I can really do this, plus I am going to take the basic quilting class at Isabella's next month." We all cheered her on and thought it would be a great idea.

"Anne, if you'll let me, I'll borrow your quilt book and attempt my binding." Aunt Julia looked again at the open book.

"Absolutely," I said, with encouragement. "Boy, if Ted only knew how this quilt book has touched all of us!"

"Speaking of Ted, have you seen him anywhere?" Aunt Julia looked up from her book.

"I have," interrupted Sue.

"Never mind, Sue." I didn't want her to gossip about Wendy being in the picture. "He came by the shop that snowy morning after the funeral. He wanted to tell me how sorry he was to hear about Aunt Marie. I thought it was very nice, but then of course he was fishing to see if I would see him again. I didn't let him go there, so he left."

"Well, that's pretty doggone nice of him, don't you think?" said Aunt Julia.

"Yes, of course," I said graciously. "Mother and I were very appreciative."

We continued organizing our thoughts about our quilting projects and decided we would try to meet once a week. We wanted to support each other since none of us were really quilters like Aunt Marie. We commented in jest on how we knew we would have to meet here in the basement so Aunt Marie and Grandmother could join us. No one would ever believe our group of quilters was six and not four. It was a good thing we all had a sense of humor about this!

Sam and I exchanged some e-mails and confirmed our dinner date with the Bakers on Friday night. I sent over flowers since it was a sit-down dinner party. Sam said he would give Uncle Jim some golf outings at the local country club for his birthday present.

I chose to wear a black skirt with a sheer white blouse with a V-neckline that had just enough cleavage showing so I could wear a special pearl drop necklace. It once belonged to one of Mother's distant relatives who had passed it on to Mother, who passed it on to me. I had a fondness for pearls and had always thought a pearl ring would make a grand engagement ring, instead of a diamond. The gems reminded me of Aunt Marie wearing precious pearls, underground. Dismissing the thought quickly, I pulled my hair straight back for a more sophisticated look. When I looked in the mirror, I saw a more maturing woman in love and smiled. All those smiles.

I couldn't wait to see Sam. Mother was admiring how nice I looked when he arrived. After a warm kiss on the cheek, he greeted Mother with a little hug. She blushed as he caught her by surprise.

"You need to come back for dinner again soon, Sam," she offered with sincerity.

"I would love that very much, but you better check with my social secretary here." He looked fondly at me.

"Soon, soon," I promised, as we went out the door hand in hand.

Uncle Jim welcomed us at the door with a great deal of merriment. I was pleased that he had accepted our relationship, even though he had told Aunt Julia that Sam was a bit too old for me and more worldly than Ted Collins. Aunt Julia looked radiant, as if the day's chores for the event simply had no effect. As a young girl, I could see how she was the men's favorite of the three sisters, like Mother always said. She wore longer hair and had a more flirtatious way about her.

She took us in the holiday-adorned living room and introduced us to Uncle Jim's sister, Christy, and her husband, Ron. Christy looked just like her brother, but a little younger. I had an instant feeling that she was more of a modest sort with her conservative black and white dress and little makeup. They had brought their daughter, Patty, who was a year younger than Sarah. The girls were no strangers and had already run upstairs and were enjoying their own time together. Aunt Julia had thought of everything for them including a wonderful, heavenly-smelling homemade pizza, which the girls would be eating in their room.

Sam and Uncle Jim made sure a glass of wine was in my hand before I could sit down anywhere. It started a whole discussion on wine and Ron seemed to be quite the connoisseur on the topic. I knew from Aunt Julia that he was Italian and had a bit of a temper, which at times concerned Uncle Jim.

"Ron has his own wine cellar and brought us wine for the dinner courses." Uncle Jim boasted. "He and Julia got together on the menu so he'd know what to bring."

"Where did you learn so much about wine?" I wanted to learn more.

"My father and grandfather had wineries in California. My great-grandfather grew grapes in Italy. I think I disappointed some family members when I didn't learn more about the business."

"I think you qualify as an expert more than any of us! This is quite good. I'll have to write down the name of this one."

"I'll try to give you a bit of the history as we try each wine this evening."

"So you have no desire to continue the wine business?" I asked.

"The labor and time are more than I'm willing to sacrifice after watching them deal with all the hard work and problems," he laughed.

Christy seemed rather quiet and went to help Aunt Julia in the kitchen. It was always interesting to me how some women melted into the wallpaper when men were speaking, as if their opinion didn't matter. Christy seemed to be that kind of woman.

Uncle Jim and Sam, of course, had plenty to talk about even though they saw each other often. Sam was sharing some information with him about a client he had seen when he was out of town. I was the type to follow the conversation rather than assume the female duties in the kitchen or try to be a good hostess. What was I thinking? I didn't have much experience playing hostess other than to occasionally help Mother get things together ahead of time for her guests. I usually entertained my friends and employees at the shop or at a nearby restaurant.

Aunt Julia was serving us delightful appetizers she had made herself. There were assorted filled puffed pastry shells with textures that melted away in my mouth. I could tell from the start that she had put a lot of thought and preparation into tonight's occasion.

We were about to be seated for dinner when Sam pulled me aside in the hallway to tell me how stunning I looked, and that he was getting quite used to the heavenly scent of my perfume.

"Let's make this a short evening here, so we have some time together," he whispered.

"That would be very nice." I kissed him on a cheek that was freshly shaved with a touch of a fragrance I had noted before. Uncle Jim came to find us to lead us into the dining room. The place cards fortunately had me sitting next to my new love. The boy-girl arrangement had Ron on the other side of me.

Aunt Julia had arranged a gorgeous table of her best china, crystal, and silver. My floral arrangement of red carnations, roses, holly, and baby's breath gave a nod to the season at hand.

"The table setting is too pretty to use!" I said with much admiration.

"It's all about the flowers, don't you think?" She grinned.

"The women in this family have exquisite taste, don't you agree?" Sam managed to tease both of us at once.

"I think we have good taste in women to start with," bragged Uncle Jim.

"I say we begin this special occasion with a birthday toast to our guest of honor this evening." Sam raised his glass.

Everyone agreed, and raised their glasses. "Here's to our good friend, brother, uncle, and husband," Sam announced. "May you have many healthy, happy years to follow!"

"Now Sam, that was so formal," Aunt Julia complained. "What would your toast have been if you were at the local pub?" She was so pretty when she laughed.

"We won't go there." He was so charming when he was droll.

In front of us was a first course of potato-leek soup with a sprig of parsley on top. The conversation started with how tasty it was and who liked to cook and who didn't. It seemed the men enjoyed the artistry of cooking more than the women. Christy, still very quiet, smiled and agreed with whatever we seemed to be saying. Sam was attentive and occasionally I caught him looking at my cleavage. Uncle Jim was the kind of guy who would have cornered all the conversation for the evening, so we knew we had to jump in or not be heard.

The second course was a soft-shell crab salad accompanied by an explanation from Aunt Julia. She got the recipe when she was last at Topsail Island in North Carolina. The wine, Ron explained, was a vintage pinot white chablis from his wine cellar. His detailed description helped us understand what we tasted.

The soft shell crabs from the beach had been frozen till they were prepared in Aunt Julia's loving kitchen. Mention of that trip sparked a conversation about favorite vacation spots. Uncle Jim and she went to the island often and one year I had joined them, so I could contribute to the conversation. Aunt Julia and Uncle Jim lit up with words of joy, talking about the walks on the beach, great restaurants, and the interesting people they had met.

I thought to myself that the two of them could recapture some of that joy again, but things had changed in the last year. Aunt Julia was convinced another woman or two had intervened. Ron and Christy said they preferred the mountains as they usually traveled west.

Sam didn't say much. He did say something to the effect that he envied everyone's memories and that he was bad about taking time for pleasure without business. He sounded a lot like me. I especially liked the combination when I went away to market to purchase things for the shop. I didn't feel guilty if I threw in good restaurants or an extra mile or two to visit something I was interested in. I loved taking a moment away from the shop to write down fresh thoughts or stories when I was in a new environment. Some of my favorite poetry was written at those away places that affected me with their scenery or activities. I had a way of looking in from the outside as I witnessed scenic views and experiences. The thought of getting away to a vacation spot sounded pretty good to me right now, as the others kept sharing their travels.

The main course was a rack of lamb with sun-dried cherry sauce, accompanied by a serving of asparagus beautifully placed on the side. It reminded me of one of those pictures you see in *Food Network Magazine*. I wasn't sure how I could manage another course of wine, but did my best to drink at least a few sips of the white zinfandel that Ron had chosen. It seemed to be one of his favorites, but why, I already had forgotten. It seemed to get the best reviews of the meal so far.

How did Aunt Julia manage to present such a delightful menu? Uncle Jim led the list of compliments that Aunt Julia received from us. She was very pleased we were impressed and I think Uncle Jim scored many points by giving her all the credit.

"When I first met Julia, I couldn't believe she was for real," Uncle Jim said, as if he really meant it. "I wasn't used to people choosing my favorite things to please me. She makes her gifts and menus very personal. Our mother did well to serve us our favorite kind of cake on our birthday, right, Christy?"

"Yes, I agree, Jim." Christy was all but expressionless. "I think we were probably lucky to get any food on the table, much less our favorites."

I felt a bit of tension. As no one knew quite what she meant, I asked Aunt Julia what her favorite dish was. She said that making her special chocolate cake gave her a great deal of pleasure, plus it was also one of her favorite desserts. I chimed in that it was one of the family favorites that we enjoyed from her.

"It will be one of two choices you'll have for your dessert tonight." She stood up to take our plates. "The other choice will have to wait for now until I hear about other people's favorite foods."

Ron did not hesitate in saying there was nothing better than a good rare steak. Sam liked fresh halibut. Christy loved any kind of ice cream. I confessed I was a dark chocolate guru, and at times really craved Aunt Julia's chocolate cake and Mother's chocolate chip cookies.

"Here is your other choice," Aunt Julia announced. "It's lemon-glazed persimmon bars. I got this recipe from Marie a long time ago." The dessert was beautifully displayed on a clear Depression glass plate that no doubt was handed down from family.

"Do you remember having these bars at her house?" Aunt Julia asked me.

"No, I can't say that I do." I was trying to think past the last sip of wine I consumed.

"She offered to bring these one time to one of our gatherings, but she never did," Aunt Julia said. "I thought it would be a nice touch in her memory."

"It sure is," said Sam and Uncle Jim at the same time.

The famous chocolate cake was served on a high-rise milk glass cake plate that Aunt Julia said once belonged to Grandmother Davis. Sounds of heaven arose from each and every one—yums and umms. Ron and Uncle Jim decided they needed a sample of both treats. Aunt Julia knew she had pleased us all.

A heavy, mellow merlot finally came out as the most perfect compliment to the desserts. I had my own theory that chocolate and merlot were orgasmic together. I said so out loud and Sam took note. "I must definitely remember the combination." He winked at me in front of everyone.

"Perhaps we should go around the table and ask everyone else what they like that's orgasmic," Uncle Jim grinned. Aunt Julia wasn't too happy with his suggestion and Christy looked abashed.

"Oh no," I laughed, feeling quite foolish and blushing more than usual.

"I'll go first and I will keep it clean." Aunt Julia took charge. "I get a massage from Tommy at the Green Spa that is the closest thing to an orgasm."

"Oh really!" Uncle Jim was suddenly serious, but the rest of us were snickering.

Christy found courage somewhere because she surprisingly spoke up about a great back rub she gets from Ron. "I never want him to stop." Her tone was all innocence. Ron smiled proudly and said she didn't like him to stop at other things as well. Giggles and suggestive noises came from all corners. Christy sheepishly blushed and fussed at him for the comment.

"There are things about your sister that you do not want to know," Uncle Jim said, I suddenly remembered he was my uncle.

I could tell we might have put Sam in a spot but he managed to share this after a slight hesitation: "I go crazy eating my mother's pot roast, and at the risk of incriminating myself, I am going to pass on my favorite orgasmic moments."

"Oh darn." Uncle Jim feigned disappointment. "Anne, this would have been a good time to find out more about this guy!"

"She already knows she's a favorite," said Sam as he leaned over to kiss me on the cheek. No one responded to avoid embarrassment. At that moment, though, I didn't care, and feeling flirtatious, kissed him back.

Ron picked up his wine glass and said he'd like to make the last toast to the incredible host and hostess for an orgasmic meal! We cheered and laughed and Aunt Julia blushed with pride.

Uncle Jim then picked up his glass, stood up at the table, and said, "This is a toast for the most beautiful and loving wife, who provided me a lovely birthday dinner with my family and friends." The ringing of crystal glasses and cheers again chimed through the room. He leaned over and kissed her on the forehead.

"Here's to the birthday boy who gave us a good excuse to get together." Sam toasted, too. The group of six had blended nicely and I was beginning to think that Aunt Julia might be all wrong about Uncle Jim.

We were the last to leave despite Sam's secret plans to leave early. He and I went to his loft at a very late hour. It was obvious the two of us had had way too much wine. Things were way too sad or too silly. We threw ourselves down on his comfy couch still wearing our coats. His place was so warm and inviting that it was very easy to relax and just enjoy the moment. Sam turned on the fire, which lit the room with a warm glow.

He commented on the fun evening and hoped I enjoyed it as well. We talked about how generous the compliments were from both Uncle Jim and Aunt Julia. No one would have ever guessed they had serious problems.

Sam gently removed my coat and laid it on the footstool nearby. He held me close and I loved every minute of it. He offered more refreshment, but I reminded him I had a work day the next day.

"I should have gone home, perhaps, but I wanted to be with you every second I could," I said, responding to his affection.

"You made the right choice, Annie," he teased.

"Hey, what's this Annie business? You've called me that more than once."

"I think it fits you." He smiled at me. "I think it brings you to a level of approachability and love. 'Anne' is a bit more formal, don't you think?"

"I can't think about that tonight. I'm way too tired. If you like calling me Annie, it works for me."

"I'll get you to work in plenty of time tomorrow, just like before," Sam promised. "I catch early plane flights all the time. Let's savor the hours and moments we have left, my precious Annie."

CHAPTER 40

⟨⟨⟨⟩⟩⟩

Just as in my last stay at the Dickson loft, Sam woke me with the sunshine of the day coming through the large window in his bedroom. I couldn't believe I smelled coffee and what might be the aroma of cinnamon rolls! Did this guy sleep? I quickly dressed in my evening's attire and walked into the kitchen. Sam was in jeans and a sweater looking adorable and neat as always.

"I feel like a hooker who didn't take the money and run soon enough."

"With this kind of schedule, I guess we won't find out if we are 'morning people' if you know what I mean," Sam teased. "I look forward to us having some time to wake up, give each other a proper good morning, and not check the clock."

"Oh, that does sound good, doesn't it?"

He handed me my coffee with a kiss on the forehead, and said we could leave when I gave the word. "I assume you want to be dropped off at home to change, right?"

I just laughed and gathered my wits about me as I put on my

coat. We went out the door like any married couple rushing to their careers.

Mother would be awake, I thought, so I would probably see her. This was not going to be comfortable for me. I guess one is never old enough to feel like a grown-up when one lives under her parent's roof. Would I be in trouble? What questions would she ask?

I entered the house bringing in the morning paper, which meant Mother was still asleep.

I went to my room, quickly showered, and dressed. When I came back out to the kitchen, Mother was in her robe, drinking coffee. It was yet another morning I didn't have time to take my morning walk. When was I going to shed the calories that were mounting up with this relationship? Last night's meal at Aunt Julia's was not a good experience for any weight watcher!

"How was the dinner party?"

"It was really great. I can't wait to tell you all about it, but not now. I have last minute flowers to prepare for the Graham wedding this morning, so I need to get going. I hope Sue shows up because I'll need her. Aunt Julia prepared an amazing dinner, and the compliments flowed between her and Uncle Jim, Mother! Uncle Jim's sister Christy and her husband Ron were there. They were so fun. I'm surprised Aunt Julia hasn't mentioned them more often." Mother listened, wanting to ask many questions, but I kept moving towards the door.

I grabbed my coat and asked, "Did anyone ever call me Annie growing up?"

She looked at me rather strangely and said that she thought Grandpa Davis always called me Annie for some reason. She reminded me that in grade school they wanted to call me Annie and that I hated it. I nodded and then remembered a bit of the teasing.

"Well, I think I just decided I kind of like it!" I laughed. I left her with a funny look on her face. Suddenly I felt like this particular grown-up was feeling okay, after all, in her parent's home.

The mood in the shop was especially festive as we prepared holly arrangements for mostly happy customers. The Christmas music continued throughout the day. I never seemed to tire of it and many times we would sing along. I was tired but ridiculously happy. Sue was in a good mood also; she continued to get encouraging news from the adoption agency. After I told her about the previous night's birthday dinner, she went back to the subject of her adoption.

"I should hear this week if I qualify, and if I do, they'll give me a time frame when this all could happen."

"What a great Christmas present that would be," Sally chimed in. This was exciting for all of us. I dared not think what we would say and do if Sue was rejected.

Kevin walked in from the wedding delivery and said they were thrilled with the flowers.

"I bet it is a beautiful wedding," I said, picturing it.

"Someday we'll be getting your flowers ready, huh, Anne?" Sue winked at Sally.

"Hey, give me a break! I had my chance with Ted and gave it up, so that may have been it for me." They didn't say anything, so perhaps they believed what I just said to be true.

We were pretty caught up with our orders, so while Sally cleaned up, Sue declared she was leaving early to go Christmas shopping.

"Yikes!" I suddenly realized I had a personal life during the season. "I really need to do that myself. When are we going to have a little work party, Kevin? We can't do it Christmas Eve because Mother is planning a get-together."

"How about we all just go to Charley's after work one night, have a few drinks, and you all bring me presents?" Sally joked. The three of them clapped in approval.

"That might work," I nodded.

After everyone left for the day, I decided to get serious and made out my Christmas list. Gift cards would indeed be the easiest program. Aunt Julia and Uncle Jim would get a dinner card from Mavericks, and then I would give Aunt Julia a gift card from the quilt shop. Sue would get a gift card from the Precious Baby Boutique around the corner and a little something personal from Brian's Jewelry store. If she got approved, I would pick out a baby charm. It was sort of a tradition for babies in our family. I still had mine, which was a pair of sterling silver baby shoes. Mother needed some new work clothes, so I would give her a card for Miss Michelle's, her favorite dress shop. So, the basic list was all done accept for Sam.

I thought I would take home some poinsettias today to sprinkle about the house. I was partial to red ones, but I would always include a white one for Mother's bedroom. She told me my father would always bring her one around the holidays, and it was always white. Poinsettias might just be the right "thank you" to send to Uncle Jim and Aunt Julia for the nice dinner last night, also.

Then there was Sam, the most important person in my life these days. What in the world would he like? He bought everything he wanted from the looks of it all. I would have to think of something personal that he didn't have. I knew I couldn't top his mother's pot roast, so cooking was out! He didn't seem to need anything, but suddenly my thoughts went to the night we were walking down Main Street and peered in the window at O'Connell's Art Gallery. We both admired many things, and pretended to pick our favorite painting in the window. If I visited the shop I'd be able to remember which painting he chose.

It wasn't that long ago, so it should still be there.

My cell phone rang and Sam's sexy voice said, "So, Annie, do you have time for me tonight, or are you pretty well sacked?"

"Well, we did have a great sales day," I bragged. "This is always a good Christmas present for me. I think I've gone above last year's receipts for the day. Everyone here was so happy about that. Sue went home early and even though I'm exhausted, I want to be with you! I'll meet you for dinner or a drink if you're up to it."

"No ma'am, I'm good. The closer the holidays get, the less people want to do business, so I had a light day. I'll come by the shop and pick you up. I need to run an errand first, so it'll be a half hour or so, how's that? Lock the door, so no one keeps you late."

I didn't remember him giving me orders before and wondered what was up with him. I agreed, though, like it was the right thing to do. It was also a sign that he was seeing patterns form as I did my business. He was paying attention. Hmmm.

It was a good half hour later when I heard him knock at the back door. It would have scared me, but I could see him through the window. Luckily I had had time to freshen up. I was falling into somewhat of a habit as far as sprucing up my appearance after a work day. I had done some of this with Ted, but not with the urgency or care that I had with Sam. I had called home to tell Mother I was meeting up with Sam. She said she was going to Sadie Andrew's house down the street for dinner.

I opened the door to let Sam in from the cold and he took me in his arms. He turned around to turn the lights off by the door. It was totally dark with exception of the white Christmas lights in the front display room. I was caught off guard with his aggressiveness and passion.

"Has anyone ever made love to you in your shop and told you

they loved you at the same time?" Sam asked as his grip on me grew tighter. "If not, I want to know now because I'd like to be the first and only!"

I was taken back a bit, but answered, "No they haven't, at least not until now," murmured between kisses.

It was an unexpected portion of an evening that started out with fireworks and ended in lovely quiet conversation and a light dinner at the bar at Charley's.

Chapter 41

I ran to get what gift cards on my list I could after church on Sunday. I knew Aunt Julia would be coming by to work on her quilt binding, so I thought it might be a good time to cut out my pieces and get started on one of the flower blocks.

When I arrived home, Aunt Julia was there and as soon as I walked in the door she said she needed an update on Sam and me. She and Mother seemed to have been in deep conversation when I interrupted them.

"I should have written you a thank-you note, Aunt Julia. I'm sending you a poinsettia instead. Will that work? The dinner party was so wonderful, and what a menu! Sam said he would have the two of you over after the holidays for something a little more casual, like pasta. It was such a fun group."

"I heard he was a good cook."

"Yes, I'll have to tell you all about it sometime," I said, rushing up to my room.

As soon as I got my clothes changed, we all went to the basement. Mother and I concentrated on what to cut first. I let her take the lead in deciding how to get started. She had gotten some advice from Isabella at the quilt shop, so she was in charge. Somehow, in the back of my mind, I felt she would be the prime quiltmaker with this quilt, since I had little time. It all seemed a little overwhelming to me. Aunt Julia brought the quilt book with her, and she showed us what she might do to get the binding just right.

"I think that looks right to me," I said, not really being the most attentive to what was going on. "I guess we could have a moment of silence, and ask Aunt Marie and Grandmother."

"Oh, stop reminding me. I don't think this is going to be very hard to do," Aunt Julia proclaimed.

The fireplace had been turned on just like before. I didn't question who may have done that. At this point, some things were best left unsaid. The doorbell rang and I went up to see who it could be. Sue was standing there with a plate full of Christmas cookies.

"I wasn't sure you were going to make it."

"I thought it would take me all day to bake these, but I finished sooner than I thought, so here I am," Sue said, ready to head to the basement. "I didn't want to miss anything. I left Muffin at home. She and the cookies in the car would not mix."

"Are there any of those yummy chocolate chip cookies?" I sniffed at the plate as I took them from her.

"Can't you smell them?" Sue joked. "I brought my quilt kit and I already have some of the strips cut. Isabella showed me how to use the rotary cutter, so we quickly cut them at the shop. She is such a dear. I'm going to drop off some cookies for her as well, as a thank you."

"Go on downstairs; I'll bring your cookies and I better make a fresh pot of coffee."

As soon as I delivered the coffee, mugs, and cookies, impatient Aunt Julia reminded me to give a Sam update.

"Okay, you guys, I'm crazy about him!" I blushed.

"I could tell that, and I think the feeling is mutual," Aunt Julia said.

"It's so very different than my long relationship with Ted. I guess I kept telling myself that I needed to 'settle' for him. I don't get anywhere to meet single people like most women my age. I don't have time to search the internet or hang out at Charley's like a lot of single girls do in this town. Meeting Sam through you and Uncle Jim was perfect! I love his loft and how he has it decorated. I can't believe this guy hasn't been snatched up by someone. Am I missing something? Is he for real? I know I've asked you this a hundred times!"

"According to Jim, he's real." Aunt Julia shrugged. "But who knows what goes on when these guys travel?"

"So does Uncle Jim think it's risky to get involved with him?" I really wanted to know.

"He doesn't say much, but I think that's a good thing, because he's outspoken about everything else."

"Uncle Jim sure was complimentary to you the other night." I hoped she had noticed.

"Yeah, I don't know what to make of it. It's almost suspicious how nice he's been lately."

"Now, stop that, Julia." Mother used a tone I had heard growing up. "Try to enjoy the fact that he's showing you some affection."

"It's not in my plan, you all." Aunt Julia had an odd tone. "I don't feel the same way about him anymore. He's picking up on me going through the motions and I think it drives him crazy. It's no fun screwing around if no one cares and isn't checking on you."

"I should have such problems." Sue shook her head. "Both of

you have someone who loves you. I don't expect it will ever happen to me, so I have to take my destiny in my own hands and become a mother instead of a bride."

"It's all cool, Sue," I said. "None of us should be complaining."

"I know this quilt I'm making will be wrapped around my child one day soon," she said with optimism.

"Is everyone done with their Christmas shopping?" Mother rearranged the colors in some of the blocks.

"I have everything but something for Sam." My consternation showed. "Give me some clues, please, please! He has everything. Do you think Uncle Jim would have any ideas? The only thing I have thought of is a piece of artwork. He's fond of Leon Watkins' work. He has one of his pieces hanging in his den. I could probably look for something like that. I was with him when he admired a piece of his that was in the window at O'Connell's Art Gallery. I also learned he loves quilts, but he's going to have to hang around for awhile to see that happen." Everyone got a laugh out of that.

"I think you're going to have to come up with something personal from you, Anne," Sue suggested. "It doesn't have to cost a lot of money. Perhaps something sentimental that would remind him of you."

"Good idea, Sue," chimed in Mother. "Perhaps a baby picture of you, Anne," she joked.

"I'll think of something," I said, now wanting to move away from the subject.

I was struggling a bit with my appliqué stitching. How in the world do people do this? Isabella showed me a stitch in the shop, but I couldn't remember exactly how it went. I had chosen a tulip bouquet for the first block because the pieces were a little larger than the others.

"This looked so easy when Isabella did this," I said.

"All the pieces are now cut, and I'll put each block in a bag so you won't get them mixed up." I was right; Mother was taking control of the project.

"It's making me crazy," I fumed. "I think I'll put it away for now."

"How do you like working at the bookstore, Aunt Sylvia?" Sue appeared to make progress on her quilt.

"We've been really busy, but they were nice enough to give me simple chores during the holiday rush. There hasn't been much time to train me, they're so busy. I gift wrap and just walk around asking people if I can help them with what they're looking for. My hours are short, so it's kind of nice while my feet adjust. I see so many people I know, and the bargains I get are wonderful."

"Yes, she is in her room reading most nights," I confirmed.

"It's right up my alley," she added. "I hope they keep me after Christmas." It was good to see Mother adding her world of activity to ours.

Aunt Julia was very intent on sewing her binding on but seemed awkward at the attempt. "I hope this looks okay." She showed us a small segment of the binding. "I love this basement quilt! It's almost totally done!"

"My dear Julia, it has to have a name, remember?" reminded Mother. "How about Aunt Julia's Fan Quilt?"

"It will always be the 'basement quilt' to me," said Aunt Julia.

"I miss the quilting itself, don't you?" Sue said, surprising us all.

We agreed that it was something we all had learned together and shared.

"The frame is in the stairway closet and ready for action on the next quilt," Mother said.

"It will be brittle and broken by the time my quilt gets done," I joked.

"Sue, yours will be done soonest," Mother observed. "Can we help you get those blocks sewn together faster, so we can get it into the frame?"

"Oh, I love sewing them myself, actually, plus I hope to have someone waiting for this, and I want them to know I made it just for them! I'll bring Aunt Marie's machine over this week, if anyone wants to help sew it together. It's getting pretty close to Christmas, but if we get the top together, we can set up the quilt frame after the New Year."

"Sounds like a plan," Aunt Julia said.

CHAPTER 42

———⊷∞⊶———

Aunt Julia and I were discussing what we would be wearing to Uncle Jim and Sam's company Christmas party coming up at the Capital Hotel in a couple of days. I had asked Aunt Julia what to expect during the evening's activities and was pleased to learn Sam and I would be going together with the two of them, although I hadn't double dated since high school. Sam had been teasing me all week about the strange people I would be meeting. Aunt Julia assured me he was correct.

Most of us were frustrated enough to be ready to depart. Aunt Julia took the rest of the chocolate chip cookies for Sarah and off they all went with their chosen projects.

The evening of Sam's company party arrived quite quickly amid all the Christmas rush. Before he picked me up, Mother was acting like I was going to the prom. She took a photo of me coming down the stairs in my Christmas red gown. It was strapless with a shear flowing skirt. I bought the gown last year when I was out of town. I was hoping to wear it last Christmas, but plans fell apart. I thought it fit me better than ever and I liked how my twisted hairdo, with a glitter strand, no less, made the whole ensemble look more glamorous and festive. Cherie, my hairstylist, did an awesome job, as always. Pearls somehow looked dull, though, leaving me to choose a diamond necklace that belonged to Mother, so it pleased her very much. My father gave it to her on their twentieth wedding anniversary.

I was hoping I didn't overdo it, but Aunt Julia had said the party was formal and that the guys would be wearing tuxedos. Mother answered the door and in walked the most handsome man I think I have ever seen.

Mother started with the oohs and aahs and I whistled until Sam blushed. He kissed me on the cheek and twirled me around like we were already on the dance floor.

"Oh, to be young again." Mother sighed and smiled at the same time. She took one more photo of us before we went out the door to pick up Aunt Julia and Uncle Jim.

She looked stunning in a black, glittery, floor-length dress. It showed off her sexy figure, which she was usually conservative about displaying. It was perfect for her long, flowing reddish-brown hair ordinarily pulled back into a ponytail. Uncle Jim saw she looked amazing, so it was going to be interesting to see how much attention she would get from him. Sam was shocked at her transformation.

"We are two lucky guys with two gorgeous girls," he said, admiration all over him.

The cocktail hour was low key, almost like a school dance that wanted to get started, but wasn't sure how. I knew some of the people there; they had come into the flower shop at one time or another. Sam was impressed at how many I knew. He seemed proud to show me off and I felt I was with the handsome prince out of a storybook. I watched his behavior with the other women there because I was sure they knew plenty about this hunk of a guy.

In the powder room, before dinner, a beautiful girl came up to me as I was refreshing my lipstick. "Hi, I'm Susan Wilshire."

"Oh, hi, I'm Anne Brown." I gave her a friendly smile.

"Yes, I know who you are." Her bluntness took me by surprise. "Sam and I are old friends. Maybe he's mentioned me to you? I saw the two of you over at Mavericks one night, and Sam acted like he didn't see me, which I thought was rather strange, because I know he did."

"So, why was that so important?" I was most curious.

"Well, it's strange, because we not only work together, but we had kind of a thing going for awhile. Don't get me wrong; I've moved on. It's not a big deal, but I just wanted you to know it's okay. I'm saying he doesn't have to ignore me. He doesn't want commitment, like most guys, and that's cool, but I didn't know he moved on because of someone else."

"Maybe he didn't end it because of someone else." I wanted to tell her she was a busybody tramp. In fact, I wanted to smack her perfectly made-up face because it was just the kind of information I was afraid to know. She too, like me, seemed younger but in a more immature and careless way. So, fear of commitment was his reason, I said to myself. I filed this in my memory card.

I stopped Susan before she went out the door of the powder room. "Susan, since you work with Sam, I guess you know Jim Baker."

"Oh, sure. Those guys are pretty inseparable," her tone was matter-of-fact.

"Have you met Julia, Jim's wife?"

"No, I haven't." She didn't even think about the question.

"What's the deal with Jim?" I fished around. "I'm just curious. Is he seeing someone else? Because I have a sense he is." She looked at me in a very strange, suspecting way, and I could tell she couldn't figure me out. After all, I was the very new girlfriend of her once-boyfriend Sam, not Jim Baker.

"Everyone knows about Jim and Brenda, so I'm surprised you don't," she said after some hesitation. "I guess it's more of a corporate secret. They're both married, but hey, it's been going on for some time, so who knows if it will ever change. I saw Jim's wife tonight for the first time and she's pretty hot. Hey, I'm sure dinner has started, so we better go. Nice to meet you, Anne, right—it's Anne?" I nodded as she flew out the door.

I sat down on the pink velvet seat to absorb what I had just heard. I know Sam was probably wondering where I was. I had to get myself together. Now I wanted to know more about this Susan and now a Brenda person, but I didn't want to ruin the evening for Sam, and especially not for Aunt Julia.

Why did I have to ask about Uncle Jim? Sadness filled me. Who were Uncle Jim and Sam? Were there more secrets in this corporate palace party? Darn that Uncle Jim, I said to myself. Didn't he have a clue what a lucky guy he was to be married to my Aunt Julia?

Then my thoughts returned to this guy that Susan said would not commit. Why hadn't Sam mentioned her to me when we talked about past relationships? Why was he keeping Brenda and Uncle Jim a secret when everyone else seemed to know about it?

Sam was full of questions when I returned. I told him I kept running into people I knew. Dinner was a blur despite the enticing courses that were served. I was drinking my share of merlot and I watched Aunt Julia and Uncle Jim with extra interest. Who is Brenda? Is she here? I wondered. I had to know before I left without asking Sam about her.

I did my best to pretend I was having a wonderful time. Sam was trying very hard to be attentive and was very affectionate on the dance floor. I decided to enjoy every moment while it lasted and didn't want each dance to end. Aunt Julia and Uncle Jim seemed to dance often. They seemed to talk most of their time together rather than dance cheek to cheek. What if Brenda was watching?

Sam asked Aunt Julia to dance, so I quickly scurried to the powder room where I had learned my previous information. It was crowded like I hoped, so I said to the older woman combing her hair, "Do you work for Martingale?" after she complimented me on my dress.

"I sure do; more years than I care to admit."

"The reason I'm asking is that I have a friend who is related to some 'Brenda' person that works here. I would like to tell her hello, but don't know her last name or what she looks like. Is she here?"

"Oh, Brenda, no, no, I don't think so. She doesn't usually come to these social things. Her husband isn't very social, I'm told."

"Does she live here in Colebridge?"

"Yes, they live in quite a lovely new development in the north part of town." She sounded as if she had been there before. "She travels a fair amount for the company, so she's gone a lot."

"Does she have children?" I continued to pry.

"I don't think so, but I could be wrong. I'll probably see her Monday, if you want me to pass on a message."

"Oh, no, she wouldn't know me. I just thought it would be neat to meet her. Enjoy your evening!" I was pleased I had obtained what I had. The lady seemed to know her, so I felt it was accurate.

Sam was talking to Uncle Jim in the bar area when I returned. "We were thinking of calling it a night." Sam received me with his usual affection.

"Oh, sure." I was happy with the idea. "Where's Aunt Julia?"

"She's dancing with one of my bosses, of all people." Uncle Jim shook his head in disbelief. "She's been quite a hit tonight."

"She's a knockout tonight," I said with pride. "I forgot what a good dancer she was, too. You better look out Uncle Jim!" He thought I was teasing, I'm sure, but I wanted him to know that he was playing with fire, big time!

We dropped them off at the curb in front of their house, declined an invitation to come in, and drove off.

I was relieved to be alone with Sam. I wasn't sure I could handle the serious conversation that would come from my news. I was feeling tired. I had acquired a headache thinking about all the players I had just been exposed to.

I couldn't bear upsetting Sam, who had been such a dear the entire night. I decided I could wait for further talk and questions until morning, when my head was clear. I couldn't spoil the evening he had so looked forward to.

CHAPTER 43

Sally opened for me at the shop the next morning because I knew in advance it would be a late night with Sam. I was surprised how well I kept the evening's secrets to myself. I wasn't surprised to meet one of Sam's girlfriends at the party, just surprised it hadn't happened sooner.

I wasn't sure how I was going to handle this business with Brenda. I certainly wasn't going to tell Aunt Julia unless I really had to at some point. Maybe it was just company gossip. Since Sam had not said anything about a Brenda, I wanted to believe she didn't exist. I didn't want Aunt Julia to put a face and name to her suspicions.

I wasn't even sure I was going to put Sam on the spot. He was being loyal to a good friend, so I had to weigh and balance that information.

The next morning, Sam and I stopped to have coffee before I had to go on to work. He had the day off, so he was relaxed and in a very good mood.

"I want to discuss Christmas weekend with you," he said. "My folks would love to meet you, Anne, and they asked me if I was going to ask you to come home for a visit. I know you mentioned having Christmas Eve with your family, and I would like to be there for that as well. My mother keeps calling, and I keep putting her off."

"Oh, I understand. I've been wondering what you'll do, and my, yes, I would really like to meet them as well! So I take it they know about me."

"Yes, I told them some time back I was dating a flower merchant. Mother loved it of course and wanted to know more."

"If it's any help for the conversation, I close the shop for inventory between Christmas and New Year's. Ideally, for me, I could handle a short visit then."

"What if we left early Christmas morning?" Sam suggested. "We could be there by noon and stay a couple of days."

"I could do that, I think." I answered with enough certainty to commit. "I just can't leave Mother with all the work of Christmas Eve, plus leaving the shop before then would be difficult."

"Super, I will call on some flight times to Chicago today." He lit up like I had just given him a new toy.

In the car we hugged and kissed, feeling closer than ever. The past now suddenly seemed unimportant. It was now going to be about the future. I couldn't believe I was going to meet his parents. Why did this seem so right? I knew already I would like them, and could even taste that pot roast I had heard about.

I arrived at the shop the same time as Sue. Sam came in to say hello to everyone since he had the extra time.

"I think you all are going to have to sit down to hear my news!" Sue was positively beaming. "I just got a call to tell me that I have been accepted as an adoptive mother!!! Do I look like a mother?"

Happiness just radiated from her.

We all jumped and cheered.

"I can't believe it Sue, congratulations!" I clapped heartily. Each of us hugged her and bombarded her with questions.

Sam said he had a feeling there would be good news when he came in the door. "That is really something to be proud of Sue," he smiled. He's kind and sensitive to my friends. Hmmm.

"They said I would probably have a little girl the first of the year! Miss Elliot in the office said it looked like she would be from Honduras. She is hooking me up with a lawyer this week because I'll have to travel there to pick her up. They advised me to take the lawyer with me in case there are any problems. They have a little girl in mind, but cannot say anything just yet. If they firm it up, I might get to see a photo! I don't know her age or anything. I can hardly believe it all!" She was bubbling all over the place.

"Oh, I can't wait till Mother and Aunt Julia know."

"I already called Aunt Julia to tell her, but I'll let you tell your mother."

"I think you should tell her," I hugged her again. "This is awesome! Have you told your parents?"

"Oh yes, they were the first to know! They are going to be grandparents! How cool is that!? I think they're still pretty shocked that a single person can do this, especially me. Goodness knows what is said between them. This sort of thing didn't happen in their generation. They seemed to be thrilled, so I hope I won't disappoint them."

"I guess Aunt Marie and Grandmother already know!" I teased, giving a glance upward. "Just think how thrilled they would be for you, Sue. This calls for a celebration! Stop by for a drink tonight."

Sam congratulated her once again before he went on to his day.

The way he reacted was another sign of how much he loved family.

That afternoon, Sue picked up the phone at the shop and told Mother the news. The excitement was catching, even for the customers coming in and out all day.

I checked back with Mother, and we decided it would be a night when the basement quilters would celebrate. We would make it simple, ordering pizza and having plenty of wine in the offering. Aunt Julia had stolen Sue's thunder by calling my mother ahead of Sue's call, but she pretended she didn't know. Aunt Julia, too, was anxious for us to celebrate. A little one in our family would be such a treasure.

I called Sam, and he was perfectly content to have the evening free when I told him our plans. He seemed to be genuinely happy for Sue. She couldn't talk about anything else all day long. Rumors, no doubt, would fly through Colebridge, and she knew there would be criticism about her being a single mother. Colebridge was progressive about many things, but still conservative on some issues. I personally had many liberal opinions that I knew I had to keep to myself because of my business.

Sue followed right behind me as we pulled into the driveway to my house. Mother greeted her with open arms and had many questions on her conversation with the agency. Sue had done her research on Honduras and had some information about the children that were being adopted from there. She said she always had a more Asian child pictured in her mind, but that a dark-skinned baby girl from Honduras would do just fine.

Sue and I happily chatted away with Mother. As soon as Aunt Julia arrived, we poured the wine as we waited for the pizza delivery. "I think we need to go to the basement to share this joy with Marie and Mother, don't you?" Mother smiled.

"Oh, I so wish they were here, especially when my baby comes."

Sue's voice filled with emotion. "I say 'baby' because she will always be my baby."

"They're pretty certain it will be a girl, right?" asked Aunt Julia.

"Yes, that was what she said. She said early on that it was much easier to get girls than boys because everyone wants a namesake. Don't they know in today's world a woman can keep her own birth name? Girls are just not desirable in most countries, I hear."

"Okay, next question." Mother was so excited for Sue. "Have you thought of a name?"

"Yes, I have. I told myself that I wouldn't make it definite until I saw her."

"Smart," I said, giving her credit. Happiness for her washed over me all over again. "I can't wait! What do you suppose Muffin will think of this home intruder?"

"Well, I've already had that talk with her, and I think the two will do just fine," she laughed.

We headed down the stairs. Mother had put up a little Christmas tree on the table since we were spending more time down there. The basement had now become more of a regular room in the house, so Mother tried to keep it orderly, clean, and decorated. The white lights were on and greenery and bows were draped down the stairway. Until this year, I didn't remember Christmas decorations extending into the basement. After all, it was a basement.

The doorbell rang with the hot pizzas ready for consumption. Mother served us as hostess and had everything prepared for our little celebration. We pounced on the two choices of pepperoni with onion and vegetarian delight. This basement crew was not about diets or healthy choices! We ate well and drank a couple of bottles of wine.

Sue was describing how she was going to redo her apartment to accommodate the new family member and then someday start looking for a small house with a yard. We all offered suggestions and discussed where nice little houses could be found. We chatted on, ignoring our early-stage quilt projects lying about the room.

Aunt Julia changed the subject to ask me if Sam and I had a good time at the company Christmas party.

"Oh, yes! How about you two? It sure looked like you were getting along well."

"Yeah, pretty surprising. I think he was actually a little jealous because of other people's attentions."

"It's no wonder, because you looked fabulous! I met someone interesting who said she was a former girlfriend of Sam's. What do you know about Susan Wilshire?"

"I think there was a Susan he once mentioned, come to think of it," said Aunt Julia. "I guess she was the last one I knew he dated before you, but frankly, I never paid too much attention to Sam's friends. I have a feeling there wasn't too much to the relationship." Mother and Sue were paying close attention to our exchange.

"Why do you ask? Did she introduce herself at the party?" Aunt Julia wanted to know more details.

"Yes, she made a real point to do so. I didn't mention it to Sam because I didn't want to spoil the evening. I wasn't sure how he would react. I know I wouldn't have appreciated someone bringing up Ted. She works at Martingale, so I guess the two of them met there."

"Well, that takes some nerve!" chimed in Sue.

"How awkward for you, Anne," Mother's look said she was concerned for me.

"Do you want me to ask Jim about her?" Aunt Julia offered.

"No, I think I'll just let it rest for now." I wanted to sound confident, whether I was or not.

We finally decided to start working on our quilting projects. Mother bragged about having all the blocks cut out for my floral appliqué. We looked at them in admiration, wondering how it would look all sewn together.

"Now if I could just get you to appliqué them, Anne," she teased.

"How in the world am I supposed to have time to do this? It takes time to run a shop, keep a jillion flowers alive, and then you add dating to that, and it's impossible!" Everyone thought this was quite funny and said I needed priorities.

"I wouldn't know about that part of life." Sue grinningly reminded us of her solo status in life. "I feel real sorry for you!" She then got serious and said she might never be attracted to anyone, or vice versa, once she became a mom.

"Oh, that just is not true," said Aunt Julia. "There is someone for everyone. You'll probably find him when you least expect it because you'll be distracted with your new role as a mother."

Sue walked over to pick up her quilt kit. She kept it near the fireplace in a charming antique basket.

"I better get busy on this before my little girl is too big for this quilt, don't you think?" She pulled it out of the basket and we could not believe what we saw!

All the pinned pieces she had arranged were appliquéd and sewn together. It was neatly folded until she opened it up and gasped in disbelief.

"Aunt Sylvia, did you sew this together?" Her tone was desperate.

"No, ma'am!" Mother was shocked.

"Oh, no, not again!" Aunt Julia looked a little pale.

Sue sat down in the recliner and held the top to her face to hide sudden tears. We went to her side.

Mother calmed our hearts and tears as always and said, "Now, look, we have here another omen that tells us we have spiritual support with our quilting. Let's think about this for a minute. They, Marie and Mother, that is, know we need to get this quilt done, and they wanted to help."

"Do you know what you're saying, Mother?" I was trying to be realistic about it all. "This means they know about Sue's adoption plans, too, not just about this quilt."

Saying that out loud, I, too, became tearful. This was just too much. I was to the point of nausea with all the events that had taken place. It was hard to always be in the right frame of mind for this craziness.

"Sounds like we need to get busy and set up the quilt frame soon, now that this top is done." Mother was taking control. "Just look at its fine workmanship." She tried so hard to keep us all calm with this spiritual madness.

I sat down with my wine and decided that if I wrote a book about our basement quilts someday, no one would believe me. We had to keep this nonsense quiet or we'd all be committed and never taken seriously.

"Did you buy a batting and backing for it, Sue?" Mother asked.

"No, but I'll do it right away." She was still sitting there in disbelief. "I know the kind I want."

"Well, when you bring the batting and backing, I'll have the frame all ready for you. You know, I think this sends a message that this little girl is going to be coming soon!"

Mother refilled our wine glasses. When she became nervous, it was her style to get busy with something. It was Aunt Julia's turn to start on her project. She went to where her quilt storage bag sat near the end table. She sat on the chair and pulled out her quilt. We observed in silence because we knew she had made little progress on her binding. Still in silence we watched as she opened the quilt. She peered at the binding, bringing it closer to her eyes. It was just like we feared, yet could not imagine. The binding was completely done on Aunt Julia's quilt! She sat back down in disbelief with misery written all over her face.

"I guess Marie or Mother didn't think I could do it by myself." She pouted. "How should I feel about this? I guess they were convinced I couldn't even finish the binding. I nearly had this sucker done, and now look!"

"Julia, I think another 'thank you' is in order." Mother sighed, unhappy with her sister's reaction. "No one has to know that we received this help. I guess they wouldn't believe us anyway."

"No, they wouldn't, Mother. What happens in this basement needs to stay in this basement."

"It's pretty magical, and yet…it's also scary down here," said Sue. "No wonder Muffin runs and sits in the corner like she's scared to death when she comes over here."

"Thanks be to the Lord and whoever finished our work!" Mother said. We raised our glasses much more hesitantly than we always did for the least accomplishment.

"This was quite a celebration you planned, Anne," said Sue. "Little did we know we would have this kind of surprise! So much for my news!"

"Yes, y'all, let's get back to the real reason we're here. We are getting a little girl in this family and we want to have a baby shower for you, Sue, just as soon as you know her age."

"I would love that!" Sue was pure joy. "You are all the best!"

"Start making your list of friends from the office, church, and the shop, of course," Mother enthused.

"If we have it in the basement, Aunt Marie and Grandmother will be able to come," I joked.

"We'll just bring down decorations and maybe they'll have it all decorated for us!" Aunt Julia used her best sarcastic tone.

"This is all crazy! I'm going home," Sue announced. "I can't take much more of this celebration!"

She took home the extra pizza, and Aunt Julia took home her finished quilt. "I can't wait to get this on my bed." At last she was seeing the bright side of the situation.

This was not the ending we expected to the party. Everyone was in disbelief and felt a mixed bag of joy and concern. Sue left her quilt top and Mother didn't waste any time saying that the day after Christmas, the quilt frame would be ready for the next quilt.

CHAPTER 44

———— ∞∞∞ ————

Christmas was coming quickly and I didn't feel I was really ready. The added commitment of meeting his parents combined with a travel list for my first trip with Sam was starting to weigh on me. I still had to go by after work and pick up the painting I was going to give him for Christmas.

Sam e-mailed that he would like to get together at the end of the evening. I did want to see him to firm up details on the flight, and since I had not met his parents, I needed guidance on what to take them. I had arranged for flowers to be sent but wanted them to have something to open. I e-mailed back that I would call him later.

We were finishing things up at the shop and decided we needed to stop and smell the roses to enjoy such a successful holiday season. Everyone was becoming preoccupied with his or her holiday plans, so productivity had gone by the wayside. Sue dropped by before closing to have a Christmas drink with us. She had a glow about her that would truly carry her through the season. She, Kevin, and Sally were such troopers throughout the holidays. They were my other family with its own joys and challenges, but I couldn't be more pleased with my employee choices for Brown's Botanical Flower Shop.

As they scurried to finish up the last of orders, they were dropping hints all over the place about needing more help. I had already made note of it, especially if I were going to make room for Sam in my life. Valentine's Day would be our next rush, so I would need to get someone trained before then.

While Kevin poured us some wine, I handed each of them a Christmas bonus check, which I did each year. They had chipped in together to buy me some updated computer items that I just kept putting off and a red and white electric teapot to keep at the shop. I was touched, as they presented the gifts to me neatly wrapped in white tissue with red bows. I thanked them with sincerity and told them to also help themselves to one of the several live Christmas arrangements we had remaining in hopes of last minute sales. We shared a few laughs about our holiday challenges and then off everyone went to catch up on their errands.

Mother was at her card club's Christmas dinner at the country club, so I planned to grab fast food on the way home after I picked up Sam's painting.

I walked to the only art gallery in town, which was owned by a sweet couple, Tim and Pam O'Connell. They had been nice enough to hold the painting when I called and had offered me a discount as well.

The street was like magic with Christmas music and the smells of fudge, cookies, marshmallows, cookies, and real live chestnuts roasting on an open fire. Santas and carolers were on every corner. Some of the shops near restaurants were still open, hoping to capture the evening's dinner crowd.

The gallery was very busy with customers when I arrived. One elderly gentleman was purchasing a very large painting of our riverfront. It was stunning. I wondered if that should have been my purchase, since Sam loved overlooking the river from his loft. It surely meant a great sale for O'Connell's.

I kept myself occupied looking at fine pieces of hand-blown glassware until they were free to help me.

"We have it all ready for you," said Pam. "I went ahead and put a bow on it. It's in the backroom. I'll go get it." Tim went over to lock the shop door.

"Sorry I have kept you so late," I said ruefully.

"Oh no, sales have kept us busy, but we are ready for a break and some dinner!" Tim said.

Pam came from the backroom and said there was something else for me to pick up. I was quite puzzled. Then Tim appeared from the back room with a different painting than I had asked him to hold for me. Behind him came Sam!

"Sam, what are you doing here?" I was flustered and confused.

"I just came by to pick up your Christmas present, and Tim said you were coming within the hour to pick up something, too, so I decided to wait."

With that said, Tim held up the wonderful watercolor painting I had admired the same night Sam admired the painting I bought for him.

"Merry Christmas, Anne!" Sam handed me the fairly large painting that I told him would be perfect in my bedroom.

"Oh, my word, Sam, thank you! This is awesome and so very beautiful! I know just where this is going! But hey, wait a minute!"

Before I gave him a hug and kiss, I set the painting on the counter and Pam handed me the painting I bought for him.

"Merry Christmas, to you, too, my love. Surprise, surprise!

Guess what this is?"

He laughed with a surprise that I hadn't been sure was possible for him. He looked it over with a big smile and leaned over to kiss my cheek.

"So much for Santa Claus!" he joked. "Ho, ho, ho!"

We both laughed and managed to embrace before Tim said, "This calls for a celebration. It's not every day we can satisfy our customers this way. We hoped it would work out like this when you both called to say you were coming this evening to pick up your paintings. We've never played Santa Claus before!"

Pam lifted a tray of champagne glasses from under the counter. Tim popped the cork and we all exchanged more Christmas cheer with each other. Sam teased Pam and Tim about not exchanging gifts themselves. They had obviously given our accidental meeting some prior thought. We lifted our glasses to wish one and all a Merry Christmas! This was indeed an unexpected Kodak moment.

"Our Christmas present is a new kitchen we just had installed last week." Tim gave Pam a little squeeze. "See what happens when you get married? You start being practical and neglect giving things to each other that are more personal."

"That's okay, I love my new kitchen!" Pam kissed him on the cheek.

"You also have the joy of spending the money on your kids." I was wry. "How old are they now?"

"Six and eleven," said Pam. "They had pretty long Christmas lists for us this year, and the older they get, the more expensive it gets."

"This was nice of you to make this exchange special, you guys." Sam took hold of his painting. "We need to let you get home, and I hope I can talk Annie into some dinner. After all, we just had

Christmas and exchanged our gifts!"

"I think it sounds great." I picked up my own painting. "You're welcome to join us if you like."

"No the kids are expecting us, and I have wrapping to do tonight," Pam said.

"Thanks so very much for everything!" Joy was written all over me. "I love this, Sam," I said, as I hugged my painting.

We took the paintings to Sam's car, and he drove down the street to my shop so I could get my car. He had made a reservation at Donna's Tea Room for dinner. It was a fine dining establishment and I was dressed pretty casual.

"Let me run into the shop and freshen up for a minute."

"Sure, take your time, but I'll come in to stay warm. You may end up doing some work, knowing you!"

I didn't turn on the lights so as not to give the impression we were open. The white Christmas lights twinkled on us. Sam waited in the retail room and I redid my makeup and put on a scarf to detract from my plain red sweater. I put on the fragrance Sam seemed to love most. When I came out of the restroom, he was there to grab me with a kiss and hug, praising my scent, and thanking me once more for the painting.

"By the way, I picked up a little something else for you," he said softly.

"Oh Sam, don't do that! I didn't get you anything else but the picture, so you're going to make me feel bad."

"I know tomorrow will be hectic at your house, so I'd like to give it to you tonight." He drew me closer to him. "You may like it enough to want to wear it to dinner."

"Where is it?" I was looking over his shoulder and side to side.

"I'm not telling," he teased. "Would you prefer we go by my

place and I could give it to you there?"

"I have to go home tonight, Sam." I backed away. "I shouldn't even be going to dinner, so if you have something I can wear to dinner, and you want me to have it before tomorrow, this would be a good time to give it to me."

"What if you don't like it?" he teased again. "I've never bought you anything to wear before."

"You certainly know me well enough by now," I assured him. "If I don't like it, you'll know it and I'll return it, so there!"

Sam pulled me over to the Christmas tree and held my face with both of his hands, holding me still for a second. He took out a small package from his coat pocket and opened the lid to what appeared to be a ring box. As he opened it, I could not believe my eyes. I was staring at a large pearl ring with two diamonds perched on each side. Of all my pearl jewelry, which I had in many shapes and sizes, I had never seen such a pearl as this. I couldn't speak. What was going on? Was he out of his mind? Was I?

Sam got down on one knee and said, "My Annie, will you marry me?"

He paused, such a dead serious look on his face, and the silence was deafening.

I stared at him, then at the ring, wondering if this was a weird kind of joke. I told myself I had better be careful how I was going to react to this in case it was a joke.

"I'm not getting up from this floor until you say yes," he threatened.

I stared at the ring again, still in the box, still in his hand.

"Sam, is this a joke, because if it is, it's not too funny." I had never been more serious and refused to crack a smile. My heart had stopped beating and I was stunned.

"I know it's soon for us to make this permanent commitment,

but I have never been so sure in my life that I've found the right person to marry. I want our families to know that this weekend when we see them. I love you, and I'm not going to let you get away from me. Do you love me? Do you want to spend the rest of your life with me?" He paused. "Or are you not sure?"

It was such a shock and yet it seemed like a dream was coming true before my very eyes, and I was afraid I was going to wake up to something else. I could tell my response to any of this was taking way too long, and I saw sadness develop in Sam's eyes. The words that I would choose right now would have a lasting impression, so I had to slowly think it through.

Still staring at the box, I said, "Sam, I do love you. I've never felt this way about anyone, I told you that. I know that my life without you would not be complete. You make me so happy! Please, get up and let's talk about this."

"No, Anne, I will not get up until you make it clear whether your answer is yes or no."

Yep, indeed he meant business. I smiled in disbelief and wished I had a photo of my tall, handsome Sam down on one knee looking so very serious. This is another Kodak moment that could go well or sour, I told myself.

"If you can accept my crazy life, and love me unconditionally, my answer is yes."

Sam got up, rubbed his one knee, and took the sparkling ring out of the box. I never saw him so serious and relieved that the right answer had come. I remained very still, to see if I really was about to get engaged. Me, Anne Brown, was really getting engaged, before the age of thirty. I had never been sure I would ever see this in my life. Sam put the ring on my finger and a perfect fit it was.

"It is absolutely beautiful, Sam!" I tingled all over. "You remembered how much I love pearls, and these diamonds truly make it divine!"

Out of the blue, tears were coming down my face. They blurred my vision as I tried to examine the ring.

"Are these tears of joy or is this a sad occasion for my single Annie?" Sam was teasing as he wiped a few tears off my cheek.

"I love you so much, but I had no idea you would consider me as a wife, especially not this soon." I wiped at my tears, too.

"I think we both felt this was something good for both of us, and I've waited long enough for someone like you. I want us to have our own place. I want a real house with a yard, garden, picket fence and the whole nine yards, but that's another discussion. I might even want to have children, if my wife feels the same way," he teased.

"Hold it." I was overwhelmed. "I can't absorb this all right now. Sam, I really didn't see this coming. It is the most exciting moment of my life." I kissed him hard, with all my heart, soul, and body could give him. He accepted my response with a hold on me that nearly crushed my chest.

I couldn't let go of him. As I snuggled in his neck, I prayed to God that I was not making a mistake and that we both were doing the right thing.

"Now I know I'm underdressed if I wear this ring to dinner."

"It looks great on you, like I knew it would." He held up my hand in admiration. "Still want to keep that reservation?"

"I'm starved and exhausted," I smiled. "But I don't think I'll sleep a wink tonight!"

CHAPTER 45

I arrived home very late. Mother was already asleep. I was on a cloud of nine times nine times nine. I went into the living room where the only light came from the Christmas village of houses that Mother had been collecting since I could remember.

I sat down in the wingback chair that my father had ownership of for as long I could remember. I could still see him leaning back into its padded corner to take a quick snooze. No one seemed to ever fill the seat that he had left empty for my mother and I. Oh, how I wish he were here now to hear my news. I would have so many questions, and no doubt he would have his opinions.

Who would walk me down the aisle to give away Daddy's little girl? Did Sam realize how young I was in spite of my independent nature? After all, I've never lived anywhere else than in the house I was sitting in right now!

Daddy died when I was only sixteen, but he left my heart full of love and admiration. Mother said I was just like him. He was such an entrepreneur, and when Mother decided to give me the money from one of his insurance policies to start my business, she knew he would have approved. I thought of him daily and hoped to make him proud of the investment and the choices I made in my career. He hadn't been able to see my business grow, and now he wouldn't be able to meet my future husband.

Would he have liked Sam? Would Sam have liked him? Tears were streaming down my face. Why cry now, for heavens sake, after all these years? I was sobbing like I'd been saving up for it. Was this breakdown a sign I wasn't really ready for all this? Was it immature to be so sentimental?

Mother had heard enough movement to come downstairs.

"Anne, is that you I hear?"

I couldn't answer her. I had to get myself together so I wouldn't upset her. As she walked slowly into the living room, she could tell something was wrong.

"Anne, what is it?"

I still couldn't speak.

"Oh Anne, is it you and Sam?" she sadly asked. "Is something wrong? Did you break up?"

She came and put her arm around me as she sat on Dad's footstool. The silence certainly was a signal to her that it might indeed be a break up.

I knew this was the moment to share with her what had just occurred. I looked at her and forced a smile, despite my tears.

"No, nothing's wrong," I choked, wiping my eyes. I held up my hand so she could see the ring shining ever so brightly in the soft glowing light.

"Oh, Anne, is this what I think it is?" She was well and truly astonished.

"Yes! I am engaged, and I'm not handling it very well."

She hugged me again and more tears poured out of my face in a complete sob.

"This is indeed sooner than I could imagine, but I could definitely tell there was something very special and serious between the two of you." Her voice was soft, just like when I was little and got hurt. "It didn't take me long to know I was in love with your father, you know." This brought a big smile to her face.

"Oh, I miss him so much!" I said as I wiped the tears away from my face. "What would he say right now, Mother?"

"Honey, he would be so proud of you. You are a wise, successful woman working very hard. You deserve to have a good man in your life and you have been so very good to me. Your parents can't pick the love of your life for you, so we trust your judgment on that. You do love him, don't you?"

"Yes, yes, I do. But it still is hard for me to believe he feels as strongly as I do. I tried not to fall so hard for him."

"That's just like you, Anne, always trying to protect yourself and being so darn independent. Sam needs you now in his life, and I don't want you to look back—only ahead."

As she admired my ring, I told her how Sam and I ran into each other at the gallery to pick up Christmas gifts and how Pam and Tim had planned for us to get there at the same time. I told her that after we had a drink with them, Sam had walked me back to the shop where he gave me the ring. I told her he wanted to break the news to her and his parents over Christmas.

"Well, you will indeed do that, making this holiday so extra special." She was full of joy. "Did you talk about how soon this wedding would be?"

"No, I told him I would have to absorb it all first. What if his parents don't like me?"

"Are you kidding!? They will fall in love with you, and if they don't, I'll tell them a thing or two! Their son is darn lucky to have a wife like you." She was holding back her own tears by now, trying to be strong for me.

"I've never lived anywhere else than in this house, Mother."

"Yes, I know, and it's time you experience all the excitement of planning a home you and Sam want to live in. It will be such fun! Hopefully you'll always be in Colebridge, so I can see you."

"I'll have to have time to 'be engaged' and let all this sink in. Plus, I'll need time to plan some kind of wedding."

"Yes indeed! And what a wedding that will be!"

"Oh Mother, I love you so. Thanks for being happy for me."

CHAPTER 46

There was plenty to do the next morning as Mother prepared a special pork loin roast for the Christmas Eve menu. She finished setting the table with her best crystal, Grandmother's china with the gold trim, and silverware that was a wedding gift from her in-laws. She had entertained all her life, but she knew this dinner would be extra special.

I had spied on many dinners that she and my father had given when we entertained his clients. Now, times were so different and everyone went to restaurants for such occasions, but my father had loved showing off my mother's good cooking and presentation. She taught me good etiquette at a very early age but gave me little cooking advice. I knew she missed having people to dinner, so the rest of the family gladly let her do much of the entertaining.

As I was drinking my coffee at the kitchen table, Sam called to see if I had gotten any sleep. He said he stayed up quite late and didn't fall asleep until close to morning. I told him I had shared our news with Mother after she heard me come in.

"She didn't expect it this early in our relationship, but she had a pretty good idea it would indeed happen."

"How does she feel about living alone for the first time?" he asked.

"We didn't get that far," I said, reminding myself it was indeed a future conversation to have with her. Such a thoughtful man! "I'm just glad she's happy for us. She wants to make the announcement before dinner tonight, is that okay?"

"Absolutely!"

"I need to get packing for our trip, but I guess you just leave a bag packed ready to go?"

He laughed. "Pretty much."

"I hope I have everything arranged at the shop. Having the shop closed for a few days helps. So you're ready to go?"

"I think so. Remember, I do this once a week sometimes. We need to leave by 8:00 a.m. to catch our flight."

"I can do that if you don't keep me up all night," I teased. "Santa Claus has already come, so I don't have to stay up late to listen for him."

"As soon as your mother signals that the evening is over, I'll be out the door tonight."

"I need to help her now with a few things here in the kitchen, so I better go."

"Later, my sweet Annie."

When I went up to my room, I hung the painting on the wall where I knew it would be perfect, and it was. Would Sam always be this observant and generous?

When Mother asked last night about when this wedding would happen, it made me realize Sam and I had to have some kind of answer. I wanted everything to be just right and perfect, with just the right size wedding, but another part of me wanted to just be with Sam now. I would have to have some time and not rush the wedding date. Maybe we would have some time to talk on the plane before we told his parents.

My stomach was churning with uncertainties, plus, tonight was, in a sense, my engagement party. I should be happier than ever before in my life. Happy? What was there not to be happy about?

Getting ready for the big Christmas Eve dinner, I chose a simple royal blue dress accented with my favorite pearl earrings. The blue color made my blue eyes pop but my impressive engagement ring was the real focus. I needed to place it on the dresser until everyone arrived or Mother's announcement would be ruined. The ring was out of the ordinary, you might say. I never imagined having such a gorgeous thing. I was so pleased it was not a large diamond. Yikes, I thought. Wearing this every day would be nearly impossible since I was constantly washing my hands and cutting flowers.

I heard people arriving and went down the stairs to greet Uncle Jim, Aunt Julia, and Sarah.

They looked fabulous and Sarah looked like a grown-up. She was about to turn thirteen next week, but she looked like an eighteen-year-old. When I complimented her, she said, "I guess I'm old enough to quilt, then."

"Yes, indeed, young lady. We'll be getting back to that after Christmas, so get your thimble ready."

Sue was the next to arrive. She, too, looked festive in a black cocktail dress. Her pretty face had gotten even prettier since her positive adoption results. She didn't dress up very often as she complained constantly about her weight and how clothes didn't look good on her. She was a great baker, though, and, sure enough, brought a cake in the shape of a Christmas wreath. We all admired her handiwork.

"I just talked to Mom and Dad and they said to wish you all Merry Christmas!"

"Oh, I wish they lived closer," Mother said, hanging Sue's coat in the closet. "I'll call them tomorrow and wish them a Merry Christmas as well."

Just as they lead the way to the living room, Sam arrived. He looked so handsome and sported a red tie in honor of the season. He brought gifts for all, which Sarah put under the tree, and a good bottle of Mother's favorite wine. He took it to the kitchen, where she was doing some last minute basting on the roast.

"Oh, Sam, should I say congratulations on a good catch?" She whispered so no one else could hear.

"I did pretty well, didn't I?" He grinned his pleasure. "I should have come to see you and ask for your blessing, but somehow I knew this daughter of yours had a mind of her own."

"Yes, I'm glad you're aware of that," she laughed in agreement. "She loves you, and that makes me so happy."

"I love her, and I appreciate your blessing," he said. They were hugging as I came in the room to give Sam a little kiss, so I included Mother, too. The clicking in my head was capturing another Kodak moment. Seeing the two I loved most in the world happy together was the best Christmas present ever!

She went into the living room, where the Christmas tree was getting many compliments. Soon they were sipping wine and enjoying the eggnog that Uncle Jim had brought. Sam and I looked out the large bay window in the kitchen to see snow beginning to fall.

"I love a white Christmas!" I leaned my head against him. "Ever since I was little, we all would make bets about whether there would be snow on Christmas morning. My father would say that Santa loved a white Christmas because he was so used to all the snow at the North Pole."

"You don't talk about him much," Sam said.

"I know," I sighed. "Somehow this holiday with you, Sam, has made me think of him more than ever. I keep wondering what he would be telling me right now. Last night, it dawned on me that he would not be walking me down the aisle!" Sam said nothing, but hugged me closer to his side. What could he possibly say, for he never knew him.

Just then we saw some of the neighbors placing lit luminaries in front of our house. It was a neighborhood tradition since I could remember. I told Sam that when I was younger, we helped out as a family. We would get them lit before we went to church every Christmas Eve so it was a beautiful sight to come home to.

"We will start our own traditions, my love, or maybe carry on some of the old ones."

Mother picked up the tiny silver bell on the sideboard and announced that we should be seated for dinner. I made a quick exit up the stairs to put on my ring. No one noticed as everyone was gathering to see where his or her assigned place card was set.

When I entered the dining room, I gave a quick tweak to the centerpiece of red roses that I had sent from the shop. Sam checked to make sure I had remembered the ring.

After we were seated, Mother stood at her place at the end of the table and said we would say a blessing and then there would be a special announcement. She led us in prayer, thanking God for the many blessings and for us to remember those family members who were not with us, including the loved ones who had passed.

In silence we fell to thoughts of Aunt Marie, who had just left us a short time ago. Were she and Grandmother looking down on us now? What would they think of the announcement Mother was going to make?

CHAPTER 47

Everyone remained quiet waiting for Mother to speak. She began by announcing that there would be a new member in our family.

"I am pleased to tell you that Sam and Anne are engaged and I couldn't be happier!"

There were the surprised reactions we expected, but there was instant clapping and congratulations coming from every direction.

"Does Sam know he's also marrying Brown's Botanical Flower Shop?" Sue said in fun.

"Yes, yes," laughed Sam. "Both of the Browns are beautiful and I am happy to have the two of them in my life!"

"Now I know why this trip to meet Sam's parents was planned!" Aunt Julia mused aloud.

"Sam, you pulled this one off without telling me!" Uncle Jim patted him on the shoulder. "I'm pleased we'll be related, but you don't have to start calling me uncle."

Sarah was the first to ask, "When? When? Oh, I can't wait!"

"We really haven't had time to talk about it, but we promise to keep you all posted." They could hear the joy in my voice. I knew this wouldn't be easy in the time to come. Family, fellow business owners, and my employees would be relentless on this topic. "It's important that the Dicksons have a reaction to all this, and that may influence our plans."

"My folks will love her to death, but they will be surprised about the engagement, no doubt."

Uncle Jim proposed a toast "to the perfect engagement" and wished us much happiness as we journeyed to our wedding date. It was almost too much to absorb. I really hadn't had time yet to envision the occasion.

Now the ring became the center of attention, as Sue was the first to ask to see it. Compliments about its unusual setting and the sparkle of the diamonds beside the pearl flew around the table. I tried to watch Sam's reaction as everyone fussed over the ring. The entire family seemed to be talking at once in all the excitement.

Sue stood up and clinked on her crystal water glass for everyone's attention. "It's now my turn to share a Christmas surprise."

We were silent immediately, wondering where the conversation was going. She pulled out a framed 5x7 photo from her purse. "I want to introduce a photo of my two-year-old daughter, Mia Marie Davis. I'll be picking her up from Honduras at the end of January. I am going to be a mother! Can you believe it?"

The cheers were loud and Mother got up from her chair to go over to hug her. The picture of a darling, round-faced, dark-headed girl with a half smile circled the table. The oohs and ahhs overshadowed any engagement ring, quite rightly, I thought. This was indeed a marvelous announcement as well as another addition to our small family. I was beaming with pride for Sue.

"Did you get to name her?" I asked. "I love Mia Marie! Wouldn't that make Aunt Marie happy!"

"Mia is what they call her now. I added Marie, because of someone we dearly love, and it really goes well with Mia. I'm glad you like it!"

"It's a beautiful name, Sue, I am so happy for you," agreed Aunt Julia. "This means she's already running around enjoying the terrible twos, as they say. I think the name really fits her. I love it, too!"

"Well this makes two new members in the family!" Mother had a big smile. Aunt Julia said how fun it would be to have a little one around again. Sarah wouldn't give up the photo once it was passed to her. She was delighted to be sure, as she questioned Sue about becoming a babysitter for her.

"Have you called your parents?" Mother asked. "They will be so delighted!"

"Yes, I called them right away, and they were so excited. Mom started crying and wanted to go with me to pick her up. I told her that was not possible, but that I was meeting with the lawyer that they assigned to me at the agency later this week. I'll also get to meet some other couples who have gone there before to pick up their children, so I'm looking forward to that. I think everything will go fine."

"Here's to Sue and Mia," Sam said as he raised his glass for a toast. We picked up our glasses to join in. The little darling in the photo was indeed the center of attention.

Mother went to the kitchen to see how her pork roast was doing, since we had delayed the timing of dinner. Uncle Jim got up from the table and starting refilling our wine glasses.

"This might be a merrier Christmas with all these toasts, so drink up!" Uncle Jim teased as he walked around the table.

When Mother sat back down, Uncle Jim said, "Now that I have the floor, Julia and I have something we want to announce!" Sarah started giggling like she already knew the secret news. The first thing I thought it might be was not good, so I prayed he did not ruin our celebration.

"On our wedding anniversary, March 2, Julia and I would like to invite you all to St. Stephens Church to celebrate the renewing of our vows!"

"You mean, like a wedding!?" Sue wasn't alone in her astonishment.

This was not going to be a good Kodak moment I said to myself. From the silent reaction, I was not the only one thinking this was pretty strange.

"It will be a small wedding, so to speak." Aunt Julia blushed. "We have been having some rocky moments for some time, but now we feel we have resolved our issues and would like to start anew. I hope you'll be happy for us." Mother's face reflected happiness and relief. The rest of us were still reacting.

"Sarah, will you be in the wedding?" Sue tried to make light of the announcement.

"Yesiree, and I get to pick out my own dress!" This made us laugh.

I was still stunned and couldn't speak. I told myself there was no way Uncle Jim's second life could have gone away this quickly. I wondered what in the world could have brought all this on. I remembered distinctly that very recently Aunt Julia said she no longer loved him!

"Well Jim, I guess you pulled one over on me." Sam shook his friend's hand.

We gave the couple compliments and best wishes, despite what most of us were really thinking. My mind kept wondering about

Brenda, Uncle Jim's long-time girlfriend at Martingale. I was going to have to find out the real story here without telling Aunt Julia I had known about her since the company Christmas party. If Uncle Jim were faking this reunion with her, I would never forgive him. I wondered if he really had come clean about his affair. What happened to create this total turnabout for Aunt Julia? What took place that she was so willing to abandon her secret plan about ending their marriage?

Mother stood up and said dinner was going to be served before the roast would be too well done. She made a toast that calmed the room for just a moment.

"Here's to Sam and Anne, and to Sue and her new daughter, and to Jim and Julia."

"Here! Here!" we cheered and clinked our glasses.

"Sylvia, if there are no other announcements," Uncle Jim said, "I'd like to make a toast to the best hostess ever!" We agreed this was indeed in order as we again lifted our glasses. Mother nodded as if she were taking a bow.

"And I would like to wish my new family a Merry Christmas." Sam lifted his glass yet again.

"And a Happy New Year," we said in unison.

CHAPTER 48

This Christmas Eve was one none of us would ever forget. I had to remind myself that this was most likely the last one I would spend in my childhood home. We had much to chat about at the dinner table. It was hard for me to attend to what everyone was saying to me as I kept glancing at my gorgeous ring.

Mother and I cleared what needed to be removed from the table after dinner before everyone went into the living room to exchange gifts. Sarah was taking pictures with her new camera, and I was delighted that some of these moments would be on film. A video of all the announcements would have really been a treasure, but I had had no idea of any surprise other than my own.

Coffee was served on the buffet with Sue's cake, Christmas cookies, and Mother's delicious peanut brittle. I watched as Sam devoured the cookies like a sweet little boy who had just been given permission to indulge. A warm loving feeling came over my heart. More Kodak film, for moments to come, would be needed to put in my memory for my new life with Sam.

He and I sat close to each other watching all the reactions to our gifts. He held my hand and squeezed it now and then as he looked at the ring and then into my eyes.

The gift cards I purchased went over big, so that was a good idea. Sam's gift to Sarah was a gift certificate to her favorite shopping mall. She could not thank him enough and I could tell he was proud of all his Christmas choices. Sue knew exactly what she was going to purchase with her gift card for the baby, and she loved the big bone for Muffin, which had a big red bow tied around it. Her dog was in the basement entertaining Grandma and Aunt Marie, so Sue went downstairs to give her the treat. Mother had a hint of shyness in her voice as she thanked me for her gift card to buy new clothes.

Aunt Julia shared that part of her Christmas gift was getting her wedding ring reset and adding more diamonds in honor of their renewed marriage. Again, I wondered to what great measures Jim went to convince Aunt Julia of his new way of life.

As I watched the love and laughter around the room, I hoped in my new life that I would always be able to spend Christmas Eve in the home of my past and share it with Mother as long as she lived. Our new traditions as a married couple might have to happen on another day, like on Christmas Day.

Mother motioned for Aunt Julia and me to join Sue in the basement. All the news we had just experienced demanded the attention of our small basement quilters' group. We took our coffee downstairs, appreciating Mother's suggestion to be together. Uncle Jim, Sam, and Sarah stayed upstairs, not really noticing we were gone.

It was the natural place to be when Mother said, "I think we should have a Christmas toast with Mother and Marie, who are in our hearts today. So much of what has just happened upstairs was shared down here, around the basement quilt."

We toasted our dearly departed, thanking them for their love and contributions, and naturally, tears started to flow. We were happy and warm, feeling their presence and their joy for us.

"I guess they don't mind it's with coffee instead of wine!" joked Sue.

As I observed us, I noticed we were standing in a circle, in the same order that we sat around our quilting frame. I could only smile inside my head as I looked at Mother, Sue, and Aunt Julia in this special moment.

"We have a baby quilt to quilt, you know, and it needs to be real soon!" said Sue.

"Thanks to someone in this room, it is ready to put in a frame. What about a wedding quilt next?" Mother looked at me with love and pride. "My only daughter is going to have to have a wedding quilt, let there be no doubt. Mother and Aunt Marie would make certain it happens, if I don't."

I shook my head and said, "Now, Mother, I have no idea when such a quilt would have to be finished."

"Good, we don't need the pressure and it will give us plenty of time to plan ahead," she said.

"What if I also want a wedding quilt?" chided Aunt Julia. We laughed and Mother said she shouldn't be greedy, as she had just gotten one.

"You'll have to get on the list, Aunt Julia," Sue joked.

We agreed that we would concentrate on meeting on Sunday afternoons or whenever we were free.

"We also have to help plan a wedding for our 'flower child' here." Aunt Julia reminded me that I had not been referred to that for a while, but when I first purchased the flower shop, I was called that frequently.

The thoughts of all the planning ahead were overwhelming and I knew my wedding plans would not be solely my own. It was something I was certain would be shared not only with the living, but also with those who already passed in this life.

"Just hold off, you all. We do not know when that will be," I chided them.

Mother gathered us closer as we entwined our arms.

"Because of Julia's quilt, we came together as a family to help and support her," Mother said with a smile. "We accomplished our mission for Julia and because of that we have been given more opportunities of love and joy in this family. There is much to celebrate and look forward to."

There were still many unanswered questions for each of us. Why did I feel not all would have happy endings? The secrets and unknowns could change the outcome of every toast we had made at the Christmas Eve dinner table.

I did know, however, that no matter where my life with Sam would take me, I would always be part of my family's love and future challenges.

There was nothing we couldn't achieve, just as we did with the basement quilt.

And the Colebridge community continues…

Coming soon…another story from
the Colebridge Community.

Don't miss…**The Potting Shed Quilt**!
A Novel by Ann Hazelwood.

1. Does Anne proceed with her engagement to Sam?

2. What puzzle do the quilters put together?

3. What "unique find" expands the number
of Anne's family members?

4. What happens at the first meeting of
the Jane Austen Book Club?

5. Do lilies and lemonade continue to
speak for the unseen?

About the Author

Ann Hazelwood has written several books for the American Quilter's Society including *100 Things You Need to Know If You Own a Quilt, 100 Tips from Award-winning Quilters,* and *100 Sweet Treats by and for Quilters.* A former quilt shop owner, Ann is an author of regional food and travel books about her home state of Missouri, and is an AQS-certified quilt appraiser and President of the National Quilt Museum's Board of Directors. *The Basement Quilt* is her first work of fiction, soon to be followed by *The Potting Shed Quilt* and *The Funeral Parlor Quilt.* Visit her at www.booksonthings.com.

The pattern for this block is available at:

**http://www.americanquilter.com/
grandmothers_fan_hazelwood**

More Books from AQS

#8156 $12.95

#7558 $12.95

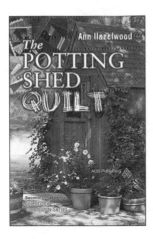

#1256 $14.95

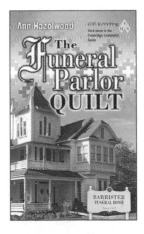

#1257 $14.95

Look for these books nationally.

1-800-626-5420

Call or Visit our website at

www.AmericanQuilter.com